VALKYRIE

Also by Kate O'Hearn

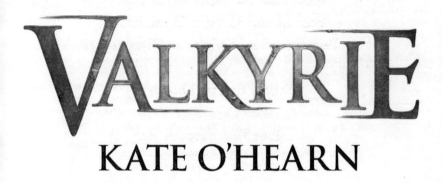

VALKYRIE

KATE O'HEARN

Hodder
Children's
Books

A division of Hachette Children's Books

A Catalogue record for this book is available
from the British Library

ISBN 978 1 444 90755 1

Typeset by Avon DataSet Ltd, Bidford-on-Avon, Warwickshire

Printed in the UK by CPI Group (UK) Ltd, Croydon, CR0 4YY

The paper and board used in this paperback by
Hodder Children's Books are natural recyclable products
made from wood grown in sustainable forests. The manufacturing
processes conform to the environmental regulations of
the country of origin.

Hodder Children's Books
a division of Hachette Children's Books
338 Euston Road, London NW1 3BH
An Hachette UK company
www.hachette.co.uk

I would like to send a special message to anyone out there who is being bullied – either in school or online.

Please tell someone – your parents, your guardians or teachers – tell ANYONE! You don't have to suffer alone . . . we do care.

And I promise you, it does get better. I was bullied at school and now I write books that travel all around the world!

This book is for YOU!

VALHALLA

If on some cold winter's night you gaze up into the darkened sky and see the glow of the Northern Lights – consider this. Those shimmering colours are not an illusion. They are the glow of the Rainbow Bridge called Bifröst. Across that magnificent bridge, far from the World of Man, you will find Asgard: Land of the Norse Gods and home of Valhalla.

Also known as Odin's Great Heavenly Hall for the Heroic Dead, Valhalla sits in the very centre of Asgard. Resting deep within the ethereal plane it is accessible from Earth only by crossing Bifröst.

Enormous in size, with a thousand spires rising high into the clouds, Valhalla hosts over five hundred entrance doors. Each door is wide enough to allow eight hundred slain warriors to pass through, marching side by side.

In ancient times, the Vikings fought valiantly to earn a seat at Valhalla. It was all they strived for. But to get there, they had to be selected by an elite group of winged Battle-Maidens, known as the Valkyries.

In the middle of the battlefield, the Valkyries would swoop down from the skies, riding their winged Reaping Mares and howling their haunted cries. Coming to Earth, or Midgard, as they called it, to choose among the dead and dying only the most valiant of warriors to deliver to Odin at Valhalla.

Arriving at Valhalla, these chosen warriors would spend their nights sitting with Odin, feasting and drinking. They would dance with the Valkyries and listen to their enchanting songs as the Battle-Maidens entertained the dead.

A warrior's days at Valhalla were spent on the training grounds outside the heavenly hall, as they picked up their weapons and gloried once again in endless battle.

This was their heaven and their paradise. In today's battles, soldiers have long forgotten Valhalla and the Valkyries that fly in to gather up the chosen dead.

Though we have forgotten them, they haven't forgotten us . . .

CHAPTER ONE

The first rays of dawn swept over the distant horizon and drove away the long night. But Freya did not welcome the rising sun. It was her mortal enemy, that would bring only sorrow. She tilted her wings and flew headlong into the fading darkness, hoping to follow the night, praying day would not find her.

But darkness betrayed her and allowed in the light. She had been flying all night, soaring high above Asgard, dreading her upcoming First Day Ceremony.

Orus, her raven companion, flew at her side and tried his best to keep up. But his wings were much smaller than hers, and despite his best efforts he lagged behind. After the long flight, he was too tired to beg her to go back. All he could do was try to stay with her and help guide her through First Day.

'Freya!' a voice called from behind her.

Freya looked back and saw her older sister Maya soaring confidently behind them. Her own raven was flying closely at her side.

'Freya, stop!' Maya called. 'Please land; we must speak.'

Orus forced more speed and caught up with Freya. 'Stop!' he gasped. 'I can't fly much longer, and your sister is calling.'

Freya looked over to her raven and saw how exhausted he was. She hadn't been fair, forcing him to fly all night. Pulling in her wings, she descended and gracefully touched down in a field of golden grain. As she folded and settled her midnight-black wings on her back, Orus landed on her shoulder. 'Don't lose your temper with your sister,' he panted softly.

'Thank Odin I found you!' Maya cried as she also landed and charged towards Freya. 'Mother's in a state. Everyone is searching for you. Where have you been all night?'

Freya used her sleeve to wipe away the beads of sweat from her brow. Now that she had stopped, she felt exhausted from the long flight. The muscles in her wings warned of the stiffness to come. 'I needed a bit of fresh air.'

'I can see that,' Maya cried. 'But why didn't you tell anyone you were going? You could have at least told me!'

'I saw you dancing at Valhalla with some of the warriors. I didn't want to disturb you.'

'You know I would much rather spend time with you than dance.' Maya softened her tone. 'Especially on the eve of your First Day.'

'I don't want to do this.'

Her sister's pale brows knitted together in a frown. 'Do what?'

'This! Today!' Freya shot back. 'My First Day Ceremony and then going to the battlefield.'

'What do you mean? You've been to the battlefields thousands of times. You have spent all of your life there. Only today you will reap your first dying warrior.'

Freya sighed heavily. 'But I hate it. I hate the warriors and I hate all the killing and wounding. Humans are bloodthirsty monsters. I don't want to touch them or be part of bringing more of them here. Asgard would be much better off without Valhalla and its dead warriors.'

Maya looked shocked. 'How can you say that? Valhalla is a wondrous place and a home to all the valiant warriors who have fallen in battle since the dawn of time! Those men have earned the right to be here. It is a great honour that we are the ones chosen to escort them. You should celebrate them and what they have achieved.'

'All they have achieved is being good killers!' Freya challenged. 'And what does that make us when we reap them? We're even better killers!'

'We do not kill!' her sister said indignantly. 'We are

Valkyries. We bring an end to their suffering and escort them home.'

'It's still killing,' Freya insisted, and her wings fluttered in annoyance. 'If we didn't touch them, they would live.'

'No they wouldn't. It is their time to die, whether we touch them or not,' Maya insisted.

'But I don't want to do it,' Freya responded as she turned and walked away from her sister. 'I don't want to touch a human or even talk to them. I have seen the warriors at Valhalla. All they want to do is kill and destroy.'

Her sister started to preen the black feathers on Freya's folded wings. 'Freya, how can I make you see that you're wrong? The soldiers of today are nothing like the warriors of the past. Most do not remain in Asgard and choose to ascend to be with their families. You'll see today when you reap your first. Talk to them. You will soon find they are nothing like the others you have seen.'

'But what if I don't want to?'

'You are a Valkyrie. Reaping is what we are born to do. You have no choice – it is your destiny.'

Freya looked at her sister and sighed. Maya was beautiful. All four of her sisters were, but Maya was the most enchanting. She was tall and lean with long flaxen hair. The skin on her sculpted face was unblemished and she had the palest pearl-grey eyes in all of Asgard. Her

6

wings were fine-boned with elegant white feathers lying neatly over each other. She was everything a Valkyrie should be, which was why most of the reaped warriors fell instantly in love with her.

Compared to Maya, Freya, the youngest of the five sisters, felt like a plough horse. She wasn't as tall, beautiful or graceful. Her wings were large and stocky. Their raven-black feathers always looked as if they could use a good grooming. Instead of pearl-grey eyes, Freya's were dark blue. And although she was the fastest flyer in Asgard, it was always Maya who attracted attention.

But for all their differences, Freya adored her older sister. Many times Freya had watched Maya with envy as she confidently approached the battlefields. Without a trace of hesitation, she reaped the warriors she was assigned to and escorted them back to Valhalla.

'Don't you ever question what we do?'

Maya shook her head. 'We do as we are intended to do. As Odin tells us to.'

'And if we don't want to do it?'

Maya put her hands on her hips and tilted her head to the side. 'Sometimes I wonder if you are even my sister. How can you not want to be a Valkyrie?'

Sitting on her shoulder, Orus whispered in her ear. 'Stop arguing. Maya cannot understand. Don't condemn her for that.'

Freya looked into the dark eyes of the raven on her shoulder. Orus was right. No one in Asgard could understand how she felt. At times *she* didn't even understand it.

'I'm sorry,' she said finally. 'I guess I'm nervous for today.'

Maya nodded and combed her fine fingers through Freya's wild, unkempt hair. 'I understand. Now come, let's get you prepared for the ceremony – before Odin sends out a Dark Searcher to find us.'

Freya and Orus followed Maya and her raven back to Valhalla. Beneath them, the Great Heavenly Hall was being prepared for her First Day Ceremony. This was to be the final ceremony for some time as there were no Valkyries younger than Freya. Everyone in Asgard wanted this ceremony to be the best ever – everyone except Freya.

In the fields surrounding Valhalla, the reaped warriors who had chosen to remain in Asgard did what they were always doing. Fighting. The clanging sounds of sword upon sword rose up in the air as fighters spent all day battling against each other until night fell. Then they would enter Valhalla and drink and sing – preparing for the next day's battle.

To Freya, it all seemed so pointless. There were so

many other things to see and do. Why these warriors should choose to fight, day in, day out, was something she couldn't comprehend.

They veered away from Valhalla and flew over the beautiful buildings that made up the main city of Asgard and back to their home. It was a magnificent mansion standing alone on a hill, surrounded by gardens that turned into dense forests.

The Valkyries lived in the most extravagant palaces, and as Freya's mother was Senior Valkyrie, she had the biggest, most opulent – second only in size and beauty to Odin's palace.

Landing on the main balcony, they found their mother pacing the large reception room. Shields and weapons of battles throughout the ages adorned the walls and the floor was lined with sheepskin rugs.

Their mother was dressed in her shining silver armour. The feathers on her wings were groomed and bejewelled and her ceremonial dagger was at her waist. Her winged helmet was cast on a chair.

'Freya!' she shouted as she charged over. Her ice-blue eyes blazed and her white wings were half open in fury. 'Where have you been? Do you realize the time? You will be late for your own First Day Ceremony! Odin will be in a rage.'

'Mother, it's all right,' Maya said calmly. 'Freya and

Orus went out for a quick flight and lost track of time. Odin need never know. If you tell him we're on our way, we'll be there shortly.'

'It will take an age to get her prepared,' her mother ranted. 'Just look at the state of her, she's filthy!' She snatched up a comb and tried to drag it through Freya's tangled blonde hair. Just look at the state of your feathers! I'm amazed you can even fly . . .'

'Mother, please,' Freya begged. She caught the comb as her mother pulled it through a large knot. 'I can do this. Just give me a bit of time.'

'Of all my children, you have always given me the most trouble. Your sisters were dressed and ready to leave at sun-up. They've already gone to Valhalla to join the honour guard. Don't you realize how important this is? You are my youngest child and the last Valkyrie. Today, finally, you will join us in the reaping. It is a great honour.'

Freya opened her mouth to protest, but her sister cut in. 'Of course Freya understands how important it is. We all do. Just give us a moment to prepare and we'll meet you at the entrance to Valhalla.'

Her mother seemed unconvinced, but nodded as she reached for her winged helmet. 'Just don't keep Odin waiting long. You know how impatient he can be.' Without a backward glance she crossed to the balcony, opened her wings and leaped off.

'Remember to bow when you approach Odin,' Orus warned. Well preened, he sat on Freya's shoulder as they prepared to leave for Valhalla.

Freya nodded her head nervously. 'I'll remember.'

Maya put the finishing touches to Freya's gold and white gown as she flitted around her. 'And try not to yawn when he gives his speech.'

'I'll try. But why does he always have to talk for so long?'

Orus leaned closer to her ear. 'To hear himself speak!' The raven started to laugh and caw at his insult to the leader of Asgard.

'Don't let Odin hear you say that,' Maya warned, swatting at him. 'Orus, you should show more respect – like my Grul.' Maya reached up and stroked the raven at her shoulder.

'Don't try to educate Orus, Maya,' Grul teased. 'He's too thick to learn anything.'

'Who are you calling thick?' Orus challenged, cawing loudly and flapping his wings.

'You,' Grul answered.

As the two ravens cawed at each other, Maya held up her hand. 'Enough! When will you two finally get along?'

'Never!' the ravens said as one.

Freya reached up and stroked Orus's smooth black chest. 'Calm down. He's just trying to upset you before the ceremony.'

'He's doing a fine job of it,' Orus muttered. 'One of these days, Freya, I'm going to show that Grul just how clever I really am . . .'

Ignoring the bickering birds, Maya finished fastening a plain gold chain at her sister's neck. 'Oh, and try to look interested when Odin tells the story of Frigha.'

'Oh no, not again,' Freya moaned. 'Why does he keep telling us the same old story every time there is a First Day Ceremony? Surely, by now, we all know it.'

'He tells the story as a warning to all of us,' Maya said. 'So no one forgets what happened to the one Valkyrie who defied him and ran away from her duties in Asgard. You remember what happened to her?'

'How could I forget? Odin had to summon a Dark Searcher to find her. Then he let loose the Midgard Serpent to punish those who helped hide her from him. Half the Earth was destroyed in his rage.'

'Yes,' Maya said. 'And then he cut off her wings and took out her eyes before he banished the Valkyrie from Asgard for all time. She was left to wander the World of Man – blind, alone and flightless. To lose our wings is a fate worse than death.'

'I know the story,' Freya said tiredly. 'You don't have to remind me.'

'I'm just saying that Odin will repeat it. You must show him respect and try not to look too bored.'

'I'll try.' Freya inhaled deeply. 'So how do I look?'

Maya took a step back and surveyed her work. 'You look beautiful. Not even Mother could find fault.'

Freya grinned and opened her dark wings. Her sister had applied fragrant oils to the feathers that had them shining brightly. In the full sunlight, the black feathers shone with rainbow iridescence.

Freya looked to Orus. 'Well, what do you think?'

'You'll do,' the raven said casually. He gave her a playful nip on the ear with his polished long beak. 'Just as long as they don't look too closely at your fingernails.' He cawed in laughter and flew off her shoulder towards the balcony. 'Now, hurry up before they start the ceremony without us!'

Valhalla had been dressed for the ceremony in the most beautiful flowers that grew in Asgard. The high walls had been scrubbed, the spires that rose high into the air all flew the flag of the Valkyries and the weapons adorning the doors had been cleaned and polished. All the grounds surrounding the hall had been groomed. There wasn't a thing out of place.

Outside the Great Hall, the slain warriors stopped fighting and gathered together along either side of the entrance to greet Freya. As she approached, they all bowed their heads.

'See, they're not so bad,' Maya whispered as she smiled radiantly at the gathered warriors.

Freya wasn't convinced. 'Just you wait. The moment we're inside, they'll go back to slaughtering each other in the name of amusement.'

Maya sighed. 'That is the afterlife they have chosen. Why must you condemn them for that?'

'Because it's foolish.'

'It is their choice,' Maya insisted.

Their mother appeared at the entrance. 'You're late,' she chastised. 'Everyone is waiting.'

'I'm sorry, Mother,' Maya said. 'But doesn't Freya look beautiful?'

Her mother was much like Maya. Tall, elegant and beautiful. 'Yes she does,' she admitted. She embraced Freya warmly.

'You are my youngest child and I am proud to welcome you into the sisterhood of the Valkyries. Come, my daughter, come and take your rightful place among us.'

Freya stood directly behind her mother, while Maya took position behind her. As they approached the wide doors of Valhalla, Maya donned her winged helmet and then placed a reassuring hand on her shoulder. 'I'm right behind you, Freya. Always.'

Grateful for her sister's presence, Freya reached up and gave Orus a stroke on the chest. 'Well, this is it.'

'Good luck,' the raven whispered. 'You'll do fine.'

As her mother led her into Valhalla, Freya felt the eyes of Asgard resting upon her. Lining the aisle leading up to Odin were all the other Valkyries. They were dressed in their full armour and wearing their winged helmets. Their wings were open in salute as they raised their swords high in the air.

Freya knew them all by name, but there were none among them that she could call friend. She was the youngest and the last in the long line of Valkyries. But this wasn't what made her different. For reasons no one understood, Freya was the first Valkyrie born with solid black feathers, as opposed to the white or grey wings of the other Valkyries. This difference made her stand out and was the subject of much talk and rumour. At times, she felt almost as if they resented her and didn't trust her. Her mother had always said that her father was a powerful warrior of dark hair and piercing black eyes. She had been told that he remained in Asgard and was one of the warriors fighting outside Valhalla. But her mother had never pointed him out.

When she was younger she would walk among the warriors and wonder if she could find him. But as time passed and she saw how brutal they could be, she lost interest. Besides, she reasoned, he could have come forward to find her. He knew her mother – surely if he wanted to meet her he could. So if he wasn't interested, why should she waste her time trying to find him?

The blasting of horns pulled Freya from her thoughts. Everyone in the huge hall stood to attention. As Freya followed her mother down the long aisle, she walked past her three sisters at the front. Their swords were held high, their armour shone and their extended wings glistened as they all smiled proudly at her.

Finally, Odin appeared with his family on a tall dais at the front of the hall and took a position to receive her. Following close at his heels were Odin's two pet wolves, Geri and Freki. At Odin's command, they sat and panted softly.

Freya's mother bowed before the leader of Asgard, stepped to the left and knelt down. Freya followed suit and knelt before Odin. Her sister bowed and then knelt on Freya's right.

'Rise!' commanded Odin.

Freya rose and stood before the imposing leader. She felt awed in his presence. Odin was a terrifying sight in his full, well-used battle armour. His wild red hair spilled out from under his large horned helmet and his red beard grew long and thick, down to his waist. His left eye socket was covered with a gold patch. It was rumoured that he had sacrificed his eye in pursuit of wisdom, but Freya didn't know if this was true or not. In his bare arms he carried his famous spear, Gungnir.

Freya had never been this close to Odin before and the sight of him petrified her. All the wild stories told about him and his strength and battle prowess now seemed possible as she stood before him.

Standing behind Odin was his wife, Frigg. She too was dressed in her golden battle armour and in her hands was the new silver breastplate that was to be given to Freya. Her long blonde hair was neatly styled in two bejewelled braids that almost reached down to her fur-lined boots. It was said she was the most beautiful woman in Asgard. Up close, Freya could see it was true. The only one who could ever rival her beauty was Freya's own sister, Maya.

Beside Frigg was Thor. He was the spitting image of his father, Odin, except for the colour of his hair. Thor's hair was long and blond; only his beard showed a trace of his father's red. Thor stood stone-faced and unmoving as his blue eyes bored into her. He was clutching his hammer, Mjölnir, in one hand and holding a newly crafted winged helmet in the other.

It was said that Thor didn't have a lot of time for the Valkyries and, by the dark expression on his face, Freya could see that this was true. What caused the animosity remained a mystery. But for as long as she had lived, Freya had done her best to avoid him and his sharp tongue.

Standing back against the wall behind the dais was Loki, the trickster and unrelated blood-brother to Odin. Unlike the other men of Asgard, he wasn't strongly built, nor did he wear armour or carry a weapon. He had long dark-brown hair and sparkling, mischievous eyes. Freya knew even less about him than she did Thor. Only that, for reasons untold, Odin tolerated his presence in Asgard despite all the trouble he liked to cause. Her mother said he was dangerous and was always warning Freya to stay away from him.

As he caught her eye, he gave her a charming grin and bowed elegantly.

Odin cleared his throat loudly to ensure he had everyone's attention. 'Welcome to this final First Day Ceremony.' He dropped his eyes and they landed directly on Freya.

'Freya, today you are the last to join your sisters in the reaping. This is a sombre occasion indeed, filled with reverence for a time-honoured tradition assigned only to the Valkyries. It falls upon you to bring only the best of the slain to me, here at Valhalla. They have earned their place among the glorious dead and share in the celebration of battle . . .'

Freya stood before Odin, trying her best to stay focused and listen to every word of his long speech, but as the moments passed it was becoming harder and harder.

To her, there was no glory in being a warrior killed in battle. It was wasteful. Where were art, music and all the other parts that made up a life? Maya kept insisting there was more to the World of Man than just fighting. But if that was so, why did Odin revere it as he did?

As her eyes drifted around the Great Hall, she saw how everyone hung on Odin's every word. How they murmured in agreement as he spoke of the glorious dead and of battles fought and won. Looking at the masses of people surrounding her, Freya had never felt more alone.

Why was she so different?

Why couldn't she feel the same way everyone else did?

A sharp nip at her ear brought her out of her reverie. She stole a quick look at Orus on her shoulder. 'Freya, stop daydreaming!' he warned softly. 'Prepare to swear your oath.'

With a quick nod, Freya turned her attention back to

Odin. She hadn't been aware of his speech and suddenly realized he was now deep into telling the story of Frigha, the runaway Valkyrie.

'It gave me no joy to blind and de-wing her,' he was saying. 'Finally she was banished from her home in Asgard. To this day, she wanders the Earth alone, lost in her shame and betrayal . . .'

On and on Odin droned, giving warning to all Valkyries that once they swear the oath, they are bound to their duties. Freya wondered if he ever stopped talking long enough to actually breathe.

Finally he offered her his large hand. 'Come forward, Freya,' he commanded.

'Go on,' Orus ordered into her ear. 'This is it!'

Freya nervously took hold of Odin's outstretched hand and stepped up on to the dais. 'Kneel, child.'

Freya opened her wings wide enough to allow her to kneel before the leader of Asgard as Odin placed a hand on the top of her head. 'Freya, do you swear to carry out your duties to the best of your abilities?'

'Say "I swear",' Orus whispered softly in her ear.

'I swear,' Freya repeated sombrely.

'Do you swear allegiance to the sisterhood of the Valkyries and promise to fulfill your obligations as one of the favoured?'

'I swear.'

'Do you swear your allegiance to me to do my bidding according to the laws of the Valkyries – bringing only the best of the best warriors to my Great Heavenly Hall, Valhalla, and leaving the others to Azrael and his Angels of Death?'

Freya hesitated. This was the one order she knew was going to be hardest to follow. Who were they to decide who was worthy or not? How could she be expected to judge someone? It was all so unfair.

'Say "I swear"!' Orus whispered. 'Freya, swear it!'

Freya could hear the sharp intake of breath from the others behind her as she hesitated.

'Answer me,' Odin commanded. 'Do you swear?'

It went against everything Freya believed, but with the pressure of her mother beside her and all of Asgard gathered behind her, Freya finally nodded. 'I swear.'

She could hear her mother release her held breath.

Odin inhaled deeply before continuing. 'Do you understand your position as Valkyrie? That you possess the power to keep the Angels of Death at bay and with a word can command them away from the battlefield. They resent this ranking, but accept it. Do you?'

'I understand and accept,' Freya said.

'Then it is by my order that I command you to arise, Valkyrie. Rise and receive your armour and sword.'

Freya climbed to her feet as Odin took her hand. He

drew her back to his wife, Frigg.

Frigg raised the new silver armour. 'By this breastplate, I give you the power of wisdom in choosing the best slain for Valhalla. May it guide you and protect you always. I welcome you, young Valkyrie.'

'Lift your arms and open your wings,' Orus softly instructed.

Freya felt as if she was in a dream as she lifted her arms and opened her wings fully. Frigg approached and placed the silver breastplate into position on her chest. The heavy armour fell down past her waist. She had never been measured for it yet, somehow, it fit the lines of her body perfectly. The leather straps were then fed around her body and under the wings at her back to be fastened at her right side.

With her breastplate in position, Frigg kissed Freya lightly on the forehead and took several steps back.

Next, Thor came forward. He put his hammer down as he lifted the silver winged helmet high above Freya's head.

'With this helmet, I grant you speed and stealth. No human eyes will rest upon you as long as you wear it. Only the dead and dying may see you as you truly are. Take this helmet and protect it. With it lies your power of secrecy.' He paused and his blue eyes threatened. 'But be warned. Never allow a living human to wear your helmet. To do so will cause the helmet great suffering and its cries will be heard in all Asgard.'

Thor took a step closer and put the silver winged helmet on Freya's head. When it was in place, Freya felt everything change. She became dizzy and light-headed. The world around her drained of colour, as though she was gazing through a dense fog. Maya always said it was harder to see with her helmet on. Freya now understood what she meant. Though the helmet made her invisible and part of the ethereal realm, it had a cost. That cost was her clear, colour-filled vision.

She felt herself starting to fall. Thor's strong arms went fast around her.

'Steady . . .' he said. 'It takes a moment to adjust.'

Freya recovered, but still felt very strange, almost as if she weighed nothing. Distracted by the strange sensations coursing through her body, Freya was unaware of the silver gauntlets being drawn up her arms or the heavily jewelled dagger being placed at her waist.

When she was fully dressed in the armour of the Valkyrie, Odin came forward again. In his hand he carried a newly forged sword. Her sword.

Freya had seen Odin perform this part of the ceremony many times, and had watched her sisters going through it. But now that it was her turn, her fear returned.

Odin lowered the sword until the tip was resting

halfway down her gown, just above her knees. He reached forward and pierced the fine fabric with the sharp tip. Then, as Freya stood perfectly still, he used the sword to cut away the lower length of the gown all the way around her body.

When he finished, the jagged edge of fabric rested against her thighs as the lower half of her beautiful gown lay on the floor in ruins. Looking down at herself, she knew this signalled the end of the life she had known. She was turning fourteen. It meant she was no longer a child, or a girl or even a young woman. She was now . . .

Valkyrie.

CHAPTER TWO

The rest of the ceremony proceeded in a kind of blur. Freya was given gifts and her first taste of mead – the strong drink of Valhalla. It was what all the fallen warriors drank and most nights left them unconscious on the floor of the Great Hall.

Freya couldn't see what all the fuss was about. Mead was bitter and left an awful taste in her mouth which no amount of water could wash away. She much preferred the fruit drinks that she was used to.

When the formal celebration ended, Freya waited outside Valhalla to prepare to join her sisters on her first reap. Everyone else retired to their homes or back to the battlefield to join in the fighting of the slain warriors. Freya watched them taking up their arms and cheer as they entered the fight. She sighed heavily. Would she ever understand it all?

Lost in thought, Freya didn't hear her mother approach until the clopping of horses' hooves was almost upon her. She turned to see her mother standing with a stunning, winged chestnut mare.

Every Valkyrie had a horse to ride to the battlefields. These special Reaping Mares were used to transport the valiant dead over the Rainbow Bridge to Asgard and Valhalla. This was the only part of the First Day Ceremony that Freya had been excited about. She loved the Reaping Mares and spent a lot of time in the stables, brushing their rich manes and grooming their feathers.

'Freya,' her mother started as she handed over the leather reins to the mare, 'this is Sylt. She is to be your Reaping Mare.'

Freya's heart thudded with excitement as she approached the tall mare. 'She's beautiful. Is she really mine?'

Her mother nodded. 'I chose her especially for you. Look at the feathers under her wings.'

Freya stroked the smooth neck of the mare and approached one of the heavy chestnut wings folded neatly on her back. Lifting it, she was shocked to find black feathers instead of brown.

'Black?'

Her mother smiled. 'Sylt is as unique to Asgard as you are, my child. Treat her well and she will serve you for all time.'

'Sylt,' Freya repeated. 'Hello, Sylt, we are going to be the best of friends.'

The mare's rich brown eyes followed Freya as she moved back to her head. As she stroked her head, Sylt nickered softly.

'Thank you, Mother. She really is beautiful.'

'Hey, what about me?' Orus complained as he flapped his wings and nipped her ear.

Freya couldn't help but smile. 'Orus, are you jealous?'

'Of that great big thing?' he blustered. 'Of course not! But I didn't spend all morning trying to look nice for your ceremony, just to be ignored because of this beast.'

Freya reached up and pulled Orus off her shoulder. She gave the raven a hug that nearly squeezed the life out of him before kissing the top of his feathered head. 'Orus, you know you will always be my first love. All I was saying is that Sylt is beautiful. And she is, isn't she?'

'She is just a horse, Freya,' he said indignantly as he wiggled free of her grip. Getting back to her shoulder, he ruffled his feathers into place again. 'There are hundreds of them in the stables.'

'Yes there are. But Sylt is unique and that makes her even more beautiful. And now she's all ours.'

'Oh, joy,' the raven complained.

Freya's oldest sister, Gwyn, approached. She was putting her sword back in its sheath and adjusting her gauntlets. 'Honestly, Freya, why you put up with that ill-tempered bird is beyond me. You should have chosen a better companion, like my own bird, Gondul.' Gwyn raised her arm in the air and a black raven soared down and landed neatly on it. It crawled up to her shoulder and settled there.

'See what I mean? Gondul loves me and would never nip my ear.'

'Perhaps,' Orus agreed. 'But Gondul doesn't have enough sense to come in from the rain. He's hardly companion material, if you ask me.'

'I didn't ask you!' Gwyn stuck her tongue out at Orus before focusing on Freya. 'Are you ready for your first reaping?'

The smile dropped from Freya's face as she was reminded of the horse's purpose and her dark mission. To bring dead warriors back to Valhalla.

Maya came up behind her, dressed in her silver armour and helmet. She had a big grin on her face. 'Of course she's ready. She's been looking forward to this for ages.'

Freya managed a strained smile as Maya put her arm around her and whispered, 'It won't be so bad. I promise. Just stay with me and do what I do. It won't be a big reaping today, just a few soldiers.'

'*One* soldier is too many,' Freya muttered softly.

Maya looked at her and shook her head. 'Just talk to

your soldier. Let him show you they aren't all bad. Now, mount up – it's time to go.'

As it was Freya's first mission, she took a position directly behind her mother's massive pearl-grey Reaping Mare. Freya was riding Sylt as they made their way to Bifröst, the Rainbow Bridge, which linked Asgard to the World of Man. Even with their wings, the Valkyrie and Reaping Mares could not leave Asgard any other way. The bridge was the only route in and out.

Maya rode her own Reaping Mare behind Freya and her three other sisters followed further back. As they approached Bifröst, the bridge's Watchman stepped forward and held up his heavy sword. He was massive in size and immensely powerful, with a head of bushy blond hair and a moustache that went down to his belly. It was said that Heimdall's hearing was so keen he could hear grass grow and his vision so accurate he could see across all of Asgard both day and night. And if Heimdall didn't want you to cross the bridge, there was little you could do to get past him.

'State your purpose,' he said formally.

'Greetings, Heimdall,' her mother responded with equal formality as she bowed her head to the Watchman. 'We come in the service of Odin. It is Freya's First Day and we journey to the reaping.'

'Be welcome and journey well,' Heimdall said as he bowed and swept his sword wide to invite them on to the bridge.

As Freya directed Sylt past Heimdall, he winked at her. 'Good luck, child.'

Freya really liked Heimdall. Often times when she was feeling particularly lost or restless, she would fly to Bifröst and Heimdall would let her go halfway across the bridge to peer down into the World of Man. He wasn't big on conversation, but that was another thing she liked about him. Sometimes they would walk out together and he would stand with her. Silent and unmoving. She often felt that Heimdall was as lonely as she was and understood all that she felt.

Bifröst was the longest bridge in Asgard and was aptly named the Rainbow Bridge. It shimmered and glistened in the many colours of the rainbow. The brightest colours were the flaming reds and oranges. From a distance, their brilliance gave the bridge the illusion of being on fire.

Once they crossed to the other side, Freya's mother commanded her mare to fly. Almost immediately, her mother started to howl with a sound unique to their kind. It preceded their arrival to the battlefields.

Freya joined in the howling as she, her mother and sisters soared high in the sky over a rocky, golden desert. A tall mountain range loomed in the distance and the sun was starting to descend behind it, casting long shadows on the ground. As Freya gazed down, she saw very little growing on the dry, dusty earth.

A shiver started down her back at the sight of smoke rising in the air. The howling of her sisters grew louder and more intense, letting her know they had arrived at the appointed place of reaping.

Down below, three military trucks in a long convoy had been blown off the road and knocked to the side. The vehicle at the end was burning brightly, while the two in front smouldered and threatened to explode. Men were pouring out of the trucks and running back to help the soldiers in the flipped trucks.

Near the damaged vehicles, others arrived from the sky. These were the Angels of Death who would take the dying soldiers not chosen by the Valkyries. They landed on the ground and folded their wings to wait for the choosing to finish.

The Reaping Mares all landed together several metres from the burning trucks. Freya climbed off Sylt and handed the reins to her oldest sister. As long as one of them touched the reins whilst wearing their helmet, the mares remained as invisible as the Valkyries.

'Are you ready?' Maya asked, coming up to her.

'She is,' Orus answered from Freya's shoulder. 'Aren't you?'

Freya felt like there was a fist in her throat. She couldn't swallow and could barely breathe. She nodded.

'Ours is the last vehicle, the one on fire. There are two soldiers in there, waiting for us. Most of the others within it are destined to survive, so be extra careful not to touch them. But there are three others who will die and are to be taken by *them*.' Maya indicated the Angels of Death.

As Freya looked at the closest angel, he bowed his head in respect to her. Freya returned the bow.

'You'll know who your warrior is when we enter,' Maya finished.

'I understand.' Somehow Freya already knew who she was meant to reap. She could feel him calling to her. There was something about him – something good and very brave. He had lived a decent life and, though he lay dying, he felt no fear. She knew they were destined to meet. In all the other times she'd been to battlefields, she'd never felt this before. She couldn't deny his call.

'Remember,' Maya said. 'As long as you wear your armour, the flames can't touch you, even if the truck explodes. We'll just go in and reap the soldiers.'

Freya took a deep breath.

'You'll be fine,' Orus said at her shoulder. 'I'm right

here with you.'

'Thanks, Orus,' Freya said as she followed her sister.

The sound of shouting and crying filled the air and the acrid smell of burning stung Freya's nostrils. Several men in camouflage fatigues rushed past her, brushing against her wings. If they felt her there, they gave no indication. They ran into the back of the truck and started to pull out survivors.

'Freya, come,' Maya called. 'Ignore them, we have work to do. The longer we delay, the more our warriors will suffer.'

Close behind her sister, Freya climbed into the back of the overturned truck. She crawled past the men struggling to get at survivors, being careful not to touch anyone as she headed towards the front of the vehicle.

The flames hadn't reached the inside yet, but the smoke had. It was thick and choking. As the seconds ticked, the heat was increasing. The sight of the moaning soldiers around her made Freya all the more resentful towards humans. How could they do this to each other?

To her right she saw a female soldier with blood on her face and hair and her arm was obviously broken, but Freya could feel she was meant to live.

'Over here,' Maya called.

Up ahead, two men lay near each other. Maya was before one of them. He was covered in blood and appeared already dead. But as Maya knelt down beside him, he opened his eyes.

'Do not fear me, brave warrior,' Maya said gently. 'I am here to bring you home.'

As she had done thousands of times before, Maya leaned forward and stroked the cheek of the soldier with her bare hand. 'Come with me now. Leave this world of suffering behind you.'

The soldier actually thanked Maya as she touched him. His eyes closed and he died. Freya could see his spirit rise from his broken body, looking just the same as he had in life. He grinned and took Maya's outstretched hand. Together they moved towards the opening of the truck.

'Have you come for me? Am I going to die?'

Freya looked down at the face of the soldier who had spoken. He was the one she was to reap. His dark skin was covered in beads of sweat. A crimson stain was spreading on his shirt.

'Yes,' Freya said. 'I am here to end your suffering.'

'You can't,' the soldier's voice rose, desperate. 'I can't die.'

Freya had heard warriors beg many times before. They would try anything to stop their death. They would plead, try to bargain or even fight. But in the end the Valkyries always succeeded.

'Please don't be afraid, warrior,' Freya said gently.

'I'm not frightened for myself,' the soldier said. 'But my family . . .' He gasped as he tried to catch his breath. 'Who will look after them? My wife . . . my girls?'

For the first time, Freya noticed the soldier was clutching something in his hand. It was his mobile phone. She had seen other soldiers with them before, but had never seen one up close. With fading strength, he lifted it to show to Freya.

'Here,' he managed to pant. 'I can't leave them.'

Freya crept closer and gazed at a photograph displayed on the mobile phone. It was the image of a dark-skinned girl, not much younger than her, holding a baby. Her face was beaming with joy.

'That's my Tamika and her new baby sister, Uniik,' the soldier said proudly, with a sudden surge of strength. 'I've never even held her. I was supposed to go on leave next week . . .' The soldier started to cough and shiver but managed to recover himself as he focused on Freya.

'Please, I must live to see my baby. I need to know they will be all right.'

He coughed again and struggled to breathe, as though his chest was filled with water. 'I'm begging you,' he gasped. 'My wife says they are in trouble. I must go back . . .'

Freya was almost too shocked to speak. This soldier

was fighting to live. Not for himself, but for his family. He was nothing like the warriors at Valhalla. As he lay dying, his only thoughts were for his family.

'I am so sorry,' Freya said softly. 'There is nothing I can do. I must bring you back with me. It is your destiny. Your time on Earth has ended.'

'What's your name?' the soldier rasped. 'I'm Tyrone Johnson.'

'I—'

'Freya, no!' Orus warned. 'You know you can't give him your name while he lives. You must wait until he is dead!'

'Tyrone,' Freya said softly. 'It is time for you to go. I am sure your family will be fine.'

'How can you be sure?' He fought to get each word out. 'Does being the Angel of Death give you insight into the living?'

'I'm not an Angel of Death,' Freya said. 'I'm a Valkyrie, chooser of the slain. I am here to take you to Valhalla. You have earned your place among the valiant dead.'

His eyes were fading with each passing moment. 'It's not valiant to die in a landmine explosion,' he coughed.

'But your heart is valiant, I can see that. You must be rewarded.'

'I don't need rewards,' he struggled. 'I need to protect

my family. Please—' He began coughing again and fought to catch his breath. Death was very near.

From the back of the truck came Maya's urgent voice. 'Freya, hurry! You must take him. Mother is waiting. Just touch him with your bare skin and bring him home.'

Freya looked back at the soldier. 'I am sorry. I cannot leave you here. It is your time. Odin commands me to bring you.'

Tyrone coughed harder and blood pooled at the corners of his mouth.

'You are suffering,' she continued. 'Let me end it for you.'

As Freya reached to touch the soldier's cheek, his gloved hands caught hold of hers. He placed his phone in her hand and closed her fingers around it. 'Take this . . . They are in danger . . . I can't die until they are safe . . .'

He started to choke, but then stopped abruptly and his eyes closed. Whether she reaped him or not would not change the final outcome.

'Do it now,' Orus said softly. 'You must take him.'

Still clutching his phone, Freya did as she was born to do. She reached out her hand and gently stroked his warm cheek. 'Come with me, Tyrone. Let me free you from your suffering . . .'

CHAPTER THREE

Tyrone Johnson was the first soldier to be reaped by Freya the Valkyrie. With his body left behind in the burning truck, he took Freya's hand and followed her to Sylt. He paused briefly to gaze back at the friends he was leaving behind. But then he did as Freya instructed and climbed up on to the Reaping Mare to start the journey to Valhalla.

When they reached Asgard, Freya spent several days with him, showing him all the things he could be part of. From the daily battles at Valhalla to the feasting, drinking, singing and dancing with the Valkyries late into the night.

But as the time passed, the soldier wanted none of it. He begged her to take him back to his family, insisting they needed him. He showed her how to use his phone to look at photographs. He told her of his life in Chicago and the pride he felt in serving his country to protect his family.

Tyrone could find no peace in Asgard. Fighting all

day and drinking all night was not what he wanted. He never gloried in battle and didn't want to kill. To stay would be torture, not paradise.

Knowing he was unhappy, Freya finally escorted him to the Gates of Ascension. Through these, soldiers could leave Asgard to go to the afterlife where those who hadn't died valiantly in battle were taken by the Angels of Death.

Standing before the gates, he turned towards her one last time. 'Forgive me for not staying,' he said softly. 'But this place isn't for me. I must find a way back to my family. I need to know what's happening.'

'When you pass through those gates, you will not be allowed back to the World of Man. Your time there is done.'

'But my family is in danger!'

Freya dropped her head. 'I'm sorry, but you cannot help them now.'

'If I can't go back, will you?' he asked desperately. 'Go to Chicago. Find my family. Protect them, somehow. Do whatever you must, but get them away from the danger.'

'I can't,' Freya insisted. 'My duties are here.'

'Please, just think about it,' Tyrone pressed. 'How can I ever find peace if I don't know what is happening with them? All I know is that there is trouble.'

Seeing the desperation in his eyes, Freya didn't have

the heart to say no. 'I will try. I promise I'll do all I can to protect your family.' Freya regretted the words the moment they left her mouth. Had she really just made a promise she knew she couldn't possibly keep?

'What?' Orus cried hysterically. 'Tell me you didn't just say that!'

Tears of relief filled Tyrone's eyes. 'How can I ever thank you?'

'There is no need,' Freya said guiltily. 'Just find your peace.'

Freya had never been through the Gates of Ascension. As a Valkyrie, she was not allowed. But watching Tyrone Johnson's radiant face as he passed through the gates and saw what lay on the other side, suddenly she envied him.

She also realized she would miss him. He was the first human she'd ever spent time with and she'd discovered he was nothing like she'd imagined. He was gentle and caring. Freya never knew her father, but the more time she spent with Tyrone Johnson, the more she wished he could have been hers.

'I told you so,' Maya said softly, coming up to her at the gates right after Tyrone ascended. 'The soldiers of today are nothing like the warriors of old. Most of them don't want to stay. We aren't needed like we used to be. There are actually too many Valkyries now, even though wars on Earth continue.'

Freya sighed. 'I feel so bad for his family. They'll never know how much he loved them.' She pulled the phone from her pocket. 'Here, look at his children.'

'Freya, no!' Maya cried in alarm. 'You can't have that here!'

'It's all right. Tyrone gave it to me.'

Fear was in Maya's eyes. 'Get rid of it right now. Throw it off Bifröst. You know it's forbidden. If Odin finds that you've brought something back from a reap, he'll have your wings!'

But Tyrone gave this to me. I didn't steal it.'

'It doesn't matter how you acquired it. We can't have anything from Earth here.'

'Why?' Freya asked.

Maya shook her head. 'I don't know. All I do know is that as long as it's here, you are in grave danger. Please, let's fly to Bifröst right now and throw it off together.'

Freya hid the phone in her pocket and shook her head. 'No, Tyrone gave it to me. It's all I have left from him. I'm keeping it.'

'Orus, talk to her,' Maya said to the raven. 'Tell her what will happen if she's caught with it.'

'I've tried,' Orus said. 'But she won't listen to me.'

'It was a gift,' Freya insisted. 'I am not throwing it away.'

Maya threw up her arms in frustration and her wings

41

fluttered in annoyance. 'You are going to be the death of me!' As she stormed off, she turned back to Freya. 'Just keep it hidden.'

Freya watched her sister go. Once again, she was overcome with emptiness. While Tyrone was with her, the feeling had stopped. Now it was back – even stronger.

'What's wrong with me, Orus? Why am I so unhappy? Why can't I be satisfied like everyone else is here?'

The raven pressed closer to Freya's neck. 'You are lonely. You've never had friends your own age. You are the youngest in all Asgard. Even Maya is much older than you.'

'Then I am doomed,' Freya said. 'There will be no more Valkyries after me. I am cursed to be alone forever.'

'That's not true. You have me.'

Freya smiled sadly at the raven. 'You know what I mean. There will never be anyone here my age.'

'You could give a soldier your name before he dies. Then when you reap him he will have to stay with you forever.'

Freya shook her head. She knew the rules. If she had told Tyrone Johnson her name before he died, he would have belonged to her and would not have been allowed to ascend. He would have become her prisoner. Just like her father was to her mother and all the fathers to all the Valkyrie. This wasn't the way she wanted to find friendship.

'I'll never give my name away. It's not fair. Especially if soldiers wish to ascend. It would be too cruel. I will only give my name away to someone who really wants to stay with me. But that will never happen . . .'

She pulled the phone from her pocket and stared wistfully at the photograph of Tyrone's daughters. 'Do you think Tamika is like her father? Would we be friends if we met?'

'What are you saying?' Orus said cautiously. 'Your voice sounds strange. You're not *really* considering going to help Tyrone's family, are you?'

'She is saying exactly that. She wants to go to Chicago to meet her soldier's daughter.'

Freya jumped at the voice behind her. She turned and saw a beaming face. It was Loki – Odin's trickster blood-brother. 'I don't blame you. The World of Man can be a very exciting place. There is always a lot to see and do and there are millions of girls your own age. Boys too. Having human friends could be just the thing to ease your restlessness.'

Orus fluttered his black wings. 'Go away, Loki. This is a private conversation.'

'Is it?' Loki said, concentrating on Freya. 'I'm sorry if I'm intruding, but I just wanted to let you know some of the wonders I have seen on Earth.'

43

The raven cawed a warning. 'Move away from him, Freya. He's just telling you this to cause mischief. He wants to see you get into trouble with Odin.'

Loki placed his hand on his chest and his face was all innocence. 'You wound me! All I want is to help Freya end her loneliness.' He focused on Freya. 'I saw how troubled you looked at the First Day Ceremony and how you grieve over your soldier's ascension. I know you can find happiness on Earth.'

Orus cawed again. 'You know Earth is forbidden to the Valkyries except on reaping missions.' The raven nipped Freya's ear. 'Don't listen to him. He's trying to get you in trouble. Loki is jealous that your mother is in Odin's favour. He will do anything to discredit her. Her youngest daughter disobeying the rules would do just that!'

'Such lies.' Loki's dark eyes sparkled. 'I want only the best for young Freya and a trip to Earth could be just what she needs.'

Freya looked from Orus back to Loki. 'What is Earth like? I mean, the parts of Earth that aren't battlefields. Is it beautiful like Asgard?'

'More!' Loki said excitedly. 'I have seen things there you wouldn't believe. Animals beyond description and so many different people. It is a wonderland.'

'Loki isn't your friend,' Orus warned. 'He won't help

you. He'll just lead you into trouble.'

'Are you going to listen to a dumb bird?' Loki said teasingly. 'Or do you want my help? I can get you past Heimdall and across Bifröst. You can visit Earth for yourself and see that I am not lying. Then you can return without anyone knowing you were ever gone.'

Freya looked away from Loki's inviting eyes. He was a troublemaker, plain and simple. But what if he really did want to help? She had promised Tyrone she would protect his family. It would mean breaking her oath and sneaking across Bifröst. If she were to try, Loki might be the only one who could help.

'Freya, no!' Orus shouted in her ear. 'He is trying to lead you astray. Don't listen – fly away!'

Finally Freya shook her head. 'Thank you for the offer, Loki, but I can't. I took the oath. I am sworn to my duty here.'

Loki bowed. 'Of course. But do find me if you ever change your mind. I would hate to see you remain here so sad and lonely. I want only to help you.'

'Thank Odin!' the raven cawed loudly as they watched Loki walking away. 'You must stay away from him, Freya. He would lead you into harm and smile as he does it.'

It was several days before there was another reaping.

With so many Valkyries available to go, they took it in turns to reap. Freya remained in Asgard to groom the Reaping Mares and work in the stables. By the time she'd finished, her own mare, Sylt, had a gleaming coat and her wings were perfectly preened.

When the Valkyries returned, for the first time ever Freya took an interest in the warriors they brought back. She counted the soldiers who arrived and was surprised to see several women among the men. She tracked their movements throughout Asgard and watched all but one pass through the Gates of Ascension. The single remaining warrior joyously joined the others to fight and drink at Valhalla.

Maya had been right. The soldiers of this age had a different attitude to the warriors of the past. Seeing this difference only added to her sense of confusion. There was only one way to figure it out. Freya had to go to Earth.

CHAPTER FOUR

'**N**o!' Orus screamed in her ear. 'You can't go.'

'I must,' Freya said. 'It's all I've thought about since Tyrone ascended. His family is in danger. He begged me to help them. How can I refuse?'

'Because if Odin finds out, he'll tear off our wings, rip out your eyes and we'll be banished!'

'You don't have to come with me,' Freya said as she packed up a small bag to take with her. 'I won't be gone long. Just enough time to find out how his family are in danger, then I'll be back. No one will even notice I've gone.'

'Freya, listen to me,' Orus begged. 'That troublemaker Loki has fed you lies about Earth. It is filled with death, war and hatred. You have seen the battlefields for yourself. They are truly ugly. Stay here. Asgard is beautiful.'

'Yes, it is,' Freya agreed as she pulled on her new breastplate, drew the straps under her wings and secured the buckles at her side. Then she attached the jewelled dagger at her waist and put her sword in its scabbard. This she clipped to her hip guard. 'But I need to see Earth for myself. The *real* Earth, not just the battlefields.'

'That is all Earth is,' Orus cried. 'One big battlefield.'

'Then I will know, and won't want to return there,' she said as she placed the gauntlets on her arms.

The raven shook his head. 'Remember the story of Frigha. We will be banished.'

'I told you, you don't have to come,' Freya said as she reached for her winged helmet.

'I'm not leaving you, Freya. We have been together for too long. Even if it means I will be blinded, de-winged and banished with you.'

Freya smiled at her raven. 'Oh, Orus, it won't be that bad. You'll see. We'll be back before we're missed.'

They waited until darkness had fallen. Freya glided silently over the small stand of trees and bushes where she had arranged to meet Loki, checking to see if it was some kind of trick. She wasn't completely fooled by his smooth charms.

Not far ahead stood Bifröst. The bridge shimmered and glowed in all the glorious colours of the rainbow. Bifröst always looked more magnificent at night as its brilliance reached high into the dark sky. Her mother once told her that on Earth, the glow of the bridge could sometimes be seen at night and was called the Northern Lights.

When Freya first went to Loki to ask for help getting past Heimdall and across Bifröst, he told her to travel in her helmet and full battle armour. She thought she stood a better chance of getting across the bridge dressed normally or even in a dark cloak, but he insisted that she would need the invisibility her helmet offered and the protection of her armour. Freya began to believe Earth really was one big battlefield if she needed the protection of her armour.

'Can you see anything?' Freya called to Orus.

'YES!' the raven cawed. 'I can see this is a terrible idea. Let's go back now before it's too late.'

'You can go home if you want to, Orus, but I'm going to do this. I need to see what Earth is really like and I promised Tyrone. I won't break my promise.'

'Foolish child,' Orus said. 'If you insist on this insane course, I am coming with you. You need me to keep you safe.'

Freya smiled over at her raven. Despite what her sisters and mother said, Orus was the best companion she could ask for.

After circling the area, they landed several metres from the place they were to meet Loki. As Orus settled on her shoulder, Freya started to look around. Every nerve in her body was alive, every sound of the night added to the sense of mystery and adventure.

'Loki?' Freya called softly.

'Hush . . .' a voice from the bushes scolded. 'Do you want everyone in Asgard to hear you?'

Freya thought she had powerful senses. But she and Orus had walked right past Loki's hiding place with no idea he was there. It was said that stealth was one of his many special talents and it was true. 'Are you ready to go?' he asked as he stepped free of the bushes and approached her.

Freya nodded.

'Your mother and sisters?'

'They're dancing at Valhalla with the warriors. They won't be home until late.'

'Good. Now, I have a powerful sleeping powder that will stun Heimdall for no more than a moment. You must use that time to fly past him. Don't look back and don't hesitate. Just fly as fast as you can across the bridge.'

'You won't hurt him?'

Loki looked shocked. 'Are you mad? Thor couldn't hurt that thick-skulled rock with his hammer! Trust me, I have used this powder many times on him to get across Bifröst. He won't feel a thing and will have no memory of anything. But you must be quick. The effects don't last long.'

'What do I do?' Freya asked.

Orus whispered in her ear, 'Forget this crazy idea and go home!'

Swatting the raven, Freya concentrated on Loki. 'How will I know when to fly?'

'Get into the air, and soar above us. With those black wings of yours, it's next to impossible to see you in the sky. Watch for my signal. The moment I drop my arm, you soar past Heimdall and straight on to the bridge. Is that clear?'

Freya nodded as knots tied her stomach. 'How can I ever thank you?'

'You don't have to,' Loki said. 'Just go and find happiness. That's all that matters.'

On her shoulder, Orus made a gagging sound. 'Oh, I think I'm going to be sick!'

'Orus, stop!' Freya said. She looked sheepishly at Loki. 'I'm sorry. He thinks this is some kind of trick so you can discredit my mother.'

Loki looked innocently at the bird. 'Once again, you wound me. I want only the best for young Freya.'

Orus cawed in anger. 'What you want is a higher ranking with Odin by removing her mother from his favour. Freya may be blind to your tricks, Loki, but I am not. You will not succeed. I will protect her.'

Loki threw up his arms and turned to leave. 'Fine.

Let's forget it. Go back to Valhalla and watch the warriors get drunk. I don't care.'

'Loki, no, please don't go!' Freya ran to catch up with him. 'Orus doesn't trust you, but I do. Please, help me get across Bifröst. My soldier's family is in danger. I must help them.'

Loki paused and turned. 'I do this for you, Freya, not Orus. If you still wish to go to Earth, I will help you.' He gave a threatening glare at Orus.

'Yes,' Freya said. 'I want to go.'

'All right, I can be generous. Take to the sky and keep your eyes on me. The moment I raise and drop my arm, you fly at Bifröst as fast as your wings will carry you.'

Freya nodded. Before Orus could say more to endanger her mission, she opened her wings and jumped up into the sky. Gaining height, she soared in a tight circle, never taking her eyes off Loki.

On the ground, Loki trotted over to the Rainbow Bridge. Heimdall was at his usual position as guard. Freya often wondered what kind of life it was for the poor, lonely Watchman. He rarely slept and never left his post. But, like the others of Asgard, he served only Odin.

Heimdall's posture changed when Loki approached. No one in Asgard trusted him and always raised their guard when he was near. In fact, very few people even liked Loki. It was only Odin's generosity that allowed him to remain.

From her position in the sky, Freya could see that one of Loki's hands was behind his back.

As the Watchman stood before him, Loki brought his hand forward and blew a powder up into his face. Heimdall staggered back and collapsed to the ground. Loki dropped his arm, giving Freya the signal to move.

'This is it, Orus!' Freya called as she tilted her wings, changed direction and flew with all her might towards the entrance of Bifröst. Freya clutched the raven in her hands as she gained more speed.

In a flash she was passing over Heimdall and flying into the bright colours of the Rainbow Bridge. She did not slow as she reached the halfway point. Nor did she look back to see if Heimdall had noticed and was chasing after her. All she wanted, all she needed, was to get to Earth.

CHAPTER FIVE

Bifröst was a living bridge. Anyone who used it to reach Earth knew they could not control where it would send them or where they would arrive. In this case, when Freya flew free of the rainbow colours she discovered that she was soaring high above Europe. Like in Asgard, it was night.

As part of her training to be a Valkyrie, Freya had studied in detail the geography and history of all the countries of Earth, including their ever-changing borders. She was trained in warfare and knew details of every battle fought since the dawn of time. She herself, while growing up, had attended many of the battlefields to watch the Valkyries work.

Setting a course, she headed towards the United States. It had been a long time since she had been to this country. Soon they were soaring over a vast ocean.

'Are we there yet?' Orus panted. 'My wings are about to fall off.'

They had been flying all night to reach Chicago. Like

Orus, she was growing fatigued. But unlike him, her larger wingspan meant she could fly longer and further without tiring, than he could. She opened her arms. 'Here, let me carry you for a while.'

Orus gratefully flew into Freya's embrace. 'I wish Bifröst had taken us closer,' she said. 'We've lost time getting here.'

'Sometimes I think that bridge knows where we want to go and does its best to send us as far away from our destination as possible.'

Freya hugged the cynical raven. 'Did anyone ever tell you you have a dark streak?'

'You do,' Orus said. 'All the time.'

They continued in silence and entered daylight. Before long they approached the boundaries of the United States. Freya knew where Illinois was, and even Chicago. But she needed help finding Lincolnwood, the town just outside Chicago where Tyrone Johnson lived.

Flying high over farmland, the landscape beneath them soon changed. Autumn-coloured fields and trees with their falling leaves of blazing reds and oranges made way for incredibly tall buildings and heavily congested streets as Chicago loomed straight ahead.

Freya pulled in her wings and landed on one of the tallest buildings. Two white metal antennae rose high above her and the rooftop was cluttered with equipment and strangely shaped structures. But it offered the perfect place to hide while she got her bearings.

'Let's take a break for a moment while I try to figure out where we're going.'

She released Orus and removed her helmet. Instantly, the sights, sounds and colours of Chicago hit her. She looked down at the busy streets teeming with people. Car horns blared, police sirens squealed and all around were the sounds of life. She saw a river cutting its way through the city with many handsome bridges crossing over it.

The sensations were nothing like she'd ever experienced before. She could sense the people's laughter, joy, sorrow, fear, hatred and love. Every emotion merged together in a great wave of feelings rising up to her.

She peered over the side of the rooftop in excitement. 'Isn't it amazing? Look at all the people. They aren't fighting or killing each other! Loki was right, Earth can be beautiful.'

Orus cawed. 'You think this is beautiful? It's filthy. The air is choked with poison and there are too many people. I can't hear myself think with all this noise. Let's go back to Asgard before we are missed.'

'You can go back if you want, but I'm not going anywhere. Not until we've seen Tyrone's family.'

Orus huffed in surrender. 'How do we find him in all of this? It's not like you can go down there and ask directions.'

'Tyrone said he lived north of the city in a place called Lincolnwood. Number forty-five, Smith Street. We can fly north and try to find it.'

'That's your suggestion?' Orus complained. 'Just fly north?'

'Do you have a better idea?'

The raven ruffled his feathers. 'Well, no, not exactly.'

Suddenly a door behind her opened and two men emerged on to the roof. Their eyes flew open when they saw her.

'What are you doing up here?' a tall, dark-skinned man with greying hair demanded as he looked her up and down.

'Yeah, kid,' said the other. 'How'd you get up here? The door was locked and the roof is off limits to the public.' He was pale and much shorter and heavier than the first man. He had a thick beard and shaved head. His bare arms were covered in tattoos.

'I flew here,' Freya answered.

'Sure you did, kid,' the tattooed man challenged her. 'And I'm the Easter Bunny. Now, get off this roof before I throw you off it.'

Freya was hit with the force of all the terrible things

he had dove. Her Valkyrie senses could see beyond his exterior into what lay beneath. This was a dangerous man. In him, Freya recognized all the things she despised about the human race.

She opened her wings, drew her sword and advanced on him. 'Are you threatening me?'

Their mouths dropped. The taller man fell instantly to his knees and lowered his head. 'Please forgive me,' he begged. 'I meant no disrespect.'

It was the shorter man who she confronted. 'I do not like people who threaten me. And I especially do not like men who hurt others for their own pleasure. You cannot hide what you are from me, human. I see right into your heart.'

'What are you?' he demanded.

'Joe, get down on your knees,' the taller man warned, and made to reach for him. 'Can't you see she's an angel? Show some respect.'

'That thing ain't no angel,' Joe insisted. 'Angels ain't got black wings and they don't carry no swords or wear no armour. This is some kind of demon straight from the gates of hell.' He focused his cruel eyes on Freya. 'And that's just where I'm sending it back to.'

Freya could feel his violent intentions long before he lunged at her.

'I am not a demon!' she fired as she stepped forward

to meet his charge.

She knew she couldn't touch him with her bare hands. One touch would reap him and risk sending him to Asgard. There could be no explaining *that* to Odin. Instead she moved quicker than his eye could follow and struck him in the jaw with the pummel of her sword.

He collapsed to the ground in an unconscious heap.

'You,' she said, pointing her sword at the taller man. 'Rise. Tell me your name.'

He gained his feet, standing much taller than her, but kept his eyes cast down to the ground. 'Curtis,' he mumbled. 'Curtis Banks.'

Freya could feel the fear coming from him. She put her sword back in its sheath. 'Do not fear me, Curtis Banks; I am not here to hurt you. I need your help.'

Curtis's dark eyes rose to hers. 'How could I possibly help you? I'm just a simple man.'

'A man who knows this area, I hope,' Freya said.

'I – I've lived in Chicago all my life.' His voice trembled.

'Can you tell me how to find a place called Lincolnwood?'

'Lincolnwood?' he repeated. 'That's not too far from here. No more than ten miles.' He walked up to the edge of the building and pointed north. 'It's in that direction – you can almost see it from here. If you follow the

Chicago river down below us, it passes right beside it. There's a bus you can catch that will take you right there.'

'I will find it, thank you,' Freya said.

'Who are you?' Curtis asked timidly. 'Why do you need to get to Lincolnwood?'

'I cannot tell you who I am,' Freya answered. 'Just know that I am here to save a family who are in grave danger. I promised their dead father, a soldier, that I would protect them. They live in Lincolnwood.'

'What kind of danger are they in?'

'I don't know. All I know is they are in trouble and there is no one to help them now that Tyrone is dead—'

'Freya, stop! Don't say any more,' Orus warned her. 'You are already risking too much speaking with him.'

'Why?' Freya turned to the raven.

'He may tell others you are here. He could endanger you.'

'He won't. I can trust him. His heart is true.'

The raven sighed. 'You are too trusting. First Loki and now this man. It will lead to no good.'

'And you worry too much.'

She focused on Curtis again. His eyes were locked on the raven. 'Can you talk to him?'

Freya nodded. 'He told me not to trust you. But I can feel what is in your heart. I know you won't betray us.'

The fear was leaving Curtis's face. An expression of

wonder rose in its place. 'Are you really an angel?'

'No,' Freya answered. 'I'm a Valkyrie.'

'A *Valkyrie?*'

Freya frowned. 'You don't know what a Valkyrie is?'

Curtis shook his head.

'We are the Battle-Maidens of Odin.'

'Who?'

'You don't know Odin?' Freya demanded in shock.

'I'm sorry, no.'

'But everyone knows Odin!'

'I'm sorry, *I* don't.'

Freya was almost too stunned to speak. Finally she looked at Orus. 'How can this be?'

'This is a different age,' the raven said. 'Perhaps they have forgotten us.'

Still in shock, she focused on Curtis. 'Our time here grows short; we must go.' As she turned to leave, Curtis called after her.

'Valkyrie, wait. Let me take you to Lincolnwood in my van. Chicago is a dangerous place. If people saw you, they might try to hurt you. Besides, if there's a family in danger, I want to help. My wife is a lawyer and my nephew is a cop. I'm sure they'd want to help too.'

She was stunned by his sudden concern for her safety and offer to help. Freya gazed down on the unconscious man and back to Curtis. She couldn't understand how there could be such kindness and yet such darkness in people.

'Thank you, but I prefer to fly. I will be fine.' She pointed at her winged helmet sitting on the roof. 'I can't be seen when I'm wearing that.'

'Is it magical?'

Freya nodded. 'You could say that.'

She walked back to him. 'You are a good and generous man, Curtis Banks. If I need your help, I will return. But if you don't see me again, please be careful. I must warn you. That man with you is very bad. He holds many dark secrets and has done many terrible things. You would do well to stay away from him.'

Curtis looked at his partner, crumpled on the ground. 'We've only been working together a few weeks, as window cleaners. Can't say I care much for his company.'

'He is very dangerous,' Freya finished. 'Now, I must ask you not to tell him what we have discussed or where I am going.'

Curtis nodded. 'I won't say a thing.' He reached forward to shake her hand. 'It has been a great honour to meet you, Valkyrie. I wish we had more time together. There are so many things I want to understand.'

Freya held up her hands and stepped back. 'My touch is death to you. But I have enjoyed meeting you too.' She reached for her helmet and drew it on. The world around her lost its colour again.

'Well, I'll be damned,' Curtis said. 'That helmet is magic. Valkyrie, are you still here?'

'I am,' Freya said. 'But now I must go. Live well, Curtis Banks.'

His laughter followed her as she walked to the edge of the building. She climbed up on the short wall and looked to Orus. 'You ready to go?'

'Finally,' Orus cawed. 'I was ready the moment we landed here.'

Freya leaped off the top of the building. She free-fell more than halfway to the ground before she opened her wings and glided smoothly through the city streets.

'Orus, come on!' she cried, laughing as she expertly dodged around tall trucks and buses. She was playing among the traffic and having the time of her life.

'Freya, fly higher!' Orus cried from above.

Surrendering to the panic-stricken raven, Freya flapped her wings and rose higher in the sky. 'I'm just having a little fun.'

'Well, don't. Are you trying to scare me to death?'

'You worry too much,' she teased as she settled on her course and followed the winding river north.

It didn't take them long to reach Lincolnwood. They had left the city behind and now soared above a less congested area. Tall buildings were replaced with houses and short, squat buildings.

Not far ahead, the sound of children's loud, excited shouts rose up to meet her as they poured out of a building surrounded by parkland. Large, yellow buses filled a parking area and as she flew above them, Freya watched children climb on to them.

Her heart pounded with excitement at the sight of kids her own age. These were the first she'd ever seen in her life. Until now, her only experiences with humans were the warriors on the battlefields or those who made it to Valhalla. Occasionally there were some very young fighters. But war had changed them. They were as brutal as the adults.

'Look at them!' she called excitedly to Orus. 'Can't you feel their joy? Their love of life?'

Orus flew closer. 'I feel trouble brewing. We are on a mission to save Tyrone's family, that's all. You can't go down there to meet them. One look at you and they will run away screaming. You are a Valkyrie – a reaper of souls. You don't belong in the World of Man. Especially near their children. You are a child of war. That must be your playground. Not here and not now.'

Freya was about to protest when frightened screams reached her ears. She could feel terror like hot breath on her face. She changed direction in the sky and followed the frightened sounds.

'Freya – no!' Orus called, following her.

Her keen eyes caught sight of a boy running as if his life depended on it. He was passing through back yards and climbing over fences, trying to get away from the boys chasing him. She could almost hear his heart pounding ferociously in his chest. But like deadly predators his pursuers seemed to know where he was going. They split into two groups, each taking a different direction.

From her vantage point in the sky, Freya could see the boy was heading into a trap with no escape.

'Freya, leave them to their business,' Orus said trying to draw her away. 'Come, we must find Tyrone's family.'

'No, I want to see.'

'Why? They are just playing. They won't hurt him.'

Freya flew closer and gazed down on the boy's pursuers. They weren't playing. This was very real. When they caught the boy, they intended to hurt him.

From high above, Freya watched the trap snap shut. The boy's tormentors charged at him from two directions behind a house. He was cornered. His cries rose up to her as a large boy shoved him against a fence and punched him in the stomach. He collapsed to the ground and rolled into a ball, begging to be left alone.

'Orus, look – it is six against one. It's not fair.'

'That's their way. We must not get involved.'

Freya looked over at the raven. 'Maya is always saying people aren't bad. That I should get to know them so I can understand them. Well, I don't understand how six can go after one or why they want to hurt him. What's happening down there isn't right.'

Tilting her wings, Freya started to descend.

'Freya, we can't get involved! Please listen to me.'

Deaf to the raven's pleas, Freya landed in the yard behind the group of boys. With her helmet still in place, she knew they couldn't see her. She stepped closer, careful not to let even a feather graze against any of their exposed skin.

'C'mon, Daisy, put up a fight!' cried the largest of the boys as he kicked his prey.

Their victim lay on the ground in a tight ball. 'Leave me alone!'

'Ah – is Daisy crying?' called the bully. He pulled back his foot and gave the boy another brutal kick in the back. Then he looked at the others. 'Pick him up. Let's show him what we think of him.'

Several gang members rushed forward and dragged the boy to his feet. They pinned back his arms and laughed as they offered him to their leader. Blood was running from the boy's nose and a large, angry bruise was already forming on his cheek and eye.

Freya's temper flared. The sight of blood and the fear from their victim was exciting the attackers further. She could feel their heated anticipation at the beating about to come.

'No more!' Freya roared. Charging forward she lifted her booted foot and with great rapidity kicked the bullies away from the boy, careful not to touch anyone with her bare hands.

A calm Valkyrie is strong. An enraged Valkyrie is almost unstoppable.

Screams filled the air as she kicked them across the yard. They huddled together like frightened sheep as they desperately searched for their unseen assailant. Finding nothing, they fled in terror, leaving their leader to face the invisible monster alone.

His eyes were filled with hatred and rage. He was much bigger than the others and stood almost a head taller than Freya. Just like the man on the roof, Freya sensed a childhood filled with violence and anger.

He was backed up to the fence, his wild eyes searching the area. He snatched his victim up before him to use as a shield against her. 'Whatever you are, show yourself!' he demanded. 'Do it or I swear I'll break his neck!'

Freya's senses told her the threat was real. The bully was just a boy himself, but was prepared to do serious harm.

'If you do that,' she warned in her most threatening voice, 'you will know terrors you never imagined possible. Release him now, or I will show you what I truly am.'

The bully's voice faltered. 'You're, you're just a dumb girl. I – I'm not scared of you. Even if I can't see you.' Still his wild eyes searched madly for her.

'You should be,' Freya warned darkly, stepping closer. 'This is your last chance. Release the boy.'

The bully continued to scan the area. Freya stood at his left, and called, 'Let him go.' Then she darted to his right and did the same.

'Last warning,' she said from the other side of the bully again.

Just as he swung round to face her, Freya struck. With one swift kick she sent him flying several metres across the yard. His victim collapsed to the ground in a weak, bleeding heap at her feet.

Freya charged over to the bully. Placing a booted foot on his arm, she applied enough pressure to let him know she meant business. 'If I ever hear of you hurting someone again, not even the Midgard Serpent could protect you from me!'

She applied more pressure.

'Freya, stop,' Orus warned in her ear. 'You'll break his arm. Leave him.'

Freya hesitated but then lifted her foot. 'Get away from here!'

The bully climbed to his feet and turned quickly to attack. His fist impacted on Freya's breastplate and she heard the bones in his wrist snap. He howled in pain and pulled his hand to his chest.

'This ain't over,' the bully roared furiously as he turned to leave. 'Whatever you are, I swear you're gonna pay for this!'

'Just go!' Freya cried as she gave him a final kick in the backside.

Furious at his defeat, he kept looking back, trying to catch a glimpse of her. Even after he had disappeared from view, Freya could still feel him lingering in the area. After a time, she felt him move away.

Alone in the yard, Freya returned to the boy. He was on the ground, weeping softly.

'Can we please leave now?' Orus asked. 'You saved the boy. Let's go.'

'Just a minute,' Freya said.

She knelt beside him, just out of his reach. 'Are you all right?'

The boy's head lifted and darted around, searching for her. Fear was showing in his eyes as he scooted back to try to escape. 'Where are you? Why can't I see you?'

Freya rose and looked around. She closed her eyes and listened to her senses. No one was in the house behind them and the bullies had all gone. They were completely alone.

Kneeling again, she removed her helmet and became visible. 'Do not fear me. I won't hurt you.'

The boy's eyes grew wide and his mouth opened and closed as though he was speaking, but no sounds came out. Finally he managed, 'You – you – you've got wings!'

'I know.'

He rose to a sitting position, his eyes darting all around.

'They're gone,' Freya said.

'Are – are you my guardian angel?'

Freya sighed and shook her head. 'Why does everyone assume I'm an angel just because I have wings?'

'What else can you be?' the boy said breathlessly. 'You protected me from them.'

'Well, I'm not,' Freya said.

The boy reached forward tentatively. 'Can I touch your feathers?'

Freya pulled her wings back. 'No! No one can!'

Her sudden movement made him back against the fence to get away.

Freya sighed tiredly. 'There's no need to be frightened of me. But you must understand. If I touch someone, or if they touch me, they will die.'

The boy frowned, not understanding. 'But you touched the bullies when you pulled them away from me.'

'Not with my bare hands. I used my foot, and that's covered by my boot. If I'd touched their bare skin with my hands or feathers, they would have died.'

'So you're an angel of death?'

Freya sat back on her heels. 'No, I'm not that either. I'm a Valkyrie.'

The confused expression on his face let her know he didn't understand. Did no one here know what she was?

'Is your name Daisy?'

'No, it's Archie,' the boy answered. He pulled a tissue from his coat pocket and started to wipe the blood away from his nose and face.

Up close, Freya could see he was her age, maybe a bit older. He had pale-blue eyes and fine blond hair. His clothing looked worn, but clean and well kept. She could feel he was a gentle, sensitive soul. Not one meant for war or battlefields.

'Why were those boys beating you?'

Archie dropped his head. 'They always have, ever since I was young. They call me Daisy, steal my money and beat me up.'

'Why?'

'Because they can,' Archie said flatly. 'There's a group

of us that they pick on. They call us the Geek Squad. We don't fit into any of the groups at school. But because we're a little bit different and get higher marks than them, they always beat us up.'

Freya shook her head. 'I don't understand. Why don't you fight back? Defend yourself?'

'I can't,' Archie said. 'I don't know how to fight.'

'You could learn. I am sure no one taught them how.'

'But there's too many of them.'

Freya frowned. 'But you just said there are others they pick on. You could unite to protect yourselves.'

'I don't really know the others in the Geek Squad. We're not friends.'

'This makes no sense,' Freya said. 'In war, if your army is smaller than your opponents, you increase its size or its skills base. It's a simple principle that has worked for thousands of years.'

'This isn't a war,' Archie said.

'It sure looked like one to me.'

Archie sighed. 'You'd understand better if you went to my school. Bullies are always picking on weaker students. It's just the way it is.'

'Then it is stupid,' Freya argued. 'The strong should protect the weak, not abuse them.'

Archie leaned against the fence and took a deep, unsteady breath. His right eye was swollen almost shut.

'Thanks for saving my life.'

'You are welcome.'

There was something about this boy that intrigued her. He was the first boy her age she'd ever spoken to, and he was so different from what she expected. There was so much more she wanted to learn from him.

At her shoulder, Orus nipped Freya's ear. 'The boy is fine. Can we go now?'

'Orus, calm down.' She pulled the raven from her shoulder and placed him on the ground. 'This is Orus. He's my companion. But he's in a bit of a bad mood.'

'I think he's amazing,' Archie said, leaning forward. 'Hi, Orus.'

'That's the first intelligent thing this human has said,' Orus remarked as he puffed up his feathers proudly.

Freya smiled. 'Orus says hello.'

'I did not!' the raven complained.

'You can *talk* to him?'

Freya nodded. 'He came from Asgard with me . . .' She stopped mid-sentence, reached for her helmet and pulled it on. 'Silence! Someone is coming.'

'Wait, please don't go.' Archie started to panic, looking around desperately. 'They could be coming back to get me.'

'I'm still right here,' Freya said. 'You just can't see me. I won't let them hurt you again.'

The sounds of voices were growing closer. 'It is two of the boys who attacked you,' Freya warned. 'They have brought others. Can you walk?'

Archie climbed painfully to his feet. It was then that Freya saw he was several centimetres taller than her, but with a slight build. He staggered and fell forward. She instinctively reached out to steady him. Her hands went around his arms but his heavy winter coat protected him from her lethal touch.

'Do you have gloves?' Freya asked. When he nodded, she continued. 'Give them to me. I can't risk touching your skin.'

Freya pulled on Archie's gloves, and then put out her arm to steady him. Holding him close at her side, she whispered, 'My helmet will keep us both hidden. Just don't move and keep quiet.'

Freya supported Archie as they stood still, watching the bullies arrive in the yard. They listened as the two attackers described in detail what had happened.

'I swear, it happened right here,' one of them claimed. 'Look, you can still see the blood from Daisy's nose.'

'Where is he?' a new boy demanded. 'Or did the invisible creature take him away?' He started to laugh and make scary cartoon sounds.

'I don't know,' said the other attacker. 'Maybe it did.'

'Well, I don't believe you,' chimed a new boy. He was

standing with his hands on his hips, looking doubtful.

'Oh, no?' the first one said. 'Who do you think broke JP's wrist? It sure wasn't Daisy. He was too busy crying and begging for his pathetic life.'

'Yeah, it was the invisible creature. She did it,' claimed the other bully.

The boys searched the yard for signs of Archie. When they moved close, Freya tensed to fight again.

'I'll tell you one thing,' the first boy said. 'Daisy had better hope that creature *does* take him away. I ain't never seen JP so mad. He says he's gonna put Daisy in the ground on Monday. Even *I'm* feeling sorry for him.'

Archie started to tremble in Freya's arms. Fear was pouring from him in heavy waves. She realized that by saving him today, she'd caused him even more trouble.

When the group of boys gave up the search and left the yard, Freya stood with Archie for several minutes.

'Where do you live?' she asked, as he gradually calmed down.

'Not far,' he said softly. 'But I don't think I can make it.'

'You can. I will help you.'

'Freya, what are you doing?' Orus whispered. 'It is unfortunate, but you can't help him. That awful boy is going to get him no matter what you do. You are here

75

to save Tyrone's family. You don't have time to help everyone you meet.'

Freya shot him a look, but said nothing as she supported Archie.

It was a long walk to his home along tree-lined streets. As this was late autumn, the leaves were falling. There was a crisp smell of winter coming on. It wouldn't be long until there was snow.

They walked in silence, but Freya could still feel the fear coming from Archie.

They arrived before a small house and Archie carefully led them up the front steps. Freya looked up at the door.

'Do you have family here who can help you?'

Archie was hesitant to answer. 'I'll be OK. Thank you again . . .' He paused. 'I don't even know your name.'

'I can't tell you,' Freya said. 'It's a rule.'

'Well, thank you anyway,' he said softly as he approached the front door.

Freya watched him pause before the door and she felt something more than fear. Something much worse – resignation. Archie knew he was going to receive a worse beating on Monday. But he wasn't going to do anything about it.

'I could teach you,' Freya finally offered.

Archie pulled his key from his pocket and put it in the lock. 'Teach me what?'

'How to fight and defend yourself against those boys.'

'What?' Orus cried. 'Have you lost your mind?'

'You would do that?' Archie asked.

Freya ignored the screaming raven at her shoulder. 'I have been around battlefields all my life. I would do it in exchange for your assistance.'

A spark of life began to glow in Archie's eyes. 'What can I do?'

'I need to find a family,' Freya said. 'I came here to help them.'

For the first time, Archie smiled. It was a beautiful smile. 'Is that what Valkyries do?' he asked. 'They help people?'

'Not quite,' Freya answered. 'But I do want to help them.'

'And me?'

Freya looked long and hard at Archie. This was madness. She had run away from Asgard to protect one family, and now she was going to take on more? But with all the hope she felt coming from him, how could she say no?

'Yes, Archie, I am here to help you too.'

Archie unlocked the front door and held it wide as he welcomed her into his home.

CHAPTER SIX

While Archie showered and changed his clothes, Freya looked around the small house. This was the first human home she had ever been in and it was nothing like her home in Asgard. It was a fraction of the size and the furnishings were very different.

Though they were old and very tired, all the furniture and objects were clean and well ordered. As she wandered round the living room, Freya discovered things she'd never seen before and was anxious for Archie to finish bathing so he could explain what they were.

Freya and Orus started to explore the rest of the house. Down a short hall she opened a door and saw a bedroom that seemed very out of place with the rest of the well-cleaned house.

In fact, it was a filthy mess. Clothes were thrown all over the floor and empty drink bottles covered every surface. The bed was unmade and the sheets were stained and smelly.

Freya didn't linger but moved on and found another

bedroom unlike anything she'd ever seen before. The walls were covered in colourful posters and there were hundreds of figurines on shelves. Hanging on the back of the door was a long, floor-length, burgundy-coloured velvet coat, while the closet was filled with strange clothes that had chains and cogs and levers all over them.

'This is my brother's room.'

Freya jumped at Archie's quiet arrival behind her. Her wings flew open in alarm and knocked several figurines off a shelf.

'Brian is really into Steampunk.' As Archie bent down to pick up the figurines, Freya noticed he was wearing yellow rubber gloves on his hands and extra layers of clothing. The only skin exposed was his face.

'You said be careful,' Archie said. He held up his gloved hands. 'I'm being *extra* careful.'

Freya was still wearing his gloves and held up her hands. 'Me too. What is Steampunk?'

Archie picked up a figurine and handed it to her. It was of a woman in a top hat that had goggles on them. She was wearing a long, open coat. Tiny cogs were on the lapels of the coat and in her hands. Under the coat she wore a corset and a long, layered skirt. 'It's a kind of style,' Archie explained. 'Where people imagine what the world would have been like without electricity, with steam still powering everything. There are lots of cogs and gears and stuff mixed with Victorian styles.'

Archie was speaking, but the words meant nothing to Freya. She continued to explore the room in fascination. 'So where is your brother?'

Archie dropped his eyes. 'He's in jail.'

'For what?'

'I bet it was murder,' Orus said. 'Looking at this strange bedroom, it has to be murder!'

Freya swatted the raven as Archie said, 'It was for breaking and entering and auto theft. He's a thief. He'll be in jail for another eight months.' Archie paused and kicked at a spot on the floor. 'Um, while you're here, you can stay in his room if you like. I mean, unless you've got somewhere else to go. Do they have hotels for Valkyries?'

'I don't know,' Freya admitted. 'Actually, I hadn't thought that far ahead. But how would you explain it to your parents?'

Archie wouldn't meet her eyes. 'That's not a problem.' He paused and seemed hesitant. 'My father left years ago. I haven't heard from him since.'

'What about your mother? Is she here?'

The pause was longer this time. 'Sort of,' he said. 'I mean, she does live here, but she's gone for a while.'

Freya could feel there was a lot more to this, but she didn't want to press. Instead, she looked around the room again. 'I like it here. I will stay.'

At her shoulder, Orus was having a fit. 'Freya, you can't stay here! If Odin finds out, he'll send a Dark Searcher after us! We must find Tyrone's family and then return to Asgard before we're missed. It doesn't matter how much you like this place, you just can't stay!'

'What's he saying?' Archie asked as he watched Orus rage.

'Not much,' Freya answered. 'Just how much he likes this room. Who is that?' She pointed at one of the posters on the wall. It showed a squat little girl dressed in the Steampunk style. She had a crooked mouth and jet-black hair with a red stripe. There was an even smaller boy with her. His eyes looked madly demented. Beside them was a brightly coloured caterpillar on a lead, wearing military boots on his many feet.

'That's Gruesome Greta,' Archie said. 'She's my brother's all-time favourite character.' He crossed the room and reached for a thin book on a shelf. Freya's eyes glowed as she leafed through the colourful pages, filled with lots of little pictures.

'This is wonderful,' she said. 'I've never seen anything like it!'

'It's just a comic book,' Archie said. 'Don't they have comics where you come from?'

Freya couldn't draw her eyes from the pages. 'We

have a few books, but they are all about war. We have nothing like this. May I keep it?'

Archie shrugged. 'Sure, my brother has lots of them. I don't think he'd miss that one.' He stepped closer and pointed at a picture. 'That's Greta's little brother, Scott, and his pet caterpillar, Cecil. I really like Cecil.'

Archie walked over to the closet. 'I bet you can find some things to wear in here. I mean, if you don't mind wearing men's clothes. It might even help hide your wings.'

Archie pulled the long, heavy velvet coat off the door. 'Here, try this on.'

Freya removed her sword, dagger, gauntlets and breastplate. She folded in her wings as tight as they would go and pulled on the coat.

It hung down past the top of her sheepskin boots and was several sizes too big for her. The arms draped down past her gloved hands. But the fullness of the back fit perfectly over her wings.

'Here, let me help.' Archie stepped forward and rolled up the sleeves. Then he lifted the collar so that it stood up around her neck. He stepped back and considered his work. 'Not bad, not bad at all. Turn around.'

Freya turned slowly and raised her hands high over her head. 'Well? Can you see my wings?'

Archie shook his head. 'Nope. You just look like

you've got a hunched back. No one would ever suspect you had wings.'

Freya looked down at herself. 'Do I look Steampunk?'

Archie laughed too. 'A Steampunk angel? Why not!'

Freya lifted a finger. 'No, Archie, a Steampunk *Valkyrie*.'

Hours later, Freya sat in Archie's kitchen as he made them salad and macaroni with cheese. She watched him in fascination as he prepared the food with the confidence of one who had done it many times before.

'Are you always alone?'

Archie nodded. 'My brother has been away two years already and my mom is rarely here. Even when she is home, it's like she's not.'

'I don't understand.'

Archie stopped what he was doing and sat at the table with her. 'It's like this,' he started awkwardly. 'My mom drinks, a lot. When it's really bad she disappears, sometimes for weeks. She doesn't call and won't tell me where she's going. But she always comes home. But sometimes, that's even worse than when she's gone.'

'How can you live like this?' Freya asked. 'Don't you have other family?'

Archie shook his head. 'I'm doing all right,' he said. 'I earn extra money by delivering newspapers in the mornings before school. And my mother gets assistance. I use her bank card to buy food and pay the bills. A social worker visits, but not very often and she doesn't seem to care that my mom is a drunk.'

Freya watched Archie as he rose and got back to work. His words were brave, but his inner feelings betrayed him. He was very lonely.

'I understand, Archie. I have seen what drink can do to humans.'

Archie turned to her, inviting her to say more.

'Where I come from, we have a place called Valhalla. Human warriors spend all day fighting, and then drink all night. My father is there, somewhere. But I've never met him. After seeing what drink does to them, I don't want to.'

'Your father is *human*?' Archie asked in shock.

Freya nodded.

'Wow,' he said softly. 'We've both got parents with drink problems.'

Freya had never thought of it that way, but he was right. They weren't so different after all.

Eating human food was something she had never experienced before. Orus was beside her, picking at his own bowl full of the cheesy macaroni and getting it all over his smooth black feathers.

When she finished, Freya sighed contentedly.

'Does it hurt having them?' Archie asked as his eyes lingered on her semi-open wings. The way she sat meant the bottom, flight-feathers rested on the floor.

Freya shrugged. 'Not really. I've always had wings, so I don't know what it's like not to have them.'

'But you can't sleep on your back or sit properly.' He pointed to the way she had to sit with the chair turned back to front to avoid leaning against her wings.

'No, I guess not. But I can fly, and that makes up for it. There is nothing better than flying really high and pulling in your wings to dive. Right before you hit the ground you open your wings and soar.'

Archie sighed wistfully. 'That sounds amazing. I wish I had wings. Then I could fly away from here too.'

'Where would you go?'

'I don't know, just away.' Archie pulled open his laptop computer. He paused. 'You said you can't tell me your name. But I have to call you something.'

Freya considered.

'Don't do it, Freya,' Orus warned. 'Don't give him your true name.'

She looked at the raven. 'I'm not going to. I'm just thinking.' Finally she nodded. 'I know. Archie, you can call me Greta, just like in the comic.'

'Greta?' Archie cried. 'Are you serious? Did you look at her? She's . . . she's . . .'

85

'She's what?'

'Well, she's not you. You're pretty – Gruesome Greta is definitely not.'

For the first time in her long life, Freya blushed. She had never thought of herself as even remotely pretty. All she was known for in Asgard was being a great flyer. It was her sisters who held all the beauty in the family. 'You really think I'm pretty?'

'Of course you are,' Archie said.

His comment was so unexpected, Freya was lost for words.

'How many times have I said the same thing,' Orus remarked.

'But, but I'm not,' Freya said, flushing. 'My sisters are the beautiful ones, not me.'

'Well, you are,' Archie said. 'So I can't call you Greta.'

'But I like that name.'

'How about I call you Gee? It's the first letter of the name, but not actually Greta.'

'Gee,' Freya repeated. 'All right, you can call me Gee.'

Archie tilted his head to the side. 'OK, Gee, if you are a Valkyrie, let's see what the Internet says about you.'

Archie started to type on his keyboard. Freya leaned forward to see what the laptop would do.

'OK, here we go,' Archie said as he started to read

aloud. 'In Norse mythology, a Valkyrie – from Old Norse *valkyrja*, "chooser of the slain" – is one of a host of winged female figures who decide who dies and wins in battle . . .' His voice tapered off as he continued to read in stunned silence.

Freya could feel a mix of doubt and confusion coming from him. 'We aren't myths and we don't always choose who lives or dies. We just collect the souls of the valiant dead and take them to Valhalla.'

'But you do go to battlefields and reap the dying soldiers?'

'That is why I am here.' Freya explained about her life in Asgard and her First Day Ceremony. She told Archie how she had reaped the soldier, Tyrone Johnson, and how he'd begged her to help his family.

'Can Valkyries do that?' Archie asked. 'Can they come here to help people?'

Orus was still on the table and cawed loudly. 'Go on, Freya, tell him how you are breaking the rules to be here and what will happen if Odin finds out.'

'What did he say?' Archie asked, watching the cawing raven.

Freya sighed. 'He told me to tell you how I'm breaking the rules by being here. Valkyries are not allowed in Midgard unless it's to reap warriors' souls. We aren't supposed to get involved in human lives. We deal with the dead, not the living.'

'What's Midgard?' Archie asked.

'This is,' Freya explained. 'I come from Asgard. Here – Earth – is Midgard and then there is Utgard, the land of the demons and frost giants.'

'Midgard,' Archie repeated. 'What will happen if you are caught out of Asgard?'

Freya hesitated. 'Odin will be very angry. It won't be good.'

Archie reached out a rubber-gloved hand and touched Freya's hand. He leaned closer to her. 'Then you must go back. I don't want you to get into trouble because of me.'

'He is intelligent!' Orus cried in shock. 'Listen to the boy, Freya. We must return to Asgard right now.'

Freya shook her head. 'Not yet. Not until I have seen Tyrone's family and found out how I can help them.' Her deep-blue eyes settled on Archie. 'And made sure those boys leave you alone.'

'Don't worry about me,' Archie said. 'I've always been picked on and beaten up. It will always be that way, even after you go. But if helping your soldier's family will get you home sooner, let's go.'

'You wish to help me?' Freya asked in wonder. 'Why would you do that?'

Archie grinned in excitement. 'Because that's what friends do.'

CHAPTER SEVEN

'*Because that's what friends do . . .*' Archie's few words affected Freya more deeply than she imagined possible. After spending most of her life looking for a friend, she had found one by complete accident. Archie knew who she was, what she did and where she came from and yet, after all that, he still wanted to be her friend.

Archie had searched for Tyrone Johnson's address.

'It's really not too far from here,' he said, looking at the map on screen. 'We could walk there in ten minutes. I bet Tamika goes to my school. I've probably walked past her in the hall a hundred times.' He looked up at Freya. 'What do you want to do first?'

'I'm not sure. I guess just take a look and see if we can discover what the trouble is.' Freya pulled on her armour and weapons.

'Are you going to let them see you?'

Freya shook her head. 'Not yet. I don't want to scare them. The moment people see me they think I'm either an angel or the Angel of Death.'

Archie scrunched up his face. 'Well, technically speaking, Gee, you are kind of an angel of death. Just one meant for the battlefields.'

'I guess so,' Freya surrendered.

The air was fresh and crisp as they walked through the darkened neighbourhood streets. Most of the homes they passed had their lights on and held a warm, welcoming glow. From each home, Freya could feel the emotions of the people inside. She was wearing her helmet, so no one saw her.

'OK, here's their street,' Archie said. Most of the houses were dark and many front yards had SOLD signs in them or were boarded up. Two looked as if they had been burned down. It seemed the entire area was moving out.

They counted down the numbers until they reached one of the few lit houses, right beside a burned-out hulk.

'Number forty-five, here it is,' Archie said.

Freya looked up at the house her soldier had lived in with his family. It was a simple, two-storey structure. The house looked like it had seen better days and was in desperate need of repair.

'Tyrone lived here?' Orus said. 'No wonder he went off to war!'

Freya swatted the bird. 'Be nice.'

From the street, Freya could hear the sound of a baby crying. 'That's Tyrone's baby daughter, Uniik. He never got to hold her. She was born while he was on the battlefield and he died before he could come home to see her.'

'That's so sad,' Archie said. 'I read that Valkyries can choose who lives and who dies. Couldn't you save him?'

Freya removed her helmet and became invisible. 'He was badly wounded. It was his time to die and I couldn't change that, even if I wanted to. I brought him to Valhalla but promised to let his family know they were in his thoughts every minute.'

Archie and Freya stood in silence as they listened to the cries of the baby. 'Stay here. I'll get in through the baby's window up there. Then I'll take a look around. I won't be long.' Freya opened her wings and pulled her helmet back on.

'Be careful,' Archie warned. 'If the family is in danger, they might have a gun.'

Freya smiled at her new friend, even though he wouldn't see it. 'I'll be careful.' She didn't bother to tell him that while she wore her armour she couldn't be wounded.

Freya leaped into the air and flapped her wings. It was a short flight up to the window of the baby's room. She gripped the sill with one hand and shoved open the window with the other.

With little effort, she hauled herself inside. Orus returned to her shoulder when she stood. Freya walked over to the crib.

Uniik was the first human baby she had ever seen up close. She was beautiful. Her dark skin was the same colour as Tyrone's. She had a head of dark curly hair and a powerful cry, bursting with life. She had kicked off her covers.

'She's cute, but a little loud,' Orus complained.

Wearing her gloves, Freya stroked the baby's face with a trembling hand. 'Shhhh, little one,' she whispered gently. 'It will be all right. Your father loved you dearly and gave his life protecting you.'

Suddenly a light came on in the room as a woman's voice cried, 'No, please, you can't take her!'

Freya's wings flashed open as she turned and was met by a pleading old woman standing in the doorway. Her dark face bore the wrinkles of a long, troubled life and her body was wasted by age and illness. 'Angel, take me if you must, but leave my granddaughter alone.'

It took a moment for Freya to realize that she was still wearing her helmet. 'You can see me?'

The old woman moved stiffly as she knelt down before her. 'Please,' she begged. 'She's just a baby with her whole life ahead of her. If you must take someone, take me. I am old and ready to go.'

'This is not good,' Orus said. 'If she can see you, she's dying.'

Freya removed her helmet. 'I'm not here to take anyone. I knew Uniik's father and promised him I would come. Do not be afraid of me.' As she helped the old woman to rise, Freya felt pain coming from her. Pain, and something else; something hovering very near. It was a feeling of impending death.

The old woman squinted up at her. 'Why, you're just a child!'

'I am old enough,' Freya said. 'I was with Tyrone Johnson when he died.'

The old woman grasped her chest and staggered back. 'My Tyrone? You were the one who took my son?'

'I did not want to,' Freya started as she steadied her. 'But I had to. It was his time. He was wounded and dying, nothing could change that. All I did was end his suffering.' She reached into her pouch and pulled out Tyrone's phone. 'Your son gave me this. He showed me his daughters and begged me to come and protect his family. He regretted that he never held his new baby and couldn't say goodbye to his wife.'

The old woman looked at the phone. Tears rose in her grey-rimmed, brown eyes and her chin quivered.

'They are united in death,' she spoke softly. 'Victoria was killed in a hit-and-run accident almost six months ago, not long after Tyrone died. They never caught the driver.'

'She is dead?' Freya looked away, unable to understand. She felt her temper rise as she learned of yet more violence. 'Is that all this world is? Violence and war? People hurting each other for no reason?'

'Sometimes it seems that way,' the old woman said. 'But it does have goodness as well.'

'Where?' Freya demanded harshly. 'I have yet to see it. All I find is pain and loss. Boys are beating up boys for no reason, and Tyrone's wife has been killed. It is all so ugly.'

She balled her hands into fists and crossed the room. 'My sister tried to tell me that people had changed. That soldiers cared more than they used to and that I was wrong to judge them so harshly.' She turned quickly on the old woman. 'But I am not wrong. All there is here is hatred and fighting!'

'I told you,' Orus whispered in her ear. 'There is no beauty in Midgard. Asgard is where you will find it.'

The old woman reached out for Freya's gloved hands. 'Please don't judge us all so harshly. Believe me, child, our world does have more. Look at my granddaughter . . .' The old woman escorted Freya back to the crib. She stroked the baby's head with a trembling, aged hand.

'So filled with life and so innocent. She will do no harm in this world. My Tamika wants to be a doctor. She will help people.'

She turned pleading eyes to Freya. 'All you have seen are the horrors. Stay a while. Soon you will learn there is beauty too.'

Freya shook her head. 'I wish I could believe you, but I find it impossible. Perhaps there are some individuals who are good. But as a whole . . .'

'As a whole, we must still find a way to live together.'

'Yes,' Freya agreed. She gazed down on the baby. Uniik had stopped crying and was reaching up to her. Freya let the baby grasp her gloved finger and smiled as she giggled and tried to pull it to her mouth. 'What will happen to Uniik and Tamika when you die?'

'You know I'm dying?'

Freya nodded. 'You could see me while I was wearing my helmet. Only the dead and dying can. And I can feel your pain. You are unwell.'

'Cancer,' the old woman sighed. 'I've got a few weeks, months maybe. But not enough time to protect my girls. They don't know yet. How can I tell them when they've lost so much already? That is my biggest fear. We have no family left and they will be all alone.'

Freya frowned. This couldn't be the danger Tyrone referred to. He didn't know his wife would die or that

95

his mother had cancer. What had he meant when he'd said they were in danger? She wondered how much worse it could get for his daughters.

'I'm Alma Johnson,' the old woman finally said.

'You may call me Greta.'

'Greta, I was about to make myself some cocoa. It helps me sleep when the pain gets too much. Why don't you come down with me? We can talk a spell. Let me try to tell you about the good of this world.'

Freya looked out the window and saw Archie down on the street. He was alone in this world too.

'I have someone with me. It's very cold out and he is shivering. May he come in?'

'Of course,' Alma said. 'Is he an angel too?'

'No, he's just a boy.' Before leaving the room, Freya looked back down on Uniik. The baby had settled to sleep. 'This is the closest to a human baby I have ever been. In sleep, I can see traces of her father's face. Tyrone would have been proud.'

Alma smiled at the baby. 'Just like her grandma.'

'If someone had ever told me I'd have an angel sitting right here at my kitchen table drinking cocoa with me,' Alma said, 'I'd have said they were crazy.'

Freya and Archie exchanged looks, but said nothing. It was easier to let the old woman believe she was simply an angel. Archie was still shivering as he grasped his steaming cup of cocoa for warmth. Freya and Orus were enjoying home-made chocolate-chip cookies.

'Tell me what happened to Tyrone's wife,' Freya asked.

The old woman sighed and shook her head. 'There's not a lot to tell. Victoria was walking home from work when a car hit her. We're sure we know who it was, but when we went to the police they said there was no evidence. It's been six months and nothing has happened to bring them to justice.'

Archie frowned in confusion. 'You said you reaped Tyrone a few days ago.'

Freya nodded. 'I did. But time moves differently between Asgard and here. A few days there means months here.' She focused on the old woman. 'If you know who killed Victoria, there should be no problem. Those people must be punished.'

The old woman shook her head and sighed. 'It is not as simple as that. We need proof, but we have none. So those people get away with murder.'

Freya frowned at Alma. 'Your son told me he knew his family was in trouble but Victoria hadn't told him what it was. He was desperate to get back to you. Even after I delivered him to Valhalla, it was all he talked about. Is this part of what Victoria was afraid to tell him?'

97

Alma nodded. 'She didn't want to worry him, but it was getting bad.'

'I promised Tyrone I would help. What can I do for you?'

'I don't think even an angel can help us,' Alma said sadly. 'They want this house and will take it by force if they must.'

'Who wants your house?' Archie asked.

'John Roberts Developments. They've bought up most of the houses on this street and the street behind us so they can build their condominiums for Chicago commuters. But me and several others won't sell. They are offering less than the value of our houses. We won't be bullied out of our homes. But they've started to burn us out. Just last week our neighbour's house burned down.'

'So we've seen,' Archie said.

'But if they are using violence,' Freya said, 'wouldn't it be better to go?'

'If we let men like that drive us away, we are surrendering to evil. With my last, fading breath, I will fight them. They won't drive my grandbabies from their rightful home. It is all they will have.'

'Even if it means you may be hurt?'

Fiery determination rose in Alma's eyes. 'Even if it means that. Good must stand up to evil or we are all lost.' She paused and her eyes faded. 'It's my Tamika I worry about. She walks to school. What if they go after her? The police won't protect her.'

'I could walk with her,' Archie volunteered. 'You don't live too far from me. I could come here right after my paper route.'

'Would you do that?' Alma asked. 'I would pay you.'

Archie shook his head. 'I don't want your money. Just to help, if I can.'

Freya looked at him in disbelief. He was being threatened by bullies and wouldn't defend himself. And yet he was offering to help a stranger who was in greater danger. Humans confused her.

'And me,' Freya finally said. 'I will go to school with you both.'

'What!' Orus cried. 'Freya, this is getting out of hand! YOU CANNOT STAY HERE!'

Freya looked at the raven on the table. 'I promised Tyrone I would protect his family. That's what I intend to do.' She looked up at Archie and Alma. 'I am going to stay here until this danger has passed. But I will need your help.'

'What can we do?' Alma asked. 'Please tell me, Angel, I will do anything.'

Freya rose and opened her large, black wings. 'Teach me how to look like a human.'

CHAPTER EIGHT

It was late in the night and Freya was wide awake. Archie had gone to bed hours earlier. In Asgard, Freya did sleep. But here, she felt no need. She decided to use the time to explore Brian's bedroom.

It was all so strange and yet wonderful. She tried on his leather trousers and a belt to keep them secured. She liked the way they felt and looked. Then she tried his heavy black boots. They were too big, but when Freya stuffed the ends with tissue they fit fine. She tried on some of his shirts, cutting slits in the back so they fell around her large, bulky wings.

Alma had said she was a dressmaker by trade and had offered to make Freya some special clothes to wear to school; Freya planned to take her up on the offer.

'Are you trying to look like a boy?' Orus complained. He was seated on the bed, pecking at the shiny buttons on a discarded shirt.

'No, I'm trying to look like a human,' Freya explained. 'And you really aren't helping.'

'Why should I help you?' the raven said. 'The moment Odin sees us, he'll have our wings.'

'He's not going to see us. We won't be here that long.'

'We've already been here too long!' the bird complained. 'Heimdall is bound to realize what happened. He'll tell Odin and he'll send out a Dark Searcher for us.'

'All you do is worry,' Freya said as she continued to go through the Steampunk clothing. 'This is exciting. I'm going to a human school, filled with human kids my own age.' She held a frilly black shirt up against herself and admired the look in the mirror.

'There are no humans your age,' Orus said. 'You are over six hundred human years old.'

'All right,' she surrendered. 'But at least I *look* their age.'

'And act it,' Orus muttered.

Freya threw the shirt over the raven as she continued to search through the closet. She felt butterflies of excitement rising in her stomach. This was a new adventure and one she'd never imagined she could be part of. Archie said he knew of a way to get her into school without too many questions. She just hoped she could stay with him. Though she had been tutored in Asgard, it sounded very different from the way Archie described a his school.

Freya and Orus spent the rest of the night going through the house. Not a cupboard or drawer went unexplored. Finally they settled in the lounge to watch television.

When Archie rose the next morning, he found Freya and Orus huddled together on the sofa watching a movie.

'I thought I'd dreamed you,' Archie said breathlessly. 'But I didn't. You're really here and you did beat up JP to save me.'

'Good morning, Archie,' Freya said as she stood, yawned and gave a long stretch that had her wings touching the walls of the room.

'Hey, I was watching that!' Orus complained when she turned off the television. The raven hopped over to the remote and clicked it on again.

Freya shook her head. 'If I am going to try to look human, we need to go back to Alma's. Some of your brother's clothes won't fit over my wings. Oh, and I need your help with this.' She tossed a box to Archie. 'I found this in your brother's drawer and want to try it.'

'Hair dye?' Archie said. 'You want me to dye your hair crimson red?'

Freya nodded.

'Why would you want to do that when your hair's already beautiful? I mean, it needs a bit of styling but apart from that, it's lovely.'

Freya shook her head. 'Every Valkyrie in Asgard has long, flaxen hair. Since I'm the only one with black feathers, I want my hair to be different too. Will you help me?'

'Sure. I think you're crazy for wanting to change it, but if that's what you want, that's what you'll get. Besides, it's what I want to do when I grow up.'

'What's that?'

'I want to be a hair stylist. And you can be my first victim!'

Before breakfast, Freya joined Archie on his paper round. She wore Brian's long velvet coat over her tunic and breastplate, and pulled on Archie's thick winter gloves. She stood on the rear axle-rod of his bicycle as he tossed the papers to the doorsteps.

'Faster!' she called in excitement as he rode his bike down a steep hill. 'Go faster!'

She was pressed up against his back, but careful not to touch Archie's skin while she tapped his shoulder to urge him to go faster.

They squealed with excitement as they wove madly through the early-morning traffic and howled with laughter at the blaring car horns.

When they arrived home, Freya climbed off the bike,

her eyes still wide with excitement. 'That was the most fun I have ever had on the ground!'

'Me too!' Archie agreed. 'I usually hate my paper route, but not today.'

After breakfast, Archie pulled on his heavy kitchen rubber gloves. 'You're still sure you want me to do this?' He was holding scissors and a comb. 'Once I start, I won't stop.'

Freya looked up at him from where she was sitting on a backwards chair, with a towel over her sholders protecting her wings. 'Are you sure you are completely covered and won't touch my skin?'

Archie showed her that he was wearing two turtleneck sweaters with the sleeves pulled down past his wrists and the thick rubber gloves. 'The only skin that's showing is my face.'

'Then go ahead,' Freya said. 'Start cutting.'

Orus moaned, 'Your mother is going to kill you! Then she'll kill *me* for not stopping you!'

'What did he say?' Archie asked.

'He wished you luck.'

'Thanks, Orus,' Archie said as he stroked the raven.

Orus huffed at Freya. 'I never realized you were such a liar.'

Two hours later, Freya stood before the bathroom mirror. Her hair had been cut to just below her shoulders and neatly styled into flowing waves. It was now bright crimson.

'Well?' Archie asked nervously.

'It's perfect!' Freya cried excitedly. 'Not even my sister could get my hair to behave.'

'You've just got to understand how hair works,' he said proudly. 'I've read lots of books on cutting and styling. I figured a Valkyrie's hair can't be that different to humans'.'

'It's magic!' Freya said, hardly recognizing herself in the mirror. 'I wish my sister could see this. I really look like Gruesome Greta!'

'No you don't,' Archie said. 'I told you, she's gross. You're not. You look like Gee.'

'Well, whoever I look like, I like her,' Freya said. 'And . . .' She paused before turning to him, stunned by the sudden revelation. Finally she dropped her eyes. 'And I really like you too, Archie. Thank you.'

At her shoulder, Orus made gagging sounds. 'Oh, please, I'm really going to be sick.'

Freya swatted him.

Archie blushed and looked away. 'You're OK too.'

'Ready to go and meet Tamika?' Archie asked. They had arranged to go to Alma's for lunch.

Freya finished getting ready. 'All done.'

As they walked down the quiet street towards the Johnsons' house in full daylight, they could see that many of the empty and abandoned houses had also been badly vandalized.

'They're doing a good job of clearing the street,' Archie observed.

Freya nodded. 'But they won't get Tyrone's house. Not as long as I am here.'

'Which won't be long,' Orus said from her shoulder. 'I hope you can save them quickly.'

This time Freya told Archie what the raven had said. 'I agree with him,' Archie said. 'I don't want you getting into trouble with Odin. I did more research last night. It says he has a big temper and gives out harsh punishments.'

'He does,' Freya agreed. 'But his temper's not as big as Thor's. He can rattle mountains when he's angry!'

Archie's eyes went wide. 'You know Thor? I've read all about him too. Does he really carry a huge hammer?'

Freya nodded. 'It's called Mjölnir. He won't let anyone touch it. Loki's taken it away from him a couple of times, but Thor always gets it back.'

'Wow,' Archie cried. 'I read about Loki too. It says he's a troublemaker.'

Freya nodded. 'He can be, but he helped me come here, so he's not all bad.'

Archie sighed wistfully. 'After everything I've read, I would really love to see Asgard. It sounds amazing.'

'It is – but I'm sorry, you can never see it. Not unless you die valiantly in battle. Valhalla is only for dead warriors.'

'Valhalla!' Archie cried. 'What's it really like?'

Freya shrugged. 'It's just a huge banquet hall where the dead drink, dance and play all night and fight all day. It is my least favourite place in Asgard.' She paused and looked at the almost deserted neighbourhood. It looked like a war had been fought and lost. 'But it seems that here is very much the same. Perhaps it is the way of most humans.'

Archie shook his head. 'Not all of us.'

Freya raised her eyebrows. 'Oh no?'

'Really,' Archie insisted. 'There are good people here too, I promise.'

Freya looked doubtful, but said no more as they approached the house.

Archie knocked and a pretty dark-skinned girl answered the door. She was shorter than Freya with her dark hair styled in long cornrows with multi-coloured beads at the ends. She wasn't much younger-looking either. Freya could easily see traces of Tyrone in her face – and she had the same cleft in her chin as him. It was Tamika.

'What do you want?' Tamika demanded. Her eyes lingered on Freya and then moved to Orus.

Archie spoke first. 'Hi, Tamika, we're friends of your grandmother's. She invited us for lunch.'

Tamika's eyes were still on Orus. 'I don't like birds. He has to stay outside.'

The raven cawed in protest.

'Orus goes where I go!' Freya's temper started to flare. Tamika was nothing like she'd expected and not the same smiling girl from the photographs on the phone. 'If he is not welcome, I will not stay.'

'Fine, go then. I didn't invite you.'

Freya turned to leave. But before she reached the porch steps, Archie caught hold of her coat sleeve. 'Gee, calm down. Remember why you're here. I'm sure Tamika didn't mean it.'

'Yes I did!' Tamika shot. 'Birds are filthy and blackbirds are evil. They don't belong indoors.'

Freya shot around in a fury. 'Orus is not filthy! And he's a raven, not a blackbird. They're not evil. I will never enter a place where he is not welcome.'

'Of course he's welcome!' Alma called as she arrived on the porch. 'You are all welcome here.' Her eyes went wide when she saw the changes in Freya. 'Why, my sweet Angel, what on earth have you done to yourself?'

Freya looked down her front, still furious at

Tamika's comments. 'I have made a few changes before I go to school.'

'But last night you said you wanted to blend in. This is not blending in! And your beautiful long hair, what have you done to it?'

'Archie cut it for me,' Freya said. 'I like it.'

'You remind me of that stupid comic, *Gruesome Greta*,' Tamika remarked unkindly.

Freya took a step forward. 'What are you saying?'

'Freya, don't,' Orus cawed. 'She is just a grieving child. Think of her dead parents and leave her be.'

'Tamika!' Alma cried. 'Your mama raised you better than that! You apologize to our guests right now.'

'I will not!' Tamika shouted. 'And I don't need babysitters to take me to school!' She turned and ran from the door. Stomping up the stairs, they heard her slam her bedroom door at the top.

Freya had felt Tamika's grief at the loss of both her parents mixed with deep-seated anger and fear.

'Angel, I am so sorry,' Alma said as she invited them in. 'Please, please forgive her. I didn't tell her what you are. Only that you are going to take her to school.'

Freya and Archie entered the house and were greeted by the welcoming aroma of home-made soup and baking bread wafting through the air.

'She is angry at the loss of her parents,' Freya said.

'And she is fearful. She knows something is very wrong with you, but is too frightened to ask you about it.'

Alma's hands shot up to her mouth. 'Oh, my poor baby. I've tried to keep my illness hidden from her.'

'Yet, she knows,' Freya said. 'I believe she also knows this house is in grave danger from the developers.'

'That I couldn't keep from her,' Alma said. 'They call all the time, making their threats against us.'

'Can I go up and talk to her?' Archie asked.

'Perhaps I should go,' Freya volunteered.

'No!' Archie cried.

Freya frowned. 'Why not? You know I would never harm her.'

'It's not that,' Archie said quickly. 'Gee, you are still getting used to things here on Earth and talking to people. Let's say she says something that you misunderstand, or she sees your wings. I don't think she could handle that yet. Please let me go.'

Freya huffed indignantly. 'I wouldn't tell her what I am.'

Alma stepped forward. 'Let Archie go.'

Freya turned to the old woman. 'Don't you trust me? Do you really think I'd hurt Tyrone's daughter?'

Fear rose on the old woman's face. 'Forgive me, Angel, I meant no disrespect.'

Archie elbowed her in the side. 'Gee, calm

down and be nice.'

Freya inhaled deeply and let it out slowly. This wasn't going as she had planned. 'I'm sorry. I just didn't expect Tamika to be so angry. Her father told me about her and I was looking forward to meeting her.'

'She's in pain,' Alma explained. 'Give her time to get to know you. She's a sweet child with a kind heart. But her heart's been badly broken.'

Freya nodded and looked to Archie. 'Go talk to her.'

When he was gone the old woman pulled on kitchen gloves. 'While we've got a moment, I can get you measured for your new clothes.'

After Alma had carefully measured Freya's wings, and while Archie was with Tamika, Freya watched Alma feed Uniik. She was enchanted by the baby and wanted desperately to hold her, but knew she couldn't.

'She is so full of life,' observed Freya.

The old woman's eyes were sparkling with pride. 'Just like her papa. I wish he could have seen how beautiful she is.'

'He wanted that too. As he lay dying, his thoughts were only of his girls, as he called them.'

Alma's eyes fogged as she sniffed. 'I just hope I live long enough to see the girls protected. I know I couldn't rest peacefully if anything happened to them.'

'Nothing's going to happen, Grandma.' Tamika entered the kitchen, followed by Archie. 'They're not going to take our home away from us.'

She lifted her sister from her grandmother's arms and started to burp the baby. Tamika's face brightened as Uniik giggled in her arms.

Alma's eyes lingered on Freya before replying to Tamika. 'Of course, child, but you know your old grandma won't live forever.'

'Sure you will,' Tamika said. She looked at Freya while gently bouncing the baby in her arms. 'I didn't mean to call you Gruesome Greta. Take off your coat – you can stay.'

Freya rose and stepped closer. With her gloved hand, she stroked the baby's head. 'I prefer to keep it on, and I didn't mind what you called me. I like Gruesome Greta. After all, that's my name.'

Tamika frowned at Archie. 'You said her name was Gee.'

Archie shuffled uncomfortably on his feet. 'That's what I call her. But her name is Greta.' He focused on Freya. 'I told Tamika about your problem. So she's agreed that we can all walk to school together.'

'My problem?'

Freya could feel a lot of emotion coming from Archie. He was very anxious. He'd obviously told Tamika something about her and was frightened she would say the wrong thing.

'Yes, Gee,' he said cautiously. 'You know, about what happened to your family in Denmark and how you are staying at my house in hiding so the bad men don't find you?

'I also told her no one knows you are here and how we're going to try to sneak you into my school under a different name.'

'Oh, *that* problem,' Freya agreed. Her eyes caught hold of Alma's and the old woman was nodding. 'Yes, well, Tamika, I hope you can help me.'

'Sure,' Tamika agreed. 'And I know how you can get into our school without any records.'

Tamika told them about a homeless boy in her class who lived with his family in a shelter. They couldn't locate his old school records, but the school had to take him anyway.

'I'll take you to school and register you on Monday,' Alma said, forming a plan. 'I'll tell them you're my brother's niece and that you've come over here to spend some time with me and your cousin Tamika.'

'Will they believe you?' Freya asked. 'I have pale skin – we don't look like we come from the same family.'

Alma nodded. 'They'll believe what I tell them. Don't you fret about that.' She paused. 'But we are going to need some kind of birth certificate for you.'

'I can do that!' Archie announced. 'I can easily do that on the computer. I can also make up a doctor's note that says you've got some rare spinal disease and are wearing a big back brace that you're embarrassed about. So you wear strange clothing to hide it. It would also excuse you from Phys-Ed.' His eyes grew even bigger as he started to extend his idea. 'I know!' he added. 'We can say that you've got a weird skin problem so you can't touch anyone or let them touch you. That way, you can wear your coat and gloves all day. And, because we're pretending you're from Denmark, if we write the notes in something that looks like Danish it'll be even easier to fool everyone!'

Archie's enthusiasm was catching as they thought more about how to hide Freya's true identity. By the end of lunch, they had created a whole story for her to tell the school.

While they used Tamika's computer to create the false documents, Alma disappeared into her sewing room to work on the cover for Freya's wings.

When they left the Johnson house in the early evening, Freya felt prepared for her first day at school.

CHAPTER NINE

Freya was restless. It was long past midnight and she still did not feel the need for sleep. Archie had already gone to bed and there was nothing left to do.

'What are you doing?' Orus asked as he watched her pull on her armour and gauntlets. Then she attached the sword to her side and walked to the back door.

'I can't stay here watching television all night,' she said. 'Let's go for a short flight. I need to stretch my wings.'

'But it's raining. We'll get soaked.'

Freya sighed. 'A little rain never hurt anyone.'

'How do you know? This is Midgard rain, not Asgard. Maybe it has something in it that will damage our feathers.'

Freya burst out laughing. 'Nice try, Orus. Now, come on, you need exercise too.'

Orus ruffled his feathers in disappointment. 'What about your helmet?'

'Not tonight. I want to see the city with my own eyes

and not have it changed by the helmet's powers.'

Rain was coming down in heavy sheets, which limited visibility to a few short metres as Freya entered the back yard.

Opening her wings, she ran and leaped into the air. With one powerful wing beat, she climbed higher in the sky. After several more beats, she was gliding over the rooftops of Lincolnwood.

'Where do you want to go?' Orus called.

Freya's eyes caught sight of Chicago's glowing skyline in the distance. 'That way,' she pointed. 'Let's go see the city.'

Knowing they had until sunrise, Freya played in the sky with Orus. She flew circles around the raven and won every race against him. By the time they reached the large city, the rain was forgotten as the two laughed from the sheer delight of flying again.

Without her helmet's protection, Freya remained higher in the sky. But her curiosity tugged at her and she couldn't resist the temptation to land on the flat roof of a building. It offered an amazing view of the city.

'Look at all the lights! It's so beautiful here at night, isn't it?' She walked around, wide eyed, taking in the sights and staring down at the world below. The rain made the streets glow in the cars' headlights.

'It is,' Orus agreed as he settled on her shoulder. 'But

I'd be feeling better if you'd brought your coat. There are tall buildings with windows all around us and we don't want anyone to see you.'

'I didn't want my coat to get wet,' Freya said. She stepped up to the edge of the flat roof and peered down at the late-night traffic. Because of the late hour and foul weather, there wasn't a lot happening on the street.

The sound of gunshots in the distance suddenly shattered the city's silence. Freya ran to the other side of the roof and peered down. 'It came from that direction!'

'Oh no,' Orus warned. 'I know what you're thinking. Don't get involved!'

'But someone may be hurt! You know what their weapons can do.'

'Freya, no!' Orus cawed as she leaped off the roof.

Freya flew in the direction of the gunshot. 'Come on,' she called. 'Let's just see what it is.'

As she flew towards the sound of the shots, they moved away from the city centre and into an area of run-down buildings. Freya opened her senses. She could feel fear from people on the neighbouring streets who were fleeing from the sounds of gunfire.

Some stood at their apartment windows peering down curiously. With the heavy rain and her dark wings, hair and clothing, Freya knew they wouldn't see her gliding silently between the buildings.

Up ahead she felt heavy waves of terror rising to meet her from two very frightened people. As she flew closer, Freya crested a building and gazed down to the street below.

She saw a man and woman cowering in the doorway of a burned-out building, cornered by three men holding guns.

Freya landed on the closest roof and drew her sword.

'Freya, you can't!' Orus warned. 'This is their world, not ours. Don't get involved.'

'But they are going to kill them. Look . . .' She pointed with her sword tip as two Angels of Death landed silently and unseen on the street behind them. Their heads and wings were held low and a great sadness was on their faces at the tragedy about to play out.

'This is their territory, not ours. Leave them be. It's their fate; you can't change it.'

Freya shot Orus a look. 'This is wrong and you know it. We can't let them kill those innocent people.' She leaped off the roof and landed on the street several metres from the attack.

Coming up behind the Angels of Death, she caught one by the arm. 'I'm sorry, you have wasted a trip. There will be no death here tonight.'

The angel's eyes grew wide. 'Valkyrie?' he said. 'There is no war here and this isn't a battleground. You have no jurisdiction or claim. What will happen here must happen. You are forbidden to intervene.'

Freya held up her sword. 'Yes, well, I was never one for following the rules. Go back now. These people will live.'

Freya charged past the shocked angels towards the group of attackers. 'Stop now or face my wrath!'

'What the . . .' one of the attackers called as he turned and saw Freya storming forward. He wiped rain from his eyes in disbelief.

With her sword held high, Freya blocked the two innocent victims with her body. She turned to face their attackers. 'I will give you one warning. Drop your weapons now and leave these people be or you will feel my sword.'

In the dimly lit street and with heavy rain pouring down, Freya was confident they couldn't see her clearly. But even if the attackers couldn't see her wings, she was certain that the victims cowering behind her could.

She heard their sharp intake of breath and felt their fear change. They were now more frightened of her than the men. Freya turned quickly to them. 'Say nothing – and, for your lives, don't touch me!'

'Are you suicidal?' one of the attackers asked as he turned his weapon on Freya and took a step closer. 'Or just plain stupid?'

'Neither,' Freya answered calmly. 'But I am sick and tired of you humans hurting each other for no other reason than personal gain. These people have done nothing wrong, and yet you intend to kill them to steal their possessions.'

'*Us humans?*' the leader called as he laughed and nudged his friends. 'And what does that make you then?'

Freya could clearly feel his thoughts. He was preparing to use his weapon against her. 'What does that make me?' she repeated as her temper flared. 'Not human!'

Freya's wings flashed open as she charged the men. Stealing a quick look back at the couple, she cried, 'Get down and stay down!'

The loud, sharp sounds of gunfire filled the air. Bullets pinged as they struck her breastplate and fell harmlessly to the ground. Odin had been right. As long as she wore the armour, nothing could harm her – no matter where it struck.

The rules of Asgard said that if she, a Valkyrie, touched a human with her bare skin, or wings, they would die instantly and be sent to Valhalla. But in all her training, she was never told what would happen if she killed a human with her sword.

Not wanting to risk Odin's wrath, Freya would do no more than wound. She wielded her sword with precision and she sliced the guns out of the attackers' hands and left the men on the wet ground, moaning and crying as they clutched their wounds. Freya leaped at the leader and pressed down on his chest with her black leather boot and placed the tip of her sword at his throat.

'Your reign of terror in this neighbourhood ends tonight, human. If I learn of you or your men attacking anyone ever again, I will not be so generous and spare your lives.'

'What are you?' the leader cried as his frightened eyes lingered on her open wings. 'I shot you, I know I did.'

'Your weapons are powerless against me. Remember my warning. Bring peace to these streets or you will face me again. There will be no second chances.'

Freya turned and left the man. She approached the two victims. 'Come,' she commanded as she walked further down the street.

Too frightened not to obey, the couple dashed past the attackers on the ground and followed Freya.

'Thank you, thank you,' cried the man. 'I don't know who or what you are, but you saved our lives.'

They were only young – not very much older than her, by Earth standards. He was handsome with sparkling eyes and pale, smooth skin, apart from a spread of stubble around his chin. The young woman was pretty and held an air of gentleness. She reminded Freya of a delicate little fawn in the woods. She could feel that they cared deeply for each other.

In that moment, Freya realized she'd never felt more alive or happy. She shared in their pure joy of existence. They all knew something amazing had just happened – even if the couple didn't know that she was a Valkyrie: a reaper of souls. But there had been no reaping tonight. Freya had saved lives, not taken them. The feeling was more intense than she could imagine.

The Angels of Death drew near. The older-looking angel spoke in a grave tone. 'Azrael will hear of this, Valkyrie. He will not be pleased. You have broken the rules and intervened where you had no right. These streets are ours.'

'Tell Azrael if you must,' Freya said softly. 'But I meant no disrespect. I just couldn't let this happen when it is within my power to stop it.'

The angel shook his head. 'You have changed their destiny tonight. They were meant to come with us. Tell them they have new lives and to make the best of them. We will be watching. If they do badly in their new lives, or if their future children do harm, the judgement will be on you.'

'I understand,' Freya said, bowing her head.

The two angels bowed, opened their white wings and took to the sky.

The man turned quickly and looked behind him. When he returned to Freya, his eyes were wide. 'What just happened? Who were you talking to? It felt like someone was standing right behind us.'

Freya nodded. 'You are correct. They were Angels of Death, here to take you with them. They have gone now.'

The young woman cried out and the man put his arm around her for comfort. 'We, we weren't supposed to be here,' he started. 'We were in our car and got lost. We came to Chicago for our honeymoon. But when we ran out of gas, those men attacked us. We didn't have time to run. If you hadn't come . . .'

'They would have killed you,' Freya said.

His fear was calming. He looked back and saw the attackers, still on the ground and clutching their wounds. In the distance the sound of sirens filled the air. It was getting closer. He offered his hand to Freya. 'You saved us, and I am eternally grateful.'

Freya took a step back. 'I am not an Angel of Death but if you touch me you will die.'

'What are you?' The man looked Freya up and down and his eyes settled on her wings. 'Those wings are real, aren't they?'

Freya nodded.

At that moment, Orus returned to her shoulder.

'Is that a crow?' he asked. 'There is a legend about crows and death.'

'Orus is a raven, not a crow,' Freya explained. 'But what we are doesn't matter. What does is that I have intervened on your behalf and broken the rules to save you. From this moment forward, you have new lives. You must take this opportunity to do good work in this world. Teach your children the same. Remember, you should not have existed beyond this night. So any harm you or your children do, I will be punished for. Don't make me regret my actions.'

'I swear,' the man promised. 'From this moment forward, we've both been changed. We won't disappoint you.'

Finally the woman nodded and spoke. 'You have our word, Angel. Thank you, thank you for our lives.'

The sounds of sirens drew closer. Flashing lights raced towards them.

'We'll be all right,' said the man as he split his attention between Freya and the approaching police cars. 'But you'd better go. You saved our lives and we can never repay that debt. But we can try to protect you. We won't tell them what really happened here. Go now, before they see you.'

Freya was reluctant to leave. But the flashing lights and noisy sirens were not inviting.

'Live well and live long,' she said as she stepped back. Freya opened her wings and jumped into the air and started to fly. When she reached the rooftop, she peered over the side and saw the couple waving at her. She waved back.

'We had better go,' Orus said.

Freya put her sword back in its sheath. She wanted to stay in this city of darkness and find more people in trouble. Helping that couple had made her feel just as good as when she'd saved Archie. These had been the best things she'd ever done in her life.

'Freya, please,' Orus begged.

'You're right,' she said reluctantly as she took to the air. Stealing one last glance down to the street where the police were climbing out of their cars, Freya decided it wasn't over. As she and Orus made their way back to Lincolnwood, she knew she would return to the city to help stand guard over its innocent people.

They arrived back at Archie's house just before sunrise. Freya was too excited to sit and watch early-morning television with the raven. She had saved lives – and it felt amazing.

Freya longed to tell her sister Maya what had happened. She imagined the good the two of them could do together and what a team they would make. She had been gone for two Earth days. But little time would have elapsed in Asgard. Certainly not long enough for her to be missed. Her only worry was Loki. Would he tell Odin what had happened? He did like to stir things up. Even though he had helped her leave and shared half the blame.

Rolling over to her side, she gazed out the window to the distant dawn. The rain was finally letting up as the sun rose. As its weak rays slowly drove back the night, Freya thought again of Maya, wondering what was happening now in Asgard.

CHAPTER TEN

It was deep in the night when Maya returned from dancing at Valhalla and retired to the room she shared with her younger sister. As she changed for bed, she noticed Freya wasn't there.

'Have you seen Freya and Orus?' she asked her raven as she settled him on his perch.

'Not since earlier,' Grul said. 'I saw them talking to Loki.'

'Loki? Why would they talk to him?' Maya crossed the room and felt her sister's bed. 'It's cold. She hasn't been here.'

'You know Freya. She's probably gone for another long flight. Orus is always putting her up to these things and leading her astray. I'm sure they'll be back soon.'

'I hope so,' Maya agreed. 'We have another reaping to attend in the morning. I don't want her to be late.'

Maya started her nightly procedure of combing out her beautiful, long flaxen hair and grooming her wings. She put fragrant oils on her feathers and preened them until they shone. As she climbed into bed, she looked over at her sister's empty place. 'Don't be too late, Freya,' she muttered softly. 'You know how angry Mother gets.'

But even as Maya lay her head down, she knew she wouldn't sleep. Freya hadn't been to bed. Grul said he'd seen her and Orus speaking with Loki earlier that evening. But Freya had no business talking to that troublemaker.

She rolled over and tried to force herself to sleep. But it didn't work. Thoughts of her sister wouldn't let her rest. Freya constantly worried her. All her life, she had been different. Somehow lost and unable to find her way. She wasn't happy being a Valkyrie and longed for more.

Though Maya tried her best to help, nothing she did could ease her sister's loneliness. Freya was searching for something in her life. But no one seemed to know what it was – least of all Freya herself.

Finally Maya gave up trying to sleep. She rose and got dressed.

'What's happening?' Grul said as he was roused on his perch.

'I'm going to find Freya.'

'Why? She's probably just out flying again, just like she did on the eve of her First Day Ceremony.'

'No, this is different,' Maya said. She reached for her

armour and pulled it on. 'Last time, I could feel her and knew where she went. But now I feel nothing – as though she doesn't even exist.'

'Freya wouldn't go anywhere,' insisted the raven. 'Orus may be incompetent and ill-tempered but he would never let her get into trouble.'

Maya shook her head. 'I know my sister, Grul. Something is very wrong. Freya has always been restless, but she's been worse since she reaped that soldier. She's distracted. She goes off flying alone and has private conversations with Loki. Something is up and I must know what it is. I won't be able to sleep until I know she's safe.'

Grul made an impatient huffing sound, but flew on to Maya's shoulder. 'Why are you wearing your armour? You don't need it here.'

Maya reached for her winged helmet. 'Because I have the strange feeling that Freya isn't here any more.'

'Do you mean, not in this house?'

Maya shook her head as she leaped out of the window and spread her wings. 'No, I mean not in Asgard.'

CHAPTER ELEVEN

It was the early hours of Monday morning and Freya was nervous for her first day at school.

She dressed carefully in clothes that Alma had made her. A slipcover for her wings and a lovely, long, chequered Steampunkesque skirt. She'd also given Freya elbow length, burgundy-coloured leather gloves so she didn't have to wear Archie's winter pair. Then she pulled on one of Brian's altered frilly tops over her breastplate.

'You are wearing your armour to school?' Orus asked. 'What are you expecting? And don't tell me you are taking your sword!'

Freya shook her head. 'Not my weapons, or my helmet. But remember, the bullies said they would get Archie today. I want to make sure nothing happens to him.'

Orus hopped across the bed and picked at a feather poking out of the duvet. 'You really like him, don't you?'

Freya paused. 'He's all right, for a human.'

Orus cawed in laughter. 'No, you really like him! I can see it.'

'You don't know what you are talking about.'

A knock at the door cut off further conversation and Freya was grateful for the interruption. 'Come in.'

Archie entered. 'I've got the papers folded and set to go. Are you ready?'

Freya nodded. 'All set.'

They delivered the newspapers in record time and found Alma and Tamika waiting for them on their front porch.

'My, my,' Alma said as she looked at Freya. 'You look lovely. Skirts suit you much better than those leather trousers. More feminine – and they hide all the right things.'

'What things?' Tamika asked. 'Grandma, Greta doesn't need to hide anything.'

'Of course,' Alma said. She focused on Freya. 'Well, Angel, are you ready for your first day at school?'

Freya nodded. 'I'm a bit nervous.'

Alma's eyebrows shot up. '*You*, nervous?' she cried. 'Sweet child, there's not a thing to be nervous about. Just follow Archie and Tamika's lead and you'll do fine.'

Getting Freya registered into the school was easier than everyone expected. No one questioned the falsified documents, and with Alma's talent for telling sad tales about the loss of Greta's family in Denmark and her long list of illnesses, by the end, the office staff were looking at Freya with great pity.

'All right, Greta Johnson,' the secretary said loudly and slowly as she handed Freya the school schedule. 'I understand you speak English?'

Freya nodded, unsure why this woman thought she was deaf and slow-witted. 'I do.'

'Good,' the secretary said slowly. 'As your great-aunt suggests, I think it's best if we keep you with Archie until you get to know your way around an American school. Will that be all right with you?'

'Yes . . . it . . . will,' Freya said with equal slowness.

Archie sniggered and nodded. 'I'll show her around.'

'Will you be OK getting home, Grandma?' Tamika asked as they walked Alma to the school entrance.

'Course I will. God gave me two good legs and I'm going to use them.'

Freya felt great warmth towards this kind old woman. 'Thank you, Alma, for everything.'

The old woman's eyes fogged. 'No, Angel, thank *you*.'

When she was gone, Tamika turned to Archie and Freya. 'We have the same lunch hour. Want to meet up?'

Archie nodded. 'Let's meet at the old oak tree in the front yard.'

Tamika nodded and smiled at Freya. For an instant, Freya saw Tyrone Johnson shining in her face and eyes. 'Good luck with your classes.'

When she was gone, Archie caught Freya by the arm. 'Well, Gee, this is it. Math is our first class.'

Hidden from inside her coat, Freya heard Orus moan, 'It would have to be, wouldn't it!'

By the lunchtime bell, Freya's head was spinning. Each class she entered seemed worse than the one before. Every time she and Archie showed the new teacher the note from the school's office, explaining her strange dress and seating requirements at the very back of the room, the teacher would give her a curious look that suggested they would have found it easier to believe she had wings.

Once they got past the class introductions, there was her lack of comprehension of what was going on. Archie had tried to prepare her, but it hadn't worked. There were four different classes in the morning, and although she had a perfect understanding of Geography, she was lost when it came to Maths, English and something called Humanities.

'I don't think I can do this,' Freya said as the lunch bell sounded. 'I've only been here half a day and already want to fly home screaming. This is nothing like my education in Asgard.'

'Don't worry about it,' Archie said. 'First days are always the worst.'

Freya leaned her forehead against her locker and sighed. 'But it's like I know nothing! I have lived over six hundred Earth years and yet I still don't understand what Humanities mean. You are already human; why do you need a class to tell what it is to be human?'

Archie put an arm around her. 'Humanities aren't about being a human, it's human philosophy, literature and language. It's not really hard once you grasp it a bit more.'

'But I'm not human,' Freya exclaimed. 'How can you expect me to grasp something I'm not?'

'I know you're not. I also know you don't like us. Maybe in the Humanities classes, you will learn why you should like humans.'

'I doubt that,' Orus called from under her coat. 'Now, will you please take me outside before I suffocate under here?'

Tamika was already waiting by the old oak tree at the front of the school. Freya opened her coat and released Orus as they joined her.

'Why did you bring him?' she asked, eyeing the raven skeptically.

'I told you before, I go where he goes and he goes with me.'

'Why? It's really weird.'

Orus stretched and flapped his wings. 'Tell her *she's* the weird one,' he cawed irritably.

They found a private place to eat, but Freya was unable to sit on the ground. With her wings restricted uncomfortably in the coat, there was no way she could get down, let alone get back up again. Instead she leaned against the school wall as she ate her packed lunch.

'What's it like living in Denmark?' Tamika asked.

Freya shrugged. 'I don't know. I don't live there.'

Archie cleared his throat loudly. 'What she means is she doesn't live there *any more*, do you, Gee?'

Freya had forgotten her cover story. She smiled weakly. 'Of course, I don't live there any more. I live here.'

Archie finished, 'But she told me it's almost the same as here. Only the language is different. Right?'

'Right . . .' Freya agreed absently. She stood up straight and became distracted by something in the air. A feeling of fear. She scanned the direction it came from. 'Wait here, I'll be right back.'

'Uh-oh,' Orus cawed. 'What are you doing?'

'Can't you feel it? Someone is very afraid.' She started to run.

'All I feel is trouble brewing. This is your first day at school. You don't want to cause trouble.'

'Gee, what's wrong?' Archie said as he caught up with her. Tamika was close behind him.

'Someone is very frightened. They are being threatened. It is the same fear I felt from you, the first time we met.'

'Gee, wait,' Archie called.

But Freya couldn't be stopped. The fear beckoned her. She couldn't resist its call. When she rounded the building, she saw the same bullies who'd attacked Archie, pressing a boy to the wall. He was Archie's age with a similar slight build. He wore glasses, but they were knocked to the ground. He was trembling with fear.

'Come on, hand it over!' the bully, JP, demanded. His right arm was in a cast from his first encounter with Freya's breastplate. But he was still able to command his gang to hurt people. 'Search him,' he ordered.

Two gang members raced to follow his orders and rifled through the boy's pockets. When they found what they were looking for, they shoved him to the ground and handed the money over to JP.

'Gee, stop,' Archie called as he caught her by the arm. 'You'll only make it worse. They will just take his money and then let him go. He's one of the Geek Squad I told you about. They pick on him because he's Jewish and wears glasses.'

Freya looked at Archie in disgust. 'What does his

religion have to do with anything? They have no right to attack him or steal his money. It's wrong.'

'Yes it's wrong,' Archie agreed. 'But that's just the way it is.'

Freya straightened her back and ruffled her wings under her coat. 'Not as long as I'm here. What's that boy's name?'

'Leo. Leo Max Michaelson.'

Freya lifted the raven off her shoulder and settled him on Archie's arm. 'Orus, you'd better wait here. I don't want you hurt.'

'Be careful,' Orus cawed as she stormed forward.

'Leo Max,' Freya called. 'There you are!' She pushed between the bullies and reached for the frightened boy's arm. 'I've been looking all over for you. You promised to help me with Math.'

'Hey, hey, hey, who are you?' JP demanded, stepping forward.

'She's the new girl I told you about,' one of the boys answered. 'The one from my English class. What a freak!' He put on a whiny voice., 'She needs to sit at the back cos she's got a bad hunch on her back. No one can touch her or she'll get sick. She's been hanging around with Daisy.'

JP approached Freya. He caught hold of her coat lapel with his unbroken left hand and leaned in close to her face. 'No one can touch you, eh? No way. If I want to touch you, I will,' he threatened.

If he moved a couple of centimetres closer, his cheek would touch Freya's face and he would die. Then her mission would be ruined. 'Back off,' she warned. 'Release me now before I lose my temper.'

JP towered over her and his eyes burned with fury. She could feel all the bad things he had done resting behind those dark, hate-filled eyes.

'Are you threatening me?' he spat.

Freya leaned further away from him. 'I don't make threats. This is a promise.'

'Look, new girl,' JP pressed. 'It's time you learned the rules here. This is my school and I run things. You'll do what I tell you. Now, hand over your money and phone.'

His hot breath on her face was making her angrier. 'And if I don't?'

'Then we're gonna have a big problem.'

'We already have a problem,' Freya said. She snatched JP's hand and wrenched it from her collar. She started to squeeze, using her Valkyrie strength.

'You run this school?' she repeated. 'Not any more. Leo Max, Archie and everyone else in the Geek Squad are now under my protection. Do you hear me?'

JP tried to pull his hand free of Freya, but she only squeezed harder. 'I have been trained in ways you could never imagine . . .' Driving him to the ground, a pained look rushed to the bully's face. 'I could break you in two without a pause. So heed my warning. You and your gang of bullies are finished at this school.'

JP looked around desperately and called to his gang for help. But when one of them came within her reach, Freya swatted him across the yard with the back of a gloved hand. Then she kicked another away with her boot.

She turned back to JP. 'Listen to me!' she cried, squeezing until the bones in his hand creaked. 'I was raised on the battlefields of war. You can't win against me. Leave the children of this school alone or I might actually let you touch me – then you'll discover the true meaning of terror!'

'Gee, no!' Archie cried frantically as he ran forward. 'That's enough. They get the message. Let him go.'

Freya looked at Archie in disbelief. After everything JP had done to him, he still felt compassion for the bully.

'Please, Gee,' he begged.

Freya gave JP's hand one more warning squeeze before releasing the bully and shoving him backwards. 'Remember they are all under my protection.'

The bully staggered to his feet as rage rose on his face. 'This ain't over, freak,' he called, clutching his left hand.

'You hear me? It ain't over. You and that boy-loving Daisy are going to pay for this.'

Freya made a move as if to chase JP and he started to run away. She looked back at Leo Max. Archie was picking up his glasses and a small skullcap from the ground and handing it to him.

'It's over,' Archie said. 'I don't think they'll bother you again.'

Leo Max pulled on his glasses. He reached for the skullcap in Archie's hand. 'Don't count on it. They've been picking on me for years.'

'Me too,' Archie said. 'What's that for?'

'It's my yamika,' Leo Max explained as he pinned the small black skullcap to the top of his head. 'I'm Jewish and I wear it as part of my religion. They're always taking it from me, until today.' His warm green eyes settled on Freya with nothing less than adoration. 'Why would you do that for me? You don't even know me.'

'I don't know you, but I do know their kind,' she said. 'I have watched others just like them for centuries. Brutalizing people and ruining lives for pleasure or personal gain. It sickens me.'

'Centuries?' Leo Max asked.

Archie quickly corrected, 'She meant it *seems* like centuries, didn't you, Gee?'

'Of course,' Freya agreed.

Orus flew from Archie's arm to her shoulder. He gave her ear a soft nip. 'If I didn't know you better, Freya, I'd say you are developing a soft spot for some of these humans.'

Freya patted him playfully.

'Wow,' Leo Max said. 'Is that your raven?'

Freya nodded. 'I don't own him. Orus is free to go where he chooses. But he and I prefer to stay together.'

'Cool!'

'So, how many other kids are in the Geek Squad?' Freya asked.

Archie shrugged as he started to reel off names. Leo Max added a couple more. In total, including Archie and Leo, there were seven.

Freya considered. 'That's enough to start with. Leo Max, I want you to find everyone in the Geek Squad and anyone else who's been picked on by JP and his gang. Tell them I want to meet them all right here tomorrow after school.'

'Why?' Leo Max asked.

'Because it's time you all learned to defend yourselves.'

CHAPTER TWELVE

Freya walked back into the school, savouring that same wonderful feeling of success. Saving Leo Max from JP and his gang was almost as good as saving the couple in Chicago.

But those feelings faded quickly as she moved from one class to another and were replaced by a sense of being lost and confused by subjects she didn't understand.

For her final class of the day, Freya was meant to have Physical Education. But when she presented her doctor's note to the teacher she was dismissed and sent to join Expressive Arts.

Without Archie at her side, Freya felt alone as she entered the classroom. Even having Orus hidden under her coat didn't help.

But soon Freya discovered that this was the one subject that she actually enjoyed.

'Greta, before you sit down,' the teacher, Mrs Breen, said, 'I'm going to ask you to sing something for the class. I need to find out what music group you should be in.'

'You want me to sing here? Now?'

When the teacher nodded, Freya inhaled deeply. She loved to sing with the other Valkyries, but had never sung to living humans before. She closed her eyes, and imagined she was back at Valhalla with Maya at her side. In the next moment, a soft and haunting song sprang from her lips; an ancient song, sung in the tongue of Asgard by all the Valkyries since the dawn of time. It told the story of a great love between a young Valkyrie and a valiant warrior. So beautiful was the warrior's face that the Valkyrie fell instantly in love with him and couldn't bear to reap him. So she went to Odin and begged for the warrior's life. Unable to grant the request, Odin took pity on the lovesick Valkyrie and told her to give the warrior her name before he died. In doing so, they could be joined together forever in Asgard . . .

As the moments passed, her confidence grew and she poured out her heart in the music. When the song was over, Freya opened her eyes. The only sounds in the classroom were gentle sniffs as tears shone in the eyes of most of her classmates.

'Greta,' Mrs Breen said softly, hardly daring to break the spell. 'That was enchanting. What is it called?'

Freya shrugged. 'It has no name. It's an old folk song my mother taught me. It's about a lonely Valkyrie from long ago that falls in love with a warrior she has to reap and the pain she suffers fulfilling her duty.' She looked around the room and saw, once again, the expressions of confusion. Did no one in this world know what a Valkyrie was?

'You have the most delightful voice,' Mrs Breen continued.

Freya looked over the class and saw everyone nodding in agreement. As she walked to her seat, she felt a warmth from the students directed at her.

When the final bell rang, Freya was surrounded by her new classmates, anxious to speak with her. She was barraged with questions about where she came from and how she'd learned to sing so well.

As they pressed closer, Freya could feel Orus squirming under the coat as he was squashed by the clinging students. His soft caws of protest turned to louder curses.

'I had better go!' Freya said quickly.

As the girls drifted away to catch their buses, Freya was left in a daze. She was so used to humans being mean to each other, it threw her off balance when they were nice.

'Let me out!' Orus cawed.

Freya opened her coat and the raven flew out. He circled the air and landed on her arm. His feathers were a mess and he was panting heavily.

'I am never hiding in your coat again!' he cawed. 'I nearly suffocated under there. And what was going on with all those girls? They nearly squished the life out of me! I was sure I was going to pass out!'

'Sorry, Orus,' Freya said. 'I didn't mean that to happen. They just came at me. I was surrounded.'

'Freya, it could have been a disaster if one of them had touched you. You mustn't let them get that near you again. But then I suppose that's the price to pay for being popular.'

'I'm not popular,' Freya insisted. 'This is just my first day. They were being friendly.'

'You had everyone in that class enchanted. Even the boys.'

'How do you know?'

'I couldn't see them, but I could hear them,' Orus said. 'You bewitched everyone.'

'I didn't mean to,' Freya said defensively. 'Besides, it's Mrs Breen's fault. She told me to sing.'

'Hey, don't get mad at me because they liked you. If anyone has a right to be angry, it's me, not you. I nearly died in your coat,' Orus huffed. 'All I'm saying is, you've spent so long hating humans that when they're nice to you you don't know what to do. Enjoy this moment, Freya. You know it can't last.'

'Why? Are you saying they're going to hate me once they get to know me?'

'No, of course not! But soon you will have to leave them to return to Asgard. Just don't get too attached to them. It will hurt when you go.'

Freya stroked the raven and considered his words. Orus was right. She was only a visitor here. She could not stay. Once Tamika's family was safe and Archie protected from the bullies, she would have to leave.

At that moment Archie and Tamika came running up to her. 'So?' Archie asked. 'How was your first class alone? Music, wasn't it?'

'Fine,' Freya said, almost too quickly. 'Everything went fine.

Freya was grateful to finally be able to take off her coat. As she and Archie sat at the kitchen table to start their homework, she stretched out her cramped wings.

'I've never kept them folded for so long,' she complained, as she massaged an ache in the long muscle of her right wing. 'If I keep that coat on much longer, I'll cripple myself.'

'Not to mention the damage it's doing to your feathers,' Orus added. 'Not that you keep them well preened anyway.'

Freya stuck out her tongue at the raven and refused to

tell Archie what he'd said.

'A few cramps are better than being seen,' Archie remarked. Then a dark twinkle rose in his eyes. 'Though I'd pay almost anything to see JP's reaction if he saw them.'

Freya grinned. 'Me too. It would almost be worth it to show him!'

Later, while Freya and Orus were tackling her Maths homework, Archie ran back into the kitchen, bursting with excitement. 'Got it!' He waved a printed piece of paper in front of her. 'This is the answer to the Orus situation.'

'What Orus situation?' Freya asked.

'Keeping him under your coat,' Archie continued.

Orus's nails clicked across the table and he hopped up on Archie's arm. 'Thank you,' he cawed. He looked at Freya. 'See? At least someone here cares about me!'

'Oh, Orus, you know I care,' Freya shot back. She picked up the paper and started to read:

Definition of Service Animal

Public Act 97-0956 (formerly HB 3826)

... The law requires schools to permit a student with a disability and using a service animal to have that service animal assist them at all school functions,

whether in or outside the classroom, and whether it
is trained or 'being trained' as a hearing animal, a
guide animal, an assistance animal, a seizure alert
animal, a mobility animal, a psychiatric service
animal, an autism service animal, or an animal
trained for any other physical, mental, or intellectual
disability . . .

Freya put down the paper. 'I don't understand.'

'It means,' Archie said, 'that since you already have a
sick note saying you wear a back brace and can't let
anyone touch you, you can take Orus to school without
hiding him under your coat. All you need is a medical
note with a forged doctor's signature – I can do that! We
can say that he's a service animal and you need him to
warn you if anyone is getting too close to you.'

'Perfect!' Orus cawed. 'No more suffocation!'

Freya reached out and grasped the raven. She brought
him up to her lips and kissed him on the end of his sharp,
black beak. 'And no more sharp claws cutting into my
side below my breastplate!'

They celebrated with macaroni and cheese . . . again.
Freya said nothing, but realized it was one of only a
couple of meals that Archie knew how to prepare. He
needed someone to take care of him. His mother
certainly wasn't.

As the evening wore on, they sat together watching television. Eventually Archie retired to bed. When he was gone, Freya pulled out her school books and started to study again.

'No going out tonight?' Orus asked.

Freya shook her head. 'I hated not understanding things in school today. I want to learn as much as I can as quickly as possible. If humans can learn this stuff, so can I.'

The next day Orus sat on Freya's shoulder as they walked into school. They received more than a few stares as they walked through the halls.

'What's going on here?' the school secretary demanded when she saw the raven. 'You can't bring that bird into the school!'

'Good morning, Mrs Bergquist,' Archie said brightly. He handed over the forged doctor's notes. 'Yesterday Greta tried coming to school without her service animal. But she became frightened when some of the kids in her music class got too near. She normally keeps Orus with her to warn of people getting too close behind her.'

Tamika nodded. 'Yes, our grandmother was going to come with us this morning, but she couldn't get a baby-sitter for my little sister. But you can call her if you want. She knows Cousin Greta needs Orus with her.'

Freya looked at Tamika in a new light. She knew the girl didn't like Orus and was frightened of birds, but yet she was speaking bravely on the raven's behalf.

'I don't know about this,' Mrs Bergquist said. 'I've never heard of a raven as a service animal before.'

Before Freya could speak, Archie pulled out another paper. It was from the Illinois General Assembly website with the statute he'd found on the Internet the previous evening. 'It says here they have just allowed miniature horses to be service animals. If *they* can enter schools, so can ravens.'

Mrs Bergquist became flustered as she read the document. 'Wait here.' She disappeared into the Principal's office.

She returned moments later. 'Dr Klobucher would like to see you.' The secretary directed Freya, Archie and Tamika into the Principal's office.

'That's fine, Cheryl,' said the Principal gently. 'You can leave us now.'

Dr Klobucher rose and closed the door after the secretary. She stepped closer to Freya with her eyes lingering on Orus. 'You have a raven as a service animal?'

She was average height with short, styled hair that reminded Freya of fine birds' feathers. But it was her kind eyes and warm smile that struck her most. They revealed a deep caring for her students. Freya's senses confirmed this. Archie had told her that Dr Klobucher was 'cool'. But as the woman stood before her, she wondered if Archie knew just how good she really was.

'Yes,' Freya agreed. 'He tells me when people are behind me and warns when they get too close.'

'Is he friendly?' Dr Klobucher asked.

Freya nodded. 'He'll let anyone touch him. He just caws if they get to close. Here, you can hold him if you like. He loves to be stroked.'

Orus gave Freya a sharp, accusing look, but allowed himself to be handed over to the Principal and endured her hand stroking the smooth black feathers on his back.

'Well, he seems friendly enough,' Dr Klobucher said, 'but I must consider the safety of all the students in the school.'

'Orus is my companion,' Freya said. 'We've been together for a very, very long time. He poses no danger to anyone here.'

The Principal handed the raven back to Freya and shook her head, laughing. 'Well, this is a first for me! Legally, I can't say no to a service animal, though this is very unorthodox. Let's try it for the rest of the week and see how it goes. But if there is a problem with the teaching staff or students, we may have to look at it again.'

'Thank you for letting Orus stay.'

'Just keep him under control and there shouldn't be a problem.'

Moments later the first bell rang. 'I'll escort you to your first class to let the teacher know what's happening and then I'll inform the others,' said Dr Klobucher.

Freya's morning classes went without a hitch. After the initial shock each class got used to the presence of the large raven on her shoulder at the back of the room.

At lunch Freya and Archie met up with Tamika and Leo Max. Orus remained on Freya's shoulder, but was glad for the treats he was handed by the others. Throughout the lunch period, students from Freya's music class came up to her. She was invited to a birthday party and asked to join the after-school Glee Club.

'You've become really popular,' Leo Max commented.

Freya shrugged. 'It's not me – it's Orus they like.'

Leo Max laughed. 'You're not serious! Greta, boys I've never met before are coming up to me and asking questions about you. They would never have done that before. But because we're friends, they want to meet you and have asked me to introduce you.'

'Why do they want to meet me?' Freya asked.

'Are you kidding?' Leo Max cried. 'You're beautiful and mysterious; everyone wants to meet you.'

Freya looked over to Archie. He said nothing but had a big grin on his face.

'I've heard Jim Gardner was asking about you,' Tamika added. 'He's the most handsome boy in school. I bet he asks you out to the dance.'

'What dance?' Freya asked.

'You know, the winter dance next month,' Tamika said. 'Everyone's going.'

'Except me,' Leo Max said sadly.

'And me,' Archie agreed.

Freya turned to Archie. 'Why aren't you going?'

'JP says if any of us show up, he'll pound us into the ground.' Archie paused and grinned again. 'But you can go – especially if Jim Gardner asks you!'

Freya was starting to feel uncomfortable by the turn in this conversation. 'Don't be foolish. Why would I go to a dance with a bunch of humans when everyone knows I don't like them?'

Tamika and Leo Max both looked at her strangely.

'Freya!' Orus warned. 'Be careful what you're saying.'

'Gee!' Archie joined in. He looked at Tamika and Leo Max. 'Ignore her, she's crazy.'

Freya finally realized what she'd said. 'Yes, I am,' she agreed. She looked at Archie. 'Sometimes I think I must have been crazy to come here.'

CHAPTER THIRTEEN

At the end of the day Freya and Archie waited outside the school. Leo Max soon arrived with a group of other students. They all looked like timid animals that had been cornered by a predator. Their eyes darted around and they looked ready to bolt.

'This is it,' Leo Max said. 'This is the Geek Squad. We've all been robbed and bullied by JP.' Leo Max turned to the group. 'Everyone – this is Greta. She's the one I told you about. She beat up JP and saved me.'

All eyes fell on Freya as if she were exposing her wings.

'Really?' a young girl asked, hardly daring to speak. 'But you're a girl! We can't fight boys. They're bigger and stronger than us.'

'What's your name?' Freya asked.

'Elizabeth.'

She was small and thin for her age but very pretty. She had long brown hair with caramel streaks and an exceptionally fair complexion that blushed easily. She kept her large grey-blue eyes cast down to the ground, not daring to look at anyone.

Freya bent down to her level. 'Elizabeth, fighting should never be the first response, but sometimes you must fight in order to defend yourself. Don't think for one moment that because you are a girl, you can't protect yourself. If someone is hurting you, or making you feel bad, you do what you must to survive.'

Elizabeth looked on the verge of tears. 'But I don't know how.'

'Me neither,' added a tall, thin boy wearing glasses. His wispy, curly hair fell long into his blue eyes, eyes that constantly scanned the area, looking for danger. Archie had told her about him. His name was Kevin and he was the smartest boy in school – but because he wouldn't share his homework with JP he was picked on the most.

'Maybe not now, but soon you will.' Freya looked at the group. 'I asked Leo Max to bring you all here for a reason. I want to tell you that you don't have to be afraid of JP or his gang any more. If you stand up to them, they will leave you alone. Now, how many of you want to go to the school dance but won't because you are afraid to?'

Everyone put up their hands.

A chubby girl stepped forward. Her face was covered in acne and she was obviously very self-conscious. Like

Elizabeth, she wouldn't raise her eyes to meet Freya.

'I really want to go, but JP said he'd hurt me if I went. He says ugly girls aren't allowed.'

Freya looked at each of them and they all nodded. 'What else has he done?'

'He's stolen two of my cell phones already,' another boy said. 'My dad won't let me have another one.'

One by one, they shared similar stories of what JP had done to them.

'While I am here,' Freya continued, 'I will protect you. If JP or any of his gang approaches you, just tell them they will answer to me. I promise you, you will all go to the dance. But I must warn you, I won't be here forever.' Her eyes darted to Archie and he dropped his head. 'When I go,' Freya said softly, 'you will have to fight for yourselves.'

'How?' the girl with acne said.

'What's your name?' Freya asked.

'Connie.'

'Well, Connie, I will show you everything you need to know to stand up to bullies.' Once again, Freya addressed the group. 'But you have to want this. I won't force you to do anything you don't want to. So if you are interested in learning to defend yourselves, meet me here tomorrow after school. We'll find somewhere to go where you can train.'

'We can use my back yard,' Leo Max offered. 'It's close to school.'

'Perfect,' Freya said.

'How much will it cost?'

Freya looked at the boy who had spoken. He wasn't very tall but he was stocky. She could feel his fear and desperation. He was young, but had already lived a hard life without any happiness.

Freya smiled gently at him. 'It won't cost you anything. If you want to learn to protect yourself, just come along and I'll teach you.'

Moments later, Tamika arrived and Freya could tell from her facial expression that something was wrong.

'That's all for today,' Freya said, drawing the gathering to a close. 'Remember, if any of you want to learn to protect yourself, meet Archie, Leo Max and me here tomorrow.'

As the Geek Squad drifted away, Freya turned to Tamika. 'What's wrong?'

'I don't know. Grandma called me. She says I have to come home right now. She said you and Archie should come too.'

'Did she say what's wrong?' Archie asked.

Tamika shook her head. 'Only to get home as soon as possible.'

It wasn't a long journey to the Johnsons' house, but it

seemed endless. Freya ached to tear off her coat and fly there. They found Alma in the living room. She was clutching papers in her trembling hands and pacing the floor.

'Grandma, what is it?' Tamika said.

Alma's pleading eyes landed on Freya. 'Angel, now I need your help more than ever.'

'What's wrong?' Freya asked.

The old woman handed over the papers. Freya could read, but she could make no sense of the complicated paperwork. 'I don't understand. What does this mean?'

'They are taking our house,' Alma said. 'Men came by this afternoon. Somehow the developers bought our mortgage from the bank. They are demanding full payment immediately or they will evict us. I don't have the money.'

'What!' Tamika cried. 'They can't do that!'

Alma nodded. 'I think they can. The papers seem to say so. I know we need a lawyer, but I can't afford one.' Her pleading eyes landed on Freya. 'Angel, tell me what to do.'

Freya looked over to Archie. 'What is a lawyer? I've heard that term before. How can they help?'

'A lawyer knows the law. They work as advocates. So if something is wrong with the paperwork, they would find it and stop the eviction.'

'Please, Angel, help us,' Alma begged.

'She can't help,' Tamika said furiously. 'Greta's got her own problems. We won't go, Grandma. They can't make us.'

Freya approached the old woman and took her hands. 'I told your son I would protect his family. I won't break my promise. Those men will not take your home.'

'Gee!' Archie cried, indicating to Tamika.

'What do you mean, you spoke to my dad?' Tamika asked. 'When?'

'What Gee means—' Archie started.

Freya shook her head. 'No, Archie, don't make excuses for me. This has gone too far. It's time we told Tamika who I am.' She looked at Orus. 'What do you think?'

The raven nodded. 'Show her.'

'Will someone tell me what's going on?' Tamika demanded.

Freya pulled off her velvet coat. When it fell to the floor, she reached back for the slip-cover Alma had made for her wings. 'I am not what you think I am. Please don't be afraid. I'm not here to hurt you.'

'What are you talking about?' Tamika demanded.

Making sure she was standing well away from them, Freya opened her wings.

CHAPTER FOURTEEN

Tamika wouldn't stop screaming.

'Maybe that wasn't such a great idea after all,' Orus admitted while Alma and Archie tried to calm her down.

'Tamika,' Freya pleaded as she pulled her coat back on, 'it's still me. You know me and you know Orus. Please, don't be frightened. We're not here to hurt you. We came to help.'

'What are you?' Tamika cried as she clung to her grandmother.

'She's an angel,' her grandmother said. 'Your father sent her to us when he died. She's here to help.'

'Angels don't have black wings and bright-red hair! She's a monster!'

Freya sighed. 'If you must know, I'm a Valkyrie. But you probably don't know what that is.'

Tamika shook her head.

Freya threw up her arms in frustration. 'I am so tired of people not knowing what I am!' She looked at Tamika.

'I was with your father when he died. All he spoke of was you and Uniik. He was so frightened for you he said he couldn't rest until you were safe. He begged me to come here and protect you. Which is what I intend to do.' Freya approached Archie. 'Give me the keys to your house. I need you to stay here with Tamika and Alma.'

'Where are you going?' Archie handed over the keys.

'I've got an idea. Hopefully, I won't be long.'

'Be careful,' Archie called after her. 'And don't expose yourself!'

Freya dashed to Archie's house. She pulled her winged helmet from the bottom of the closet and put it on. Then she reached for her dagger. She went out to the back yard, carrying her coat.

'Freya, talk to me,' Orus begged. 'What are you doing?'

Freya stopped. 'This is all about money and greed. I can't fight that, not with my powers. We need a lawyer. And we both know a good man who is married to one.'

'You're talking about the man we met when we first arrived!'

Opening her wings, Freya launched herself into the sky. 'That's right. Curtis Banks offered to help and that's just what we're going to ask him to do.'

* * *

Freya headed into Chicago. It was late afternoon, but the sun was still bright enough that she needed the protection of her helmet.

They flew towards the building they'd visited when they first arrived in Chicago. Freya and Orus circled it a couple of times but did not see the window cleaner. Moving from that building to the next, they scanned it too. And then the next. Finally, Freya's face brightened. She saw Curtis Banks on a suspended scaffold, cleaning a high-level window.

But he wasn't alone. A young man was working closely beside him.

Freya soared up to the roof and landed. She stepped to the ledge and peered over. 'How do we let him know we're here without his companion seeing?'

'Leave it to me,' Orus said. He leaped off the building and headed down the side to the scaffold. Landing on the railing beside Curtis Banks, he started to caw.

Curtis jumped at the sight of the raven, while his companion cried out in surprise. The older man's first instinct was to swat the bird away. Orus was thrown off the railing, but flew right back. He caught the man by the sleeve and looked up.

When that didn't work, Orus flew up to Curtis's shoulder and cawed loudly in his ear. Once again, the raven looked up.

This time it worked. Curtis reached for the controls and pressed a button that lifted the scaffold. Orus flew off his shoulder and returned to Freya.

She was still leaning over the side. 'Curtis Banks! It's me, the Valkyrie. I need to speak with you!'

At the top of the tall skyscraper, the winds were high. But not so high that Freya's voice couldn't be heard.

'Did you hear something?' Curtis's workmate said, looking around wildly as they arrived at the top. 'I swear I heard someone calling your name.'

Curtis shook his head. 'It's just the wind playing tricks. You get used to it. Just like you get used to some of the crazy birds that go after us. Let's take a break.'

Curtis climbed out of the scaffold and pulled some money from his pocket. 'Here, kid, go downstairs and grab us some coffee and maybe a doughnut or two.'

When he was out of sight, Freya pulled off her helmet. 'I'm so glad I found you.'

'Valkyrie, is that really you?' Curtis asked, squinting at her.

When she nodded, he continued, 'You look so different. Your hair, your dress . . . Where's your armour and sword?'

Freya knocked on her breastplate. 'It's still here, just under my shirt. I've left my sword and gauntlets at home.'

Curtis shook his head and chuckled. 'You know,

I told my wife all about you. She thought I'd been drinking. Said I was seeing things. But you ain't no apparition.'

'Not quite,' Freya said. She stepped closer. 'Curtis, do you remember I told you why I was here?'

'To help that soldier's family?'

She nodded. 'But it's worse than I thought. I can't do this on my own. I really need your help.'

'What can I do?' Curtis said.

Freya filled him in on how the soldier's wife had been killed in a hit-and-run and that they suspected it was the developers. She told him that Alma, the girls' only living relative, was dying of cancer and that their home was being threatened. 'I can fight,' Freya added. 'I was raised on a battlefield. But this is a different kind of battle.'

Curtis shook his head. 'That's so much tragedy for one family, it doesn't seem fair.'

'I remembered you said that your wife is a lawyer. Could she take a look at the paperwork? Maybe there's some way that she can help?'

Curtis looked around. 'Look, my shift is almost over. Why don't we head back to your friend's house and let me see those papers? Then I can talk to my wife.'

'There's something else. They need money to pay off their house.' Freya held up her dagger and pulled the blade from the cover. She handed over the heavily jewelled, golden scabbard. 'I've heard that humans treasure jewels and think this might be worth something. I wanted to give it to Alma to sell, but she'd never accept it. But if you sold it for me, I don't think she'd refuse the money to pay off the house. But will it be enough?'

Curtis's eyes went wide. 'That looks enough to buy half of Chicago! Valkyrie, are you sure you want to sell this?'

'What good are cold stones unless they can help someone?' Freya remarked. 'I don't care about the jewels – Asgard is filled with them – but I do care about Tyrone's family.'

'I can sell it for you,' Curtis said. 'But it sounds like those developers want more than money. They want that property.'

Freya dropped her head. 'I know. If this doesn't work, I'll have to do it my way. I don't want to hurt them, but to stop them, I will.'

'Let's hope it won't come to that.'

Freya paused, struck by his kindness. 'Why are you helping me?'

'Because it's the right thing to do,' Curtis said. 'Besides, I owe you. After your warning, I kept my eye on that guy I was working with. I saw a few things I shouldn't have and called my nephew. I told you he's a cop. Well, it turns out, Joe was wanted for murder. He was one nasty piece of work.'

'He was,' Freya agreed.

'Someone is coming,' Orus warned.

'Your friend is coming back,' Freya said as she pulled on her helmet.

'Let me send him home. Then we'll take my van to your friends' house.'

Freya had never ridden in a human vehicle before and hoped never to do so again. Trying to sit in the front of the van was more painful than she could have imagined. She needed to keep her coat on to hide her wings, which meant she had to sit on them in order to fit in the front seat.

Every bump and turn caused her pain in the bones and muscles of her constricted wings.

'You OK?' Curtis asked as he helped her from the van when they arrived at the Johnsons' house.

'I will be,' Freya complained, 'once I get this coat off!' She paused. 'Curtis, here they call me Greta. Would you do the same?'

'That's not your real name, is it?' he asked as he followed her up to the house.

'No,' Freya answered. 'But I like it.'

When they knocked, Tamika answered.

'Are you all right?' Freya asked her tentatively. 'May I come in?'

Tamika nodded sheepishly and stepped aside to let her pass. 'I'm really sorry, Greta. You just scared me when you showed me your . . .' She paused and looked at Curtis.

'Wings,' Freya finished. 'This is Curtis. He knows all about me.'

Curtis laughed. 'I wouldn't say *all* about you. But I've sure seen plenty.' His eyes landed on Tamika and he smiled brightly. 'Greta here has told me all about you and your baby sister.'

A sad smile crept to Tamika's lips. 'Greta, were you really the last to see my dad?'

Freya nodded. 'He was a very good man. He earned a place in Valhalla, but wanted to go on to be with the rest of your family.'

'So he's with my mom?'

'I believe so,' Freya said as she walked into the house. Freya introduced Curtis to Alma. She was busy feeding Uniik. When she finished, Curtis asked to hold the baby.

'My wife and I never had kids,' he said, making funny cooing sounds to the baby. 'Nearly broke our hearts. Now we're too old to adopt.' As Uniik started to cry he reluctantly handed her back to Alma. 'Show me those papers Greta told me about – maybe I can help?'

Alma handed over the paperwork. As Curtis read every page, he shook his head. 'I'm no expert, but something feels wrong with this paperwork.'

'Of course it's wrong,' Tamika said. 'They're trying to steal our house.'

Curtis smiled at her. 'Well, we aren't going to let them, are we?' He looked towards Alma. 'My wife is a lawyer. Can I bring her around to take a look at these?'

Alma shook her head. 'I can't afford a lawyer.'

'She won't mind. She loves a cause,' Curtis said. 'I promise it won't cost you a dime.' He held up the papers. 'Men like these gotta be stopped before they take over the world.' He stood up. 'I better get back – but I'll speak to my wife tonight.'

As he made for the door, he leaned closer to Freya and whispered, 'I'll take care of that other thing we discussed. I'm sure my wife can find a buyer for the jewels.'

'Thank you, Curtis.'

He grinned. 'Don't thank me yet; this fight is just getting started.'

CHAPTER FIFTEEN

Maya had spent half the night soaring in the skies over Asgard. It was still a long time before dawn but she couldn't find her sister anywhere.

Finally she headed to the one place she prayed Freya hadn't gone: Bifröst. The Rainbow Bridge was shimmering brightly in the cold, clear night. At the entrance, Heimdall stood guard.

Maya landed before him. 'Greetings, Heimdall.' She bowed her head formally.

'Greetings, Valkyrie,' Heimdall responded, as he also bowed to Maya. 'There is no reaping this night. What calls you to Bifröst?'

'Heimdall, you are a friend of Freya's.' Maya approached him gently.

The shy Watchman smiled and nodded. 'She comes here often, though usually it's late at night. We walk out on Bifröst and watch the human world. Most times, we do not speak. I can feel a great sadness in the child. She is restless. I do what I can, but nothing seems to calm her troubled mind.'

Maya nodded. 'I know what you mean. Did you see her tonight? Has she come this way?'

Heimdall frowned. 'Not tonight. Why? What concerns you?'

'I can't find her,' Maya explained. 'I came home from Valhalla and she wasn't in her bed. I've searched everywhere. Normally I get a feeling for where she is. But now I feel nothing. I fear something may have happened to her.'

The Watchman's fair eyebrows knitted together in a frown. His face revealed he was deeply troubled.

'What is it?'

Heimdall shook his head. 'It may be nothing, and I beg you not to tell Odin. But sometimes I have episodes. I am at my post one moment; the next I am on the ground. Nothing around me has been disturbed and I have seen no one. You know I require very little sleep and am certain I have not dozed off. But when I wake, I find a fraction of time has passed.'

'Did you have a similar episode tonight?'

Heimdall nodded. 'It wasn't long. But I awoke on the ground again.' He paused and rubbed his chin. 'Wait, I remember. Loki was here not long after; he said he caught me sleeping on the job and that he was going to tell Odin.'

'Loki?' Maya said. 'What did you say to him?'

'I told him if he said one word to Odin, I would squish him like a bug.'

Maya bowed again. 'Thank you, Heimdall. You have been most helpful.'

Maya turned to walk away, now convinced something was wrong. First Grul saw Freya with Loki, and then Loki was at Bifröst causing grief for Heimdall. It was too large a coincidence for such a short time.

'Maya, wait!' the Watchman called.

The ground around him shook as Heimdall jogged over to her. 'Go to the stables. The Reaping Mares are bound to their riders. Take Freya's mare. She can lead you to your missing sister.'

Maya felt like an idiot for not thinking of that first. Sylt was devoted to Freya, just as her own mare, Hildr, was devoted to her. 'Thank you, Heimdall. I shall do that.'

Opening her wings, Maya and Grul launched into the air and flew to the stables. Sylt's stall was at the very end. Just as Freya was the youngest Valkyrie, Sylt was the youngest Reaping Mare.

'Easy,' Maya said as she entered the stall and stroked the mare's smooth chestnut head. 'Sylt, I need you to find Freya.'

The mare nickered softly.

'Freya,' Maya repeated as she put the reins on the mare and climbed up on to her back. 'Take me to Freya.'

Sylt nodded her head and pulled at the reins. She trotted out of the stables, opened her large dark wings and took to the air.

Moments later, she landed before Bifröst. Sylt pawed at the ground, shook her head and snorted in distress. None of the Reaping Mares would dare cross the Rainbow Bridge without permission. To do so would mean their death.

Moments later, Heimdall reappeared. 'It is as I feared,' said the Watchman. 'I believe your sister may have crossed Bifröst without leave to do so. This is a grave offence. Odin will be furious.'

Maya climbed down from Sylt and knelt before him. 'Please,' she begged. 'Please, let me pass. I must see if this is true. If Freya has left Asgard, Sylt will lead me to her. I will bring her back. Odin need never know.'

'You want me to lie to Odin?' boomed the Watchman.

Maya quickly shook her head. 'No, Heimdall, not lie. But if he doesn't ask, please don't tell him. I know you care for Freya please help me find her.'

'Freya is one of the few who is nice to me,' Heimdall said. 'She cares not that I am a lowly watchman.'

Heimdall was a mystery. He was born of nine maiden mothers and had no known father. This caused much suspicion to most in Asgard. But he had always been exceptionally loyal to Odin and was happy to take on the mantle as Watchman of Bifröst when asked. Once Heimdall befriended you, he was your friend forever.

'Please,' Maya continued, 'I do not ask that you come with me. Only that you let me cross Bifröst to see if she is in Midgard.'

Heimdall looked at the sparkling Rainbow Bridge and then back to Maya. 'I will do this,' he said, 'on one condition.'

'Anything,' Maya said. 'Just ask.'

Heimdall's cheeks reddened. 'I like your sister very much. She has such spirit. But you are the fairest Valkyrie in Asgard. If I let you go, will you dance with me at Valhalla?'

Maya was stunned into silence. She had no idea he'd even noticed her, let alone wanted to dance with her.

'Does my request repulse you?' he asked, sounding wounded.

'No,' Maya said quickly and truthfully. 'Not at all.'

'Then do we have an agreement?' he asked.

'Don't do it, Maya,' Grul warned. 'It will lead to disaster.'

Without hesitation, Maya nodded. 'Of course, Heimdall. If you let me pass to search for Freya, I will gladly dance with you at Valhalla and be happy for it.'

Heimdall gave Maya the biggest, brightest smile she had ever seen. He bowed respectfully to her. 'Then we are in agreement. You may pass. But be sure to return before sunrise. Odin would have my head if he knew what I was doing.'

Maya climbed back up on Sylt. 'No, Heimdall, it will be my head – and my wings, and my eyes – if he finds out.'

'Stay safe, Valkyrie,' he called as Maya directed Sylt on to the Rainbow Bridge.

CHAPTER SIXTEEN

Freya was getting the hang of school life. She was even starting to enjoy some of her assignments. She had just written a History essay on the American Civil War. Freya had attended all the battles in the war, and was confident she had aced it. She took her seat in class eagerly anticipating getting the assignment back with a high grade. But as soon as Mr Powless, the history teacher, entered the class, he asked Freya to stand.

'Greta, I was most entertained by your essay. What was it about the assignment that you didn't understand?'

'I understood everything,' Freya answered frowning. 'You asked for a description of a battle during the Civil War, I described the Battle of Gettysburg.'

'What you gave me is pure fantasy.' He waved her essay in the air. 'Here you talk about the casualties.' Mr Powless cleared his throat and started to read it out loud. 'At the end of the third day, the overall battle was drawing to a close. The air was heavy with the stench of blood, filth and gunpowder. Men's cries could be heard rising high in the sky and drowned out the roaring of the approaching Valkyries.

'On that final day, there were more Valkyries on the battlefield than living soldiers. With only twenty-one warriors earning a place at Valhalla, we spent our time causing mischief with the weapons, teasing the men and misdirecting cannon fire.

'All told, in the Battle of Gettysburg thirty-five thousands fighters were wounded and eight thousand, nine-hundred and fifty-two warriors killed. Of those, seventy-nine were reaped by Valkyries and delivered to Valhalla while the remainders were left to the Angels of Death.'

Mr Powless lowered the essay. 'If I could give points for originality, you would get a perfect score. However, this is History, not creative writing. Not only are your descriptions of the battle scenes inaccurate, your figures are wrong. You didn't separate your casualties into losses on each side.'

'The specifics don't matter,' Freya defended herself. 'Dead is dead. It doesn't matter which side they fought for. They all died and valiant warriors from each side earned a place in Valhalla.'

The class laughed and Mr Powless's face went red. 'Of course it matters. We learn from these statistics, and plan better strategies.'

'Humans learn nothing from war!' Freya fired back. 'I could cite all the losses in all the battles throughout time, and still humans would not change.'

Mr Powless went back to the blackboard and snatched up a piece of chalk. 'All right, you claim you can give me statistics? Fine. Let's stick with the Civil War for now. Give me the details of the Battle at Antietam!'

'Deaths or overall casualties?'

'Both!'

Freya stated the statistics of the battle, including soldiers reaped by the Valkyries. Mr Powless scribbled her answers on the blackboard.

He turned on her. 'The Battle of Shiloh?'

Freya recited figures and Mr Powless recorded the casualties and deaths on the blackboard, ignoring the figures about the Valkyries and Angels of Death. His writing became more and more erratic.

He turned to face her again. 'All right, let's move away from the Civil War. There was a battle fought at Little Bighorn. What can you tell me about that?'

'Gee,' Archie whispered frantically. He pulled on her coat sleeve. 'Stop it!'

'Not this time. I may not know a lot about humans, but war is the one thing I do know. My figures are correct.'

Freya stated the details of the battle between General

George Custer and his men against the Cheyenne and Lakota tribes. 'Chief Lame White Man was reaped and delivered to Valhalla. He is still there and is very much respected by all the warriors.'

Mr Powless shook his head. 'Let's talk World War II and the Battle of Stalingrad.'

Freya confidently recited the figures of one of the worst battles in the war. When she finished, her teacher stood back from the battle statistics on the blackboard. 'Wrong, wrong and wrong,' he cried, crossing out each answer. 'These are all wrong and your essay is an embarrassment!'

'You are the one who's wrong!' Freya shouted indignantly. 'I was there. I saw them with my own eyes!'

'Gee, enough!' Archie cried.

'Freya!' Orus cried as he gave her ear a sharp nip. 'Stop now. Say nothing more!'

Mr Powless raised a shaking finger to the door. 'Get out. Get out of my classroom right now. Go to the Principal's office. I will be there in a few minutes.'

CHAPTER SEVENTEEN

Freya waited outside the Principal's office and listened to her history teacher ranting. When he came out of the office, he glared at her but said nothing.

Dr Klobucher appeared at the door. 'Greta, please come in.'

Freya entered the office feeling as though she had been summoned to stand before Odin.

Dr Klobucher sighed. 'Normally I like to give new students a few weeks to get settled. But in the short time you've been here, I have received complaints about you from several teachers. You are argumentative in class and constantly correct them.'

Freya opened her mouth to protest, but the Principal held up a warning finger. 'Right from the start I've felt something's not right. I've tried to be tolerant and sensitive about your situation but you are putting me in a very difficult position. None of the paperwork you've supplied is genuine. I have more questions about you than answers and unless you tell me the truth about yourself right now, you are facing expulsion.'

'Please don't do that,' Freya started. 'I am not ready to leave here yet. People are depending on me.'

The Principal leaned closer. 'Then talk to me. Tell me who you are. Where are you really from? Are you a runaway? Whatever it is, we can deal with it. But I can't help if I don't know what's wrong.'

'I can't tell you,' Freya said.

'You don't have a choice. You either tell me right now, or I'll call Mrs Johnson to collect you.' The Principal walked round her desk and softened her voice. 'Greta, whatever it is, I will understand. I have been in teaching for a very long time. There is nothing you could tell me that I haven't heard before.'

'Believe me, you've not heard this.'

'Let me be the judge of that.'

Freya was trapped. There was no way out. She rose and reached for the buttons on her coat.

'What are you doing?' Orus warned her. 'This isn't a good idea.'

Freya's hands trembled as she opened her coat and let it fall to the floor. 'My essay wasn't wrong, Dr Klobucher. I know those figures are correct because I was there . . .'

The principal shook her head. 'You've lost me. What do you mean you were there?'

'The reason I can't sit properly in a chair isn't because

of my back or a brace. It's because I *am* a Valkyrie and I have these.' She pulled off the slip cover and extended her wings.

Freya was prepared for screaming, or even the woman begging for her life. But there was none of that. Dr Klobucher stood very still and silent for several moments. Finally she lifted her hand and reached out to touch a wing. Freya pulled it back and folded it tightly.

'Please don't touch. If you do—'

'I'll die,' the Principal whispered dreamily. 'Valkyrie: a reaper of souls from the battlefield. Also known as the Battle Maidens of Odin. I studied Norse Mythology in university. You are death itself.'

Freya shook her head. 'I am not death, but I am a Battle Maiden of Odin who delivers the dead to him.'

Dr Klobucher staggered back. Freya caught her before she fell. At her touch, the Principal flinched.

'Please don't be afraid of me, I'm wearing my gloves,' Freya said. 'And I never take them off in school.'

'H-how?' the Principal stammered. 'I don't understand. Why are you here? Why would you choose my school?'

Freya assisted Dr Klobucher back to her chair and then covered her wings. As she pulled on her long coat, she started to speak filling her in on everything: the threat to Tamika's family and how JP was terrorizing

Archie and the weaker students at school.

'We have a zero tolerance policy toward bullying,' the Principal said. 'But I know it happens – especially off school property. I've been trying to work with JP for years. He's a very troubled boy.'

'He's dangerous,' Freya said flatly. 'While I am here, I'm going to teach the Geek Squad how to stand up to him.'

'I can't condone violence – especially from you. This is a school matter.'

'Not violence,' Freya corrected. 'Defence. I will teach them to look out for each other and how to keep from being victims. I will not always be here to fight their battles.'

'You can't fight their battles!' Dr Klobucher insisted. 'You're a Valkyrie! You could kill someone.'

'I am well aware of that. But I have no intentions of killing anyone.'

'You may not intend to, but it could happen. One mistake is all it will take. I'm sorry, but I can't allow a Valkyrie to run loose in this school.'

'Please don't ask me to leave,' Freya begged. 'I'm careful. I have Orus with me to keep everyone away. I wear gloves and my coat. No one can touch my bare skin.'

'How can I risk it?'

Freya leaned over the desk. 'Dr Klobucher, I know you are a good woman. You care about everyone here; your staff and your students. I am a student. I may be unusual, but I am still just a student. Please, help me find a way to stay just a little while longer. Just until Tamika, Archie and the Geek Squad are safe.'

The principal looked down at Freya's essay. 'Is this really true? Were you there?'

Freya nodded. 'I have been to every battle fought over the past six hundred years.'

Dr Klobucher raised her eyebrows. 'If you have been through all those wars, it is no wonder you want to stay here.' She paused. Finally, she nodded. 'I must be insane to be considering this, but OK, I'll help you. You may stay in school if you promise to be extra careful and keep a low profile. You are not to argue with your teachers, even if they are wrong. And if you make one mistake, just one, you must go. I am risking everything to allow you to stay. Please don't disappoint me.'

Freya beamed with relief. 'I promise. You'll see. We can make this work. No one will ever learn the truth about me.'

CHAPTER EIGHTEEN

While Archie slept, Freya felt restless. After her tense afternoon she needed to work off her anxieties and flying always helped. She changed into her leather trousers and black boots. She took her sword and breastplate and grabbed her long velvet coat.

'I'm going for a flight,' she announced to Orus. The raven was on the sofa watching television.

'You can't,' Orus cried. 'They're about to start a Judge Judy Marathon. I can't miss it.'

'What's a Marathon?' Freya asked.

'I don't know,' the raven replied excitedly. 'But I want to see it. *Judge Judy* is my favourite show.'

'Fine, stay here, Orus. You don't have to come everywhere with me.'

The raven muttered under his breath and released the remote. He flew off the sofa and landed on her shoulder. He nipped her ear. 'If I don't go, who's going to keep you out of trouble? Although I think it's a little late for that!'

Soaring through the night sky, Orus flew close to Freya. 'I thought you had done enough. You're going to teach the Geek Squad to fight, and you are helping Tamika's family. How much more do you want to do?'

'It's not that I want to do anything,' Freya lied – she loved helping innocent people in trouble and hoped she could again tonight, 'but, unlike you, I can't just sit watching television all night. And I'll go crazy if I keep reading my school books.'

'What's wrong with television?' Orus demanded.

Freya looked at the raven and laughed. 'Don't get me started!'

When they reached the main downtown area of Chicago, Freya swooped closer to the rooftops. She focused her senses on finding traces of fear or people in distress. She was barraged with emotions, but none of them particularly threatening.

Then she changed direction and headed to the part of town where she had encountered the couple in danger the other night. She immediately sensed the change. Raw and sinister emotions hit her from every angle. The landscape had changed too. She and Orus were flying above a neighbourhood of damaged and burned-out buildings . . . when suddenly they heard rapid gunfire.

'Not again!' Orus cried. 'Is there any point in me asking you to ignore it?'

Freya grinned at him. 'Nope!'

Flying in the direction of the shooting, her ears picked up the sounds of different weapons. Mixed in with the gun battle were police sirens.

'The police are here already,' Orus warned. 'You mustn't be seen.'

'You really do worry far too much,' Freya teased. Up ahead the gunshots grew louder and more frequent. 'It sounds like a war.'

Then they saw it. Two police cars were parked askew on the street. Officers were crouched behind their open doors, firing into the shell of a burned-out building.

Freya landed on the rooftop across the street. She peered into the building. 'In there,' she called to Orus. 'Look, they have weapons.' Her eyes moved back to the street. There were four police officers. They were badly outnumbered, but still brave in the face of danger.

She sensed at least fifteen men inside the building, shooting at the police. Focusing in on one of them, she felt fear and then determination to keep the police out at any cost. There was something hidden inside the building they didn't want the police to find. Something they were prepared to kill for. Reaching deeper, Freya finally understood.

'They're drug dealers,' she told Orus. 'This is where they're hiding it. They will kill the police to keep them out so they can move it from here.'

'Freya, you can't go down there. This is too big for you. You'll be hurt, or captured.'

'We can't just stay here and watch.'

On the street, she heard a strangled cry. An officer was hit and fell to the ground. As his partner ran round the car to help them, she too was struck down.

Freya looked at the raven. 'See what I mean? They won't stop until everyone is dead.'

'Uh-oh,' Orus called. 'Speaking of death, look who's just arrived.'

An Angel of Death landed close to the first fallen officer.

'Wait here,' Freya said to Orus.

'I'm coming with you,' the raven insisted.

'Orus, you're not wearing protective armour. Just stay here and warn me if more police arrive.'

Freya grabbed her coat and leaped off the building. Silently, she glided down the street, half a block from the gun battle. She folded her wings, pulled on her coat and drew her sword.

When she reached the police car, she saw there was nothing she could do for the first fallen officer. The Angel of Death was already doing his job.

'You shouldn't be here, Valkyrie,' the angel warned as he rose. The spirit of the dead officer was standing beside him, staring in wonder. 'This is our territory. Azrael will be furious.'

'I know. But still, here I am.' Freya left the angel and ran over to the policewoman lying in the road. Out in the open, she was an easy target for the criminals in the building. But when she saw Freya, she held up her hand.

'Get back,' she warned through gritted teeth. 'This is police business.'

Freya felt her intense pain and could see that she had been shot in the side of her torso. 'I'm here to help you.' She easily lifted the woman and carried her to safety behind the police car.

'Go, get away from here,' the officer cried. 'You could be hurt. I'll be fine.'

But Freya could see that she wouldn't. Blood was pouring from her wound. If Freya didn't act quickly, the woman would bleed to death. She covered the gunshot wound with her gloved hand. 'If I leave you, you will die. Just be still.'

Freya searched for something to wrap around the wound. But there was nothing. She reached under her coat and tore off her blouse, exposing her silver breastplate. She ripped it into pieces and covered the bullet hole, applying pressure.

The woman officer squinted at Freya. 'Are you wearing body armour?'

Freya nodded. 'It keeps me safe.' She looked up and saw that another Angel of Death had landed. She was walking closer to them. There was a confused expression on her face when she spotted Freya crouching over the fallen officer.

Freya held up her hand. 'Stop! I am sorry, Angel, but this woman will not die. You have wasted your journey.'

'Valkyrie, you cannot do this,' the angel said softly. 'It is her time. I must take her.'

Freya shook her head. 'I was too late for that man, but not her. Please tell Azrael that I have claimed this human for myself and say that she will live.'

'Who are you talking to?' the policewoman asked fearfully. 'You said Azrael. I know that name. He's the Angel of Death.'

'Not quite,' Freya corrected, turning back to the officer. 'He's the top Angel of Death, but there are others who serve him. Now, just stay calm. She will not take you tonight.'

'You must not get involved,' the angel said, stepping closer. 'I am here for this woman. I must take her.'

Freya looked back at the angel. 'She is young, with her whole life ahead of her. Give her that life. We both know she's a good woman. This world needs more people like her. If you must claim a life, go into that building and take them.'

'You know we do not touch their kind.' The angel spat in disgust.

'What's happening?' The officer's voice was tight with fear. 'There's someone here – I can feel them.'

'Calm yourself. Here, touch my arm,' Freya offered her arm. 'Then you can see her.'

The young officer touched Freya's covered arm. She gasped in wonder at the sight of the Angel of Death standing close by.

'She's so beautiful,' the officer said, calming. Tears of joy rushed to her eyes.

'Do not be afraid, my child,' the angel said directly to the officer. 'I am here to bring you home.'

Freya shook her head. 'No, you're not. She's going to live.'

'This is not right, Valkyrie,' the angel said. 'You can't be here. There will be consequences. Azrael—'

'I know,' Freya finished. 'Azrael will be furious with me. But I will take that chance. I outrank you. Just leave this woman be and return home.'

The angel nodded and bowed. 'So be it.' She opened her wings and flew away.

'Where's she going?' The officer sounded disappointed.

'Back where she belongs. This is not your moment to die.'

The officer's eyes focused on Freya. 'Who are you?'

'I'm someone who is tired of all the killing humans do.'

An agonized cry filled the air. Freya looked up and saw another officer fall to the ground. She looked behind him and didn't see any angels. He would survive his wounds.

She peered up into the building. The men inside were moving – she sensed they were planning to bring the battle to the street. If they succeeded, it was unlikely the officers would survive.

'Listen to me,' Freya said quickly. 'Those drug dealers are intending to come out here and kill everyone. I can't let that happen. Please keep pressure on your wound and don't move. Although the Angel of Death is gone, it won't take much to bring her back.'

Freya rose, but the woman caught her arm. 'No! Please don't go. I don't know who you are or where you came from, but that armour of yours won't protect you. Please, stay with me. Others are on their way.'

Freya removed the officer's hand. 'By the time they get here, it will be too late. Stay here and live. I argued for your life tonight. From now on, please do all the good you possibly can.'

'I – I don't understand any of this,' the officer said.

'You don't have to.' Freya rose and reached for her sword. 'Just live a good life.'

She darted across the street towards the building. Bullets continued to fly and she heard a ping as one cut through her coat and hit her breastplate. They were being fired from within the building.

Once inside, she opened her senses fully. She instantly felt three men descending the stairs from the upper floor where more men were firing down at the officers. Feeling too constricted, Freya shrugged off her coat and freed her wings.

She lifted her sword and charged up the stairs, releasing the Valkyrie cry used when approaching the battlefield. The sound rattled the entire building and momentarily halted the gunfire.

The men on the stairs saw her charging towards them with her sword held high. Using their sudden confusion to her advantage, Freya launched into battle. Within the tight confines of the stairwell, she slashed at them with her sword until they tumbled down the stairs. Soon they were all lying in a heap at the bottom.

She charged up to the next floor. To the right she saw a room with shabby furniture and several metal barrels with fires burning brightly. It appeared the men were living here. She heard a shout from another room, followed by the appearance of two men in the hallway ahead.

Freya ran at them, this time with her wings open

fully, and howled with all her might. The men dropped their weapons and covered their ears at the horrific sound. Disarmed, Freya was able to kick them to the ground, leaving them unconscious.

'Freya!' Orus called as he flew through a broken window. 'More police are here. There are hundreds of them and they're surrounding the building. Get out before they see you!'

'Not yet – there are more men upstairs. Orus, they don't want to be caught. They're going to kill everyone to protect their drugs. I won't let them hurt the police.'

'That's it – you are crazy!' Orus cried. 'If we survive this, I'm telling your mother you're completely insane.'

'Come on,' Freya called as she launched into a run. 'They're this way.'

Finding the remaining men wasn't as easy as finding the others. They had separated and spread out across the remaining floors. But one by one Freya hunted them down. She cornered the final criminal in a small room on the top floor. As he fell to the ground, she heard a new voice.

'You in there, freeze!'

Freya turned and saw two police officers entering her level. Holding torches, their guns were raised and pointing right at her. 'Drop your weapon!'

Freya lowered the sword and put it back in its

scabbard. 'I'm on your side. Look around you. I've stopped all these men. If you search, you'll find this is where they are storing their drugs.'

The officers were checking on the unconscious men as they cautiously advanced on her.

'We don't approve of vigilantes around here,' the officer said. 'You are under arrest. Now, take off that sword and raise your hands where I can see them.'

Freya looked around. She was in the remnants of a room with no windows. If she was going to get out of here, she would have to get past the police.

'Please,' she said. 'I don't know what a vigilante is, but I'm here to help. These men were shooting people outside. They wanted to kill everyone to keep their drugs safe. I had to stop them.'

'If you really want to help, start by removing that sword. This is your last warning. Do it now!'

Another officer entered the level. 'You ain't gonna believe what some of those guys are saying. They claim an angel attacked them. Said she got black wings and all—' He stopped when he noticed Freya in the room. 'Whoa, who've we got here?'

'A vigilante with a sword,' the first officer said. He focused on Freya. 'I won't tell you again. Surrender your weapon.'

'C'mon, kid, do what we tell you,' the new officer said

kindly. 'You're too young to be caught up in any of this.'
As he approached, his eyes landed on something resting
on the floor. He bent down to pick it up.

Freya realized too late what it was. A large, black
flight feather. It was one of hers.

'No! Don't touch that!' she cried.

But she was too late. He had already picked up the
feather. The instant his bare hand touched the Valkyrie
feather, his eyes rolled back in his head and he collapsed
to the ground.

'No!' Freya howled.

Orus moved. He launched himself at the remaining
officers and pecked at their heads and faces. 'Run, Freya!'
he cawed. 'Get out of here!'

Reacting instantly, Freya ran. She pushed through
the officers struggling against the raven. She could hear
them cursing and calling for help. Soon other officers
appeared and blocked her exit.

'Stop!' they shouted as they raised their weapons.

With no recourse, Freya opened her wings and let out
the loudest Valkyrie howl she'd ever made.

The police clutched their ears and collapsed to the
ground as Freya darted past them and ran to the closest
window. Without pausing, she leaped through the glass
and opened her wings.

On the street, she heard the hysterical voice of the

woman officer she had helped. Freya looked down and saw her being assisted by others. She was pointing up and screaming.

'That's her, that's her – there she is!'

The sounds of gunshots followed Freya as she gained height in the sky and flew as fast as she could from the area.

CHAPTER NINETEEN

Freya was frantic. She was on a rooftop, not far from the burned-out building. Pacing back and forth, she searched the skies for Orus. She shouldn't have left him there, fighting the police. But he'd insisted, ordering her to go.

Her hands were shaking and she felt sick with remorse. An innocent man was dead because of her. It didn't matter that he was most likely in Asgard and would be treated well. All that mattered was that in touching her feather she had killed him. Did he have a wife and children? What would happen to them? In her desire for excitement and wanting to help, she had destroyed a good man and his family.

'Freya,' Orus called.

'Over here!' Freya cried, frantically waving her arms in the air. 'Orus, I'm here!'

'Thank Odin!' Orus flew straight into Freya's outstretched arms. 'I thought for sure we were done for.'

Freya clung to the raven, grateful that he was unharmed. 'I'm so sorry. You were right. I should have left when you told me.'

She released the bird and leaned heavily against the roof ledge. 'Orus, I killed him . . .' Her voice was no more than a whisper.

'Who?' the raven demanded. 'Freya, who did you kill?'

'That man, the police officer. He picked up my feather and died.'

Orus's claws clicked on the ledge as he hopped up to her. 'He did not die.'

'Wha-what?'

'Freya, this is why I was late getting back to you. I knew you would be upset, seeing him collapse like that. So when I escaped the officers, I flew up into the rafters and watched them. They checked him. His heart was beating and he was breathing steadily. He was unconscious but will live.'

'How is this possible?'

'I thought you knew? Freya, when you shed your feathers, they lose their killing power. It had only just come away from you, so it retained some power, but not enough to kill him.'

Freya nearly collapsed with relief.

'Come on, Freya,' Orus said gently. 'Let's go home.'

'We can't go back to Asgard yet — we promised to help Tamika.'

'Not Asgard,' Orus said. 'Our home with Archie.'

It was nearly dawn when Freya and Orus made it back to Lincolnwood. They had just landed in the back yard and entered the house as the first rays of dawn arrived.

Freya was still shaking. It had been a bad night and they had come so close to being caught. It would be a long while before she'd risk going out again. She walked into the kitchen to make herself a snack when she heard a sharp banging at the back door. This was followed by a loud whinny and a scraping sound.

'It can't be . . .' Freya called to Orus. 'That sounds like Sylt!' She ran to the door and threw it open.

Standing before her was her Reaping Mare with her sister on its back.

'Maya!' Freya cried. She stood back and invited her sister and the horse into the house. The wings on Maya's helmet grazed along the ceiling as Sylt clopped through the hall. The mare's sides brushed against both walls and her right wing tip swept everything off a small table sending it crashing noisily to the floor.

There was barely enough free space in the lounge to hold the large mare.

'Thank Odin we found you!' Maya leaped down from

the horse and landed on the sofa. She approached Freya, but then stopped short.

'What have you done to yourself?' She looked her little sister up and down. 'Why are you dressed as a man? Freya, what has happened to your hair?'

Freya threw her arms around her sister and held her tight. 'I'm so glad you're here!' she cried. 'I've missed you and have so much to tell you.'

Archie staggered into the lounge, rubbing his eyes and yawning. 'Orus, turn down the television, I can't sleep . . .'

'Archie,' Freya called excitedly. 'Come here. I want you to meet my sister!'

'Sister?' Archie mumbled.

Maya removed her winged helmet, and she, Grul and Sylt became visible. Stunned, Archie stumbled backwards and tripped over a side table.

Freya started to laugh and went over to him. 'It's all right,' she called, helping him up. 'They won't hurt you.'

Archie's mouth was hanging open as he looked at the large flying horse in his lounge. 'Is that Pegasus?'

'Who?' Freya asked.

'Pegasus – you know, from the Greek myths. He's a flying horse who lives on Olympus.'

Freya shook her head. 'No, this is Sylt. She's my

Reaping Mare. Now, come here – I want you to meet my sister. You can call her Mia.'

Archie approached Maya in her shining silver armour. She was taller than Freya and her hair was in two long braids. Her elegant white wings were folded neatly on her back. She was clutching her winged helmet in her hand. 'You're Gee's sister? Are you a Valkyrie too?'

Maya frowned. '*Gee?*'

'That's me,' Freya said. 'He calls me Gee.'

A dark expression crossed Maya's face. 'What's going on here? What have you told this human of us?'

'Everything,' Freya said. 'I've been living with Archie and we go to school together. He knows all about me. He's teaching me to be human.'

Maya shook her head in disbelief. 'But you're not human, you are Valkyrie!'

'I know,' Freya said. 'But you were the one who told me I had to get to know them to understand them.'

'Yes!' Maya cried. 'By talking to the warriors at Valhalla! I didn't mean for you to come here and pretend to be one! Have you completely lost your mind? Do you have any idea what Mother will do when she finds out? Especially when she sees what you've done to yourself?'

'I like how I look,' Freya defended. She looked down her front. 'It's called Steampunk. And I like living here with Archie. I don't care what Mother thinks. All she worries about is pleasing Odin! I could never live up to her expectations anyway. I'm not beautiful like you, or as graceful as the others.'

'Of course you're beautiful,' Archie cut in. 'Everyone at school thinks so.'

'Don't help her, human,' Maya shot as her pale eyes flashed fury.

'That's enough,' Freya said to her sister. 'I'm glad you are here. But Archie is my friend. I won't let you talk to him like that.'

'Your *friend*?' Maya exclaimed. 'What is wrong with you?'

'Nothing! For the first time in my long life, I have a friend. Yes, he's human, but so what. Orus is a raven and he's my companion. You have Grul. What about Sylt? She's part of my life too. What difference does it make what they are? It is how we feel that matters!'

'But I'm your friend,' Maya said.

Freya's shoulders sagged. She had wanted Maya to see her new life, but now that she was here it was all going wrong.

'You're my sister,' Freya started. 'And you know I love you, but we aren't the same. You love dancing at Valhalla with the warriors. I don't. You are content to stay in Asgard, I'm not. I yearn to know more, see more and do more. I want to understand these humans and the reasons for the things they do. No one in Asgard can understand that, let alone explain it to me. So I came here to see for myself.'

Archie was standing between the two Valkyries while they argued. Finally his eyes settled on Freya. He started to frown. Leaning closer, he caught hold of her open coat.

'Gee, is that blood?' he asked. 'What are those holes in your coat?'

Maya stopped lecturing her sister and leaned closer. 'He's right. These are bullet holes.' She sniffed the patch of red. 'That's human blood. What have you been doing?'

Freya's eyes darted between Maya and Archie.

'Tell them,' Orus said. 'They'll find out anyway.'

Freya sighed. 'It's been a bad night and I need some cocoa.' She left the lounge and headed into the kitchen. 'Anyone else thirsty?'

The sun was up fully by the time Freya finished telling Archie and her sister the events of the past evening. Like her, Maya sat on a back-to-front chair and let her wings hang open.

Sylt was standing in the entrance to the kitchen, enjoying a bowl of apples. On the table the two ravens glared at each other.

'You left a feather behind!' Maya cried. 'Do you have

any idea how dangerous that is? Even away from our bodies, our feathers retain power. This is the World of Man. They might find a way to use that power against us, or against each other. Didn't Mother ever tell you about that?'

'I know!' Freya cried. 'But by the time I saw it, the policeman was already picking it up!'

'This is a disaster,' Maya said. 'We must get it back.'

'You can't,' Archie added. 'Not if the police have it. Besides, after tonight there's no telling what will happen to it. Especially if they realize it caused the officer to collapse.'

Maya rose from the table and reached for Freya. 'If there is nothing we can do to retrieve the feather, then our only recourse is to get away from here as quickly as possible. Come, we'll fly back to Asgard and hope nothing further happens with it.'

Freya remained seated. 'I'm not going back,' she said. 'At least, not yet.'

'What? Of course you are. Now, say goodbye to the human and let's go.'

'I have a name,' Archie challenged. 'It's Archie, not Human. And if Gee doesn't want to go, she doesn't have to.'

Maya stepped closer and loomed above him. Her white wings opened in threat. 'This is not your concern, huma— Archie. My sister does not belong here.'

Archie rose and stood before the tall Valkyrie. 'What are you going to do about it? Touch me? Kill me?' He offered his bare hand to her. 'Go ahead! I don't have much of a life here anyway. And I'd love to see what excuse you give Odin for me showing up in Asgard!'

'Archie!' Freya warned.

Maya's mouth hung open in shock. She looked to Freya and then back to Archie. Finally she burst out laughing. 'Very good,' she said softly. 'You have spirit. I like that. But whether you like it or not, my sister will return with me.'

Once again, Freya shook her head. 'I will return to Asgard. But only after I have finished what I came here for. Tamika's family is still in danger. Archie and the Geek Squad still need to learn how to defend themselves. And . . .'

Maya frowned. 'And . . . ?'

'Tell her,' Orus cawed.

'Tell me what?' Maya demanded.

Freya sighed. 'And we all want to go to the school dance together.'

'What?' Maya sat down again in complete shock. 'I can almost understand your desire to protect Archie and the others. But I can't believe you are risking everything to attend a school dance!'

'It matters,' Freya said. 'I really want to go. For the first time in my life, I am meeting people my own age. I like them and they like me. What's wrong with that?'

'Because they're not your age,' Maya insisted.

'You know what I mean,' Freya argued. 'Anyway, I have things to finish before I go back. Nothing you say or do will change that.'

'Fine,' Maya said, rising. 'I can't force you to return. But I will tell you this. In the morning we are going on a reaping. If you are not there, Odin will notice. He will ask questions. I will do what I can to distract him. But eventually he will realize what has happened. Then there will be no stopping him. Promise me you will be back before then.'

Archie looked out the window. 'But it's dawn already.'

Maya shook her head tiredly. 'Dawn in Asgard, not here.'

'I will,' Freya promised. 'The dance isn't that far off. Then I will come back and no one need ever know I've gone.'

'It is too late for that,' Maya said. 'I know, Heimdall knows and, worst of all, Loki knows. He is the one you must worry about.'

'But Loki helped me get away. If he tells anyone, he'll be placing himself in danger.'

'When has that ever stopped Loki?' Maya asked.

Before she left, Maya warned Freya not to use her winged helmet again. Every time she wore it, Odin and the others in Asgard would be able to tell where she was.

With that agreed, Maya put on her own helmet. After one final plea to get Freya to join her, she sadly shook her head and left.

When she was gone, Archie approached Freya. 'What did Mia mean when she said there would be no stopping Odin? Stopping him from what?'

Freya hesitated.

'Tell him,' Orus said.

Freya inhaled deeply. 'Odin is very strict. I told you we aren't allowed to leave Asgard without permission. If Odin finds out that I've gone, he'll send a Dark Searcher after me and then he'll release the Midgard Serpent on Earth.'

Archie's mouth hung open. 'Midgard Serpent? That sounds bad . . .'

Freya took a seat and invited Archie to sit.

'The last time a Valkyrie left Asgard without permission, Odin was furious. He sent out this large, dark creature to capture her. I've never seen one, but I've heard they are horrors beyond imagination. When the Dark Searcher was through with the Valkyrie, he gave her back to Odin, who punished her by cutting off her wings and blinding her. Then he banished her to Earth to wander alone for all time.'

Archie sat speechless, just staring at her.

'Go on,' Orus prodded. 'Tell him about the Midgard Serpent. He is human and deserves to know what Odin will do to Earth if he finds out.'

'And,' Freya continued hesitantly, 'after that, Odin released Loki's son, Jormungand – the Midgard Serpent – from his prison. He commanded him to punish those who had helped the Valkyrie. The Midgard Serpent is a terrible monster who can devour worlds. The last time he was released, he destroyed half the Earth. The only thing that stopped him from devouring it all was Thor. The two hate each other. But it takes all of Thor's strength just to subdue him.'

Silence filled the kitchen.

Finally Archie spoke, his voice no more than a faint whisper. 'Gee, your sister is right, you must go back – right now.'

'I can't,' Freya said. 'I promised Tyrone.'

'You must,' Archie insisted. 'It's too dangerous. Go back before Odin finds out.'

It felt like someone had just punched her in the stomach. Archie was telling her to leave. His face was red and he was growing angry. His emotions were coming at her in waves too fast for her to understand.

'Don't you like me any more?' Freya asked in a shallow voice.

'What?' Archie demanded.

'Is that why you want me to go? You don't like me and have been waiting for a reason to send me away!'

'Is that what you think?' Archie cried. 'That I don't like you?'

Freya couldn't face him. Instead she just nodded.

'Gee, no.' Archie moved his chair closer to her and took her gloved hands. 'You're the first friend I've ever had. I care more for you than I've ever cared for anyone in my whole life! You mean everything to me.'

'Then why are you sending me away?'

'I don't want to,' Archie insisted. 'But you must go back. I couldn't bear it if Odin did to you what he did to that other Valkyrie. It will kill me when you leave, but I'd rather lose you now, knowing you will be safe, than see you hurt.'

'But I won't be hurt,' Freya insisted. 'Archie, time moves differently between Earth and Asgard. It is still the same night that I left there, while days and days have passed here. There is plenty of time for me to do what I came here for. Asgard's dawn is still Earth-weeks away.'

'But, Gee, if you get hurt, I couldn't bear it.'

'I won't,' Freya insisted. 'And I know I've got to go

back – but can't we have just a little more time? Please, Archie, let me stay.'

'Do you promise you'll be safe?'

Freya nodded. 'I promise. Just a little while longer, that's all.'

Archie nodded. 'All right, as long as you are safe.'

Freya and Archie realized they had another big problem. A problem that looked like a horse, but one that had black- and chestnut-coloured wings.

'If my mom comes home and sees her she'll have a fit!' Archie said as he stroked the mare's soft muzzle.

'But if Sylt returns to Asgard she could be used to lead others to us. Look how easily Maya found me. Keeping her here is the only way. Besides, your mother hasn't been home since I arrived. Perhaps she won't return until I've gone.'

Archie didn't look convinced. 'What do we feed her? I don't have a lot of extra money to buy straw or hay or whatever she eats. What about exercise? She can't spend all the time in the house.'

'Simple,' Freya said. 'During the day while we're at school, we can hide her in your garage. We'll leave bowls of whatever we eat and water. Then at night I can take her out to find grains and grass and other food. We can do this, Archie, I know we can.'

Archie was stroking the mare's neck. 'I've never ridden a horse before.'

'Then tonight, after it gets dark, if you want you can ride her while we go find food.'

CHAPTER TWENTY

After school Freya stood in front of the Geek Squad in Leo Max's back yard for their first self-defence session. There were even more kids than Freya first met and she was now faced with eleven students. Mostly boys, but both Elizabeth and Connie were there too – looking just as frightened and anxious as everyone else.

Archie and Tamika were also there, anxious to learn how to defend themselves. But unlike the others, they weren't nervous and offered encouragement to everyone else.

Freya spoke first about the importance of staying close together. She spoke of strength in numbers and how even the smallest army can succeed in battle with strategy, skill and stealth.

Then one by one she took them through the basics she had been taught in her early life about self-defence. A Valkyrie had to know how to fight. In the distant past, when they arrived at battlefields, occasionally they would encounter a hostile force that did not welcome them.

The armies would raise their weapons and take on the winged warriors.

The Valkyries always won.

Freya taught them to use anything within reach as a weapon. Failing that, she showed them how to kick in such a way as to bring down even the biggest frost giant. She taught them about pressure points and how to take on opponents much bigger and stronger than they were.

Despite the seriousness of the training, there was a lot of laughter too. Freya delighted in watching the group of misfits coming together. Friendships were being forged and they were learning to watch each others' backs.

When the first training session drew to a close, Freya was touched by their gratitude and waved to them as they dispersed. They were now proud to call themselves the elite members of the Geek Squad.

'That was so cool!' Archie cried as he practised kicking all the way to Tamika's house. 'Just let JP try something. He's in for a big surprise!'

Tamika was also practising her kicks. 'Take that, Mr Developer! You want to steal my house? Try this!'

Their laughter continued as they reached Tamika's house. An unfamiliar car was in the driveway. 'That could be Curtis,' Freya suggested.

She was right. Inside the house they found Curtis and his wife sitting in the lounge with Alma. Curtis's wife

cradled Uniik in her arms. Her face was glowing as she
gazed down on the baby.

'Greta!' Curtis cried when he saw her. 'Come, I want
you to meet my wife. This is Carol.'

Curtis's wife stood. Her dark eyes were wide and
curious and carried a trace of fear. They lingered on the
lumps at Freya's back. Curtis had told her everything
and she was trying to see her wings.

'Do you want to see them?' Freya offered.

Carol blustered. 'I – I don't want to be rude.'

'It is not being rude, you're just curious.' Freya
removed her coat and freed her wings. 'See,' she said,
opening them, 'just ordinary wings.'

As Carol inhaled, Curtis reached out and took Uniik
from her shaking hands. 'It's all right, you get used to
them real quick. Soon you'll even forget she's got them.'
He winked at Freya. 'Except for when you try to get her
into a car. Then that's all you hear about.'

He put on a high and teasing voice: '*My wings* this . . .
and *my wings* that . . .'

Archie started to laugh. 'You sound just like Gee!'

Freya also laughed. 'I don't sound like that!'

'Sure you do,' Tamika added.

Before long everyone was laughing and the tension
was broken.

When they settled, Carol told Tamika what she'd

told her grandmother earlier. That she was starting to investigate the developer. She'd heard rumours around town about him, but so far no charges against him had stuck.

'Is there nothing you can do?' Freya asked.

'I'm only just getting started.'

'You be careful,' Alma warned. 'These are bad men who will kill to get what they want.'

Carol's dark eyes sparkled. 'That's just the kind of challenge I like.' She opened her briefcase and pulled out an item. It was Freya's scabbard. The gold casing was intact, but all the jewels had been removed. Carol handed it back to her.

'I hope you're not offended, but the real value was in all those jewels, not the scabbard itself. I'm arranging their sale. We'll receive more than enough money to pay off this house. I'll set up an account for the balance.'

Alma frowned. 'What money? Angel, what have you done?'

Freya smiled at the old woman. 'I asked Curtis to take my scabbard and sell it. The money will pay for your house.'

'Angel, no,' Alma cried. 'That's yours; I can't take it!'

'You are not taking it from me,' Freya said. 'I am giving it.'

'No, it's wrong.'

Freya looked over to Curtis. 'I told you she wouldn't want to take it.' She crossed to the old woman and knelt awkwardly before her chair. 'Please, Alma, accept this from me. I want to do it. Those jewels meant nothing to me, but they will protect you, and that means everything.'

'But it's too generous,' the old woman said. 'You are giving me all your money.'

'Not all,' Carol cut in. 'Just a fraction of it. Greta is very wealthy.'

There was a sharp intake of breath from everyone in the room.

'Gee,' Archie cried. 'You're rich!'

Freya shrugged. 'I don't want the money. Split it up between Alma and Tamika, Archie and you and Curtis.'

'Angel, you can't do that,' Alma said.

'You all need it more than me,' Freya insisted. 'Alma, you can pay for Tamika's and Uniik's education.' Her eyes settled on Archie. 'And you can open your own hair salon and maybe learn to cook more than macaroni and cheese.'

'You're giving it all away?' Carol asked. 'Why?'

'Because we don't use human money in Asgard; it has no value there.'

Curtis rose and approached Freya. 'Are you sure about this? It's a lot of money.'

'Absolutely.' Freya focused on Alma again. 'But I

would be grateful if we could use a bit of it to buy some fabric. I need some more clothes for school. Would you help me?'

The old woman rose painfully to her feet. 'Angel, I have been waiting to hear you say those words! I would love to make you more clothes.'

'I know exactly what you're doing, Angel.' Alma looked at Freya as she helped the old woman prepare dinner.

'What?' Freya asked as she chopped vegetables.

'I know, and I am truly grateful.'

Putting down the knife, Freya looked at the old woman. 'I really don't understand.'

'Yes, you do. The moment you found out I had cancer, you were thinking of Curtis and his wife for Tamika and Uniik.'

'You're busted!' Orus laughed, using his new favourite expression from television.

Freya sighed and pulled out a chair for Alma to sit. 'I promised your son I would see his girls protected. He didn't know what the danger was at the time, but his family was all he thought about. And I know how much you've been worrying about them.'

Alma shook her head. 'The thought of my two girls in care is more than I can bear.'

'Tamika is just as frightened,' Freya said. 'She knows

you are very ill. Though she doesn't say anything, she is terrified for Uniik. She thinks they will be separated.'

'So you thought of Curtis Banks.'

'Not at first,' Freya admitted. 'But from the moment I met him, I knew he was a good man. It was only when I saw him the second time that I put it all together. He and his wife have no children, but desperately want them. Tamika and Uniik have no parents and you are ill. It seems the perfect match.'

The old woman chuckled. 'I may not be an angel with the power to know people's hearts, but I have lived a very long time and met a lot of people. The Bankses are good folk and would care for my girls.'

Freya tilted her head to the side and smiled. 'There isn't an Angel of Death beside you just yet. Take the time you have left to get to know Curtis and Carol better.'

'I don't have to – I already know,' the old woman said. 'But I will take this time before I go to let Tamika get to know them.'

After dinner, Archie could barely contain his excitement. He practically skipped along the pavement.

'Are you that happy about the money?'

Archie shook his head. 'Nope. Tonight you said you'd let me ride your winged horse. I can't wait!'

Freya laughed. 'Then let's get home and we can go.'

Sylt had been made comfortable in the garage. But she nickered excitedly when Freya approached her.

'Are you ready to fly?' she asked the mare. She looked at Archie and saw his eyes were wide and filled with anticipation.

'All right, Archie, I want you to start stroking her neck and then move down to her wings. Sylt has never been ridden by a living human before. She may be a bit nervous. But if you reassure her, I'm sure she'll be fine.'

Archie did everything he was told to do. Before long, Sylt opened her wings and invited him up on her back. Freya helped hoist him up.

Archie offered his hand. 'Are you coming up too?'

Freya shook her head. 'I've got my own wings that I need to stretch. Besides, I can't risk my hair or something else touching you. But I'll be right beside you all the way.'

'Me too!' Orus added.

They took off from the back yard.

Climbing high in the night sky, Freya felt all of Archie's emotions. Fear and great joy all mixed together as he learned to use the reins to direct Sylt in the air.

They headed over the Chicago skyline. And despite everything she felt rising from the street, Freya remained with Archie. The police would have to take care of the criminals by themselves for one night.

They flew away from the Chicago area and towards the open fields and farms of central Illinois. Freya watched Sylt closely. When the mare opened her nostrils and started to sniff, she knew they had found somewhere for her to eat.

Soaring closer to Archie, Freya watched the excitement in his eyes. He was having the best time of his life. She hated to end it, but Sylt needed food. Finally she called over to him to let him know they were going down.

As Freya tilted her wings and descended, the Reaping Mare followed. They touched down in the middle of fields that had recently been harvested. Archie slid off the mare and hugged her neck. 'Sylt, you're the best!'

Sylt turned her head back to him and neighed. Then she focused on eating what was left after the harvest.

'I can't believe it!' Archie cried. 'I've never had so much fun in all my life.'

Freya laughed. His face was flushed from the chill of the night air and the excitement. He could hardly stand still. 'Can we go out again tomorrow night?'

'Sure. We'll have to do it every night. Sylt needs food and exercise. But, Archie, we can't be out as long as this each time.'

'Why not?'

'Because you're human. You need to sleep!'

'I'm not tired.'

'You will be.'

Archie was still stroking Sylt as she munched on the grain. 'Gee, you sure are pretty when you fly. That's the first time I've ever seen you do it.'

Freya grinned. 'I love flying. Sometimes late at night in Asgard, Orus and I would go out until it was light.'

'I'd sure like to see that.'

'I really wish you could,' Freya admitted.

It was getting very late when they brought Sylt back to the garage. Despite the hour, Archie was wide awake. 'I can't wait for tomorrow night,' he said brightly. 'That was too cool. Best ride I've ever had.'

CHAPTER TWENTY-ONE

Life over the next few weeks entered a blissfully quiet routine. Curtis and Carol spent more time at Tamika's house as they worked to stop John Roberts Developments. A strange calm had descended from the developers and Carol was getting nervous. Her research showed that the developer was not easily stopped. The fact that the house had now been paid off, with Freya's money, meant nothing to them. It wasn't the house they wanted, but the land that it stood on.

Archie started to join Freya for short patrols of the Chicago streets at night. While Archie remained with Sylt and Orus on the rooftops, Freya would fly down to stop muggings and robberies.

Before long there were whispered rumours about a costumed, winged avenger patrolling the dark streets of Chicago. Archie delighted in cutting out newspaper articles about it and reading how the police were calling it a hoax – while the victims *and* criminals were claiming it was true.

At school, Freya's grades improved. She stopped arguing with her teachers and focused on her studies. With the threat of Freya's retribution still in the air, JP and his gang of bullies seemed to be leaving everyone alone.

Despite the calm, the afternoon training sessions with the Geek Squad continued. Freya marvelled at the changes in her students. They had learned how to defend themselves. But more than that, it was their growing confidence and joy that touched her the most. As the days and weeks ticked by, the Geek Squad began to get very excited about the upcoming winter dance.

'Greta, come quickly! JP's gang is going after Archie again. The whole Geek Squad is there. It's a big fight!' Tamika shouted as she ran up to Freya, who was waiting for Archie outside the school.

They ran round the building. Up ahead, Freya saw Archie fight back against one of JP's gang. Leo Max was beside him, fighting with another gang member.

Elizabeth was trying to pull one of the bullies off Connie. She was using the kick Freya had taught her. With one blow, she drove them away.

Freya stopped running and slowed to a walk.

'C'mon!' Tamika called, trying to drag her along. 'Before they hurt them!'

'No, wait,' Freya said. 'Look at the Geek Squad. They're standing up to the bullies. All of them are working together. I can feel they aren't frightened any more.'

'But they could get hurt!'

'They've already been hurt,' Freya said. 'I can't get involved. They have to do this for themselves.' Freya pulled the raven from her shoulder and handed him to Tamika. 'Here, hold Orus for me. If this gets out of hand, I'll join in. But let them go for a moment.'

Tamika had long ago conquered her fear of Orus. She held on to the large raven as she and Freya approached the fight.

'Come on,' Orus cawed, flapping his wings. 'Get them, Archie! That's it, Leo Max, hit him!'

More and more kids surrounded the fight and cheered them on as the Geek Squad all joined in to protect their new friends. Freya strained to see JP among his fighting gang, but he didn't seem to be there.

She stood back, watching her students proudly. They were using all the moves and self-defence techniques she had taught them to protect themselves. Their days of being victims were over.

Suddenly a powerful blow cut across her back. Freya was knocked to the ground. This was followed by a second, more powerful strike across her wings.

Howling in pain, Freya looked up to see JP looming above her with a baseball bat.

'Not so tough now, are ya, Freya?' He lifted the bat and brought it down again.

Freya raised her arm and blocked the blow. The bat struck her painfully in the wrist.

'Gee!' Archie cried when he saw her on the ground. 'Leo Max, look! JP's got Gee!'

Archie fought free of the boy he was wrestling, charged over to JP and tackled him to the ground. Leo Max was right behind him and jumped on top. When Kevin joined it, JP was pulled away from Freya.

Freya used this opportunity to climb to her feet. Her wings felt like they were on fire and screaming to be freed from the coat. The armour she wore protected her from serious injury, but it didn't stop the intense, bone-searing pain of the bat's blows to her wings.

Gang members came to JP's aid and pulled Archie, Leo Max and Kevin off their leader. Within moments, JP was back on his feet again and holding the baseball bat. He moved straight in on Freya.

'This is it, Freak, you're gonna die!' he threatened.

'And you are too stupid to live!' Freya responded as she prepared to take him on.

At that moment Mr Powless arrived. The History teacher saw JP with the bat, advancing on Freya. He grabbed JP's arm to stop him, but JP turned quickly and raised the bat to the teacher.

With little time to think, Freya jumped in front of her History teacher and took the blow. It struck her full in the chest. The twanging sound of the wooden bat meeting her silver armour rang out.

It startled JP for a moment. In that time, Freya caught hold of the bat and wrenched it away from him. 'I have had enough of you, *human!*' she shrieked in rage. Tossing the bat aside, she lunged forward and caught JP by the coat. Hoisting him easily over her head, she let out a loud Valkyrie howl as she threw him across the yard.

'Wait here!' Freya ordered Tamika and Orus. 'It's time I finished this!'

Freya charged at the bully and, tearing off a glove, exposed her bare hand. But just before she could reap him, Archie darted in front of her.

'Gee, no!' he cried. 'Stop – everyone's watching you!' He caught her by her coat and turned her round. Archie held up the glove. 'They're all watching. Here, put it back on before they see.'

Everyone in the yard was staring at her.

'Please,' Archie begged. 'Don't expose yourself, not now! It's over. Mr Powless saw what happened. JP will be expelled. He won't be allowed back here. We won!'

Orus returned to her shoulder. 'It's over, Freya,' he cawed. 'Calm down.'

Freya was shaking with rage. Her wings were agony and her arm was swelling from the blow. She wanted desperately to share that pain with JP.

'Greta!' Dr Klobucher ran between the gathered students. When she saw Freya's bare hand, her eyes became fearful. 'What are you doing?'

'Nothing,' Freya muttered tightly as she pulled the glove back on. 'JP attacked us.'

'I just heard. Are you all right?'

Freya nodded. 'I am. But he got me right where it hurts.'

The Principal leaned closer and whispered, 'Your wings?'

Freya nodded.

'I've got to stay here with JP. We've called the police and they're on their way. I don't want you here when they arrive.' The principal turned to Archie. 'Would you take Greta inside and see that she's OK? Then get her home.'

'Sure,' Archie agreed. 'Come on, Gee, let's get you inside and see the damage.'

'I'll come too,' Tamika offered.

Everyone was staring at Freya as she stormed down the school's hall. Word of the big fight was spreading faster than a wildfire and all the students wanted to see her. Stopping at the girls' bathroom, Archie shoved open the door. 'Is anyone in here?'

When no one answered, they walked in.

'Stay at the door,' Archie instructed Tamika. 'Don't let anyone in, including teachers.'

Freya was already pulling off her coat when Archie came up to her.

'Nice and easy,' he said gently, helping her.

'Stand back,' Freya warned as she reached for the slip-cover. When it came away, she put both hands on the edge of the sink and leaned forward as she slowly opened her wings. The pain was intense. Freya started to tremble as she carefully extended them fully. She sucked in her breath as the pain soared.

'Gee, you're bleeding!' Archie cried as blood dripped to the floor. 'JP broke your wing!'

'Let Orus look,' Freya said.

The raven flew down to Archie's arm and inspected Freya's wing. He leaned forward and carefully went through all the feathers until he found the problem.

'Here it is. It's a ruptured blood feather,' Orus explained. 'It needs to come out now.'

Freya explained, 'My wings aren't broken. Orus says it's a ruptured blood feather. That's a new feather that's just emerging. The feather shaft is full of blood when they're new. I've got to pull it out or the bleeding might not stop.'

She looked back at Archie. 'Move further away from me – this could be messy.'

When Archie was standing next to Tamika, Orus directed Freya's hand back to the broken feather. It hurt to even touch it. She closed her eyes, gritted her teeth and caught hold of the shaft. Fighting to keep in the cries of pain, Freya wrenched the feather out.

Her hands were shaking as she inspected the damaged black feather. 'It takes ages to grow primary flight feathers.'

Archie peered at the broken feather shaft. 'Wow, no wonder it hurt. That's thicker than my finger!'

'Let me see,' Tamika called. She came forward and looked at the damaged feather. 'Yuck, that's gross.' She pulled paper towels from the dispenser. 'We'd better clean up that blood before someone sees it.'

'I'll do it,' Freya said quickly. 'My blood is as deadly as I am – you can't touch it.'

'Are you going to be all right?' Archie asked.

Freya nodded as she started to clean the floor. 'My wings are bruised and I won't be flying for a bit. But other than that, I'm fine.'

Tamika shook her head. 'I was so scared when I saw JP hit you with the bat. But I was even more scared when you took off your glove.'

Freya looked down. 'I shouldn't have done that. If Archie hadn't stopped me, I'm sure I would have killed him.'

'JP in Asgard?' Archie said. 'I wonder what Thor would do to him.'

'Thanks to you, we'll never have to find out.'

When the floor was clean, Freya put the soiled tissues in her pocket. 'We'd better get out of here before the police arrive.'

As she started to draw on her coat, Archie held up the slip-cover. 'What about this?'

Freya caught hold of the silky fabric cover. 'I'll carry that for now. I don't want too much touching my wings at the moment. My coat is bad enough.'

Out in the hall, they found the Geek Squad waiting. Leo Max had a swollen lip and a bruise on his cheek, but he was grinning from ear to ear. It appeared everyone in the Geek Squad had some kind of injury. But they were all happy.

'We did it!' Leo Max cheered. 'We showed them! They won't bother the Geek Squad ever again!'

Despite the pain in her wings, Freya chuckled. 'You sure did. I am so proud of all of you.'

Elizabeth came up to her and shyly tapped her on the arm. 'I'm not afraid any more, Greta.'

Freya wanted desperately to hug the little girl. She could feel the great change in her. 'I saw what you did for Connie. You were very brave!'

Elizabeth blushed at the compliment.

'What about you?' Leo Max asked. 'JP hit you with the bat. Are you OK?'

Freya nodded. 'I'll live. But what happened to the other members of his gang?'

'They ran away,' Kevin cheered. 'We actually chased them for half a block! It was their turn to be afraid. It was so awesome!'

Kevin was the most changed of all her students. He now had confidence and was using his academic skills to tutor the others with their subjects.

'We should go out and celebrate!' Leo Max said. 'Everyone come to my house; we can order pizza!'

Freya smiled but shook her head. 'You all go. My back hurts. I want to go home and rest.'

'Me too,' Archie said.

Freya, Tamika and Archie watched the members of the Geek Squad walking proudly down the school hall, sharing in their victory.

CHAPTER TWENTY-TWO

Back in Asgard, Maya had only been in bed for a short time when loud, angry voices disturbed her rest. She sat up when she realized who it was.

'Is that—' Grul asked sleepily from his perch.

'Odin!' Maya cried. She leaped from her bed and reached for her robe.

Maya entered the living area and saw her mother and three sisters standing before the leader of Asgard. Her mother was wearing her light robe and her long braids hung down to the floor. She was wringing her hands and trembling.

Her sisters were still dressed in their gowns and looked as though they had only just arrived from Valhalla.

Odin's face was stormy as he stood before them. Loki was standing right beside him with a self-satisfied smile on his thin lips.

The moment Maya laid eyes on him she knew he was causing trouble.

'Where is she?' Odin demanded. 'I do not like to be

disturbed during my sleep with news of a runaway.'

'Freya has not run away,' her mother cried. She caught sight of Maya and ran to her. 'Maya, would you please fetch Freya. Loki insists she has fled Asgard.'

Maya shot a threatening look at Loki.

He raised his eyebrows in surprise. Then he smiled slyly back at her and his dark eyes sparkled. He seemed to realize that she knew what was going on – and that she wasn't going to say anything. Finally he directed his attention to her mother.

'You are wrong, dear lady. Earlier this evening I saw her and Orus flying across Bifröst with my very own eyes.'

'That is impossible,' Odin said. 'Heimdall would never allow it.'

'Yes, well, Odin, I do hate to tell you this,' Loki said snidely, 'but Heimdall isn't as reliable as you think he is. I often catch him sleeping on duty. Why, this very night I found him lying on the ground and snoring like thunder. He threatened me when I told him you would be angry.'

'That's a lie,' Maya shot. 'Heimdall would never do that. He is loyal to Odin and his duties!'

Loki gave Maya another teasing smile. 'Anyone who is content to spend an eternity watching a bridge can't be trusted. How do we know that he won't allow the frost giants to cross into Asgard to destroy us all? He barely speaks to anyone. Who knows what he's thinking or what plots he's hatching?'

Just as Odin opened his mouth to defend Heimdall, Loki continued, 'But if you insist Freya is here, show her to us and we can end this.'

'If you are so frightened of frost giants, what does that say about your very own wife, who happens to be a frost giantess?' Maya countered. 'Are you suggesting that we can't trust her and that she shouldn't be welcomed in Asgard?'

'You leave my wife out of this, Valkyrie,' Loki shot as his dark brows knitted together in a threat.

'Enough!' Odin shouted. 'I will not have this bickering.'

'Great Odin,' Maya pressed, 'are you going to let Loki disturb your rest and lead you around like a mule? He is causing trouble and you know it!'

A shadow crossed Odin's face. 'I do not like your tone, child. Loki told me he saw your sister cross Bifröst without leave. I have no cause to doubt him.'

'But this is Loki!' Maya insisted. 'You know how he likes to cause trouble. He's only doing this to discredit Mother.'

'Maya . . .' her mother warned.

Maya was desperate to save her little sister and would

do anything she could to convince Odin of Loki's treachery.

'Look what he did to your own son,' she pressed. 'Everyone knows it was Loki who gave Thor's hammer to the frost giants. Then he convinced Thor to dress as a woman and pretend to be the new bride of their leader to get it back. Thor was humiliated and it nearly started another war with them!'

'Maya, stop!' her mother cried, as her pale cheeks went red with embarrassment. 'It was never proven that Loki stole Mjölnir and gave it to the frost giants. And it wasn't just Loki who convinced Thor to dress as a woman, we all did. It was the only way to get his hammer back without going to war.'

'No, it was Loki!' Maya insisted. She looked desperately to her three sisters for support, but they said nothing. They were too frightened of Odin to speak.

'Stop!' Odin boomed. 'If it is true that Loki is causing trouble, prove it. Bring your sister to me. However, if she has fled Asgard, it is she who is in a great deal of trouble.'

Loki grinned, knowing he had won. 'Yes, Maya, prove me a liar and trickster. Produce your little sister, Freya.'

Maya was trapped. She didn't know what she could say to protect Freya. She cursed Loki with her eyes.

But if she said more and told Odin it was Loki who had helped Freya cross Bifröst, that wouldn't help her sister.

'She's not here,' Maya finally admitted, trying to sound casual. She looked at her mother. 'You know how Freya loves to go flying with Orus at night? Especially before a reaping? Do you remember the First Day Ceremony?'

Her mother nodded. 'Yes, of course! Odin, Freya was nearly late for her own First Day Ceremony. Maya found her halfway across Asgard. My youngest daughter has a wandering spirit. She often goes out flying alone.'

'I told you she's not here,' Loki teased as he clung to Odin's arm. 'She's gone to Midgard to be with the humans.'

'She wouldn't do that,' Maya's mother cried. 'She knows the penalty for leaving without permission! Please, Odin, give us some time to find her. She and her sister are very close. If anyone can find her, it will be Maya. Please let her go. You'll see. Freya is just out for a short flight.'

The smile on Loki's face broadened. 'Yes, Odin, why don't we let Maya go? I am sure she can lead us straight to Freya – in Midgard!'

Maya felt the noose tightening around her neck. 'I can only find her by flight.' She turned hate-filled eyes on Loki. 'And you don't have wings, you're grounded. You can't follow where I go.'

Loki used his shape-changing abilities to turn himself into an eagle, then a hawk and finally a large black insect. When he returned to his normal shape he smiled again. 'I can follow you anywhere you go, Valkyrie. But I don't have to. Freya is not in Asgard. She has gone to the human world to live among them. She hates it here and she hates Odin!'

'Enough!' Odin shouted.

He approached Maya and his eyes were as red as his hair. He raised a threatening finger to her. 'Go now. Fly. Find your sister. But if you do not return with her before the Valkyries gather for the reaping at sunrise, you know what I will do.'

Maya's mother brought her hands to her lips. Her wings were quivering in fear. 'No,' she whispered softly.

Odin nodded. 'You have but a short time, Maya. Find your sister, bring her to me or, I swear by my sword, I will send out a Dark Searcher to find her and unleash the Midgard Serpent on Earth.'

Maya was frantic. She dashed to her bedroom, picked up her winged helmet and flew out the window. Checking that Loki wasn't following her, she headed straight for Bifröst.

Heimdall was at his post and his face showed alarm when she landed before him. 'Maya? What brings you back here so soon and dressed like this?'

Maya realized she was still dressed in her nightgown. 'It's Loki,' she cried. 'He's betrayed us and told Odin that you were asleep on duty and allowed Freya to cross Bifröst. I have been commanded to bring her back before the Valkyries leave for the reaping, or he'll send out a Dark Searcher to find her and release the Midgard Serpent!'

'No!' Heimdall cried. 'This is my fault. Freya will be punished when the crime was mine. I must tell Odin.'

'It was Loki, not you!' Maya insisted. 'But all is not lost yet. I have until dawn to find her. Please, I beg you, let me cross Bifröst. I will go to Midgard and bring her right back. Then we can go to Odin together and tell him of Loki's treachery.'

Heimdall nodded and stepped aside. 'Go, find your sister. I will do what I can from here.'

Filled with relief, Maya went up on her toes and kissed the Watchman lightly on the cheek. 'Thank you, Heimdall. I will be back soon.'

'Fly safe, Valkyrie!' Heimdall called as Maya leaped up into the sky.

CHAPTER TWENTY-THREE

'I've never been hit in the wings before. I didn't think it would hurt so much.'

Freya, Archie and Tamika walked slower than usual as they made their way home.

'We'll put ice on them when we get home,' Orus offered. 'That will get the swelling down.'

'I'm sorry,' Archie moaned. 'This is all my fault.'

Freya frowned. 'Why? You didn't hit me.'

'Because JP was using me as bait. I should have known when his gang went after us and he wasn't there. Ever since you proved you were stronger than him, he's been waiting to get you.'

Freya stopped. 'Archie, this wasn't your fault. And I'm not hurt. Just bruised, that's all. It will take more than a baseball bat to hurt me. Remember, I'm a Valkyrie. We've been shot at and blown up since wars on Earth first started. We've had arrows fired at us, cannons, rifles and hand grenades. As long as we wear our armour, we can't be seriously injured.'

The words had only just left her mouth when they heard the heavy gunning of an engine. They turned and saw a large, blue pick-up truck jumping the kerb and driving along the pavement – straight at them.

Freya had only seconds to see JP behind the wheel. Hatred burned in his eyes and she felt murder in his heart. He wasn't going to stop.

Tamika screamed. Freya knocked Orus off her shoulder and tried to push Tamika and Archie away. Tamika landed on the ground away from the vehicle, but Archie didn't. He and Freya both received the full impact of the truck's front end.

Freya was knocked high in the air. She instinctively tried to open her wings, but couldn't. Their strength managed to tear off the closed buttons, but the coat itself would not give to free them enough. She crashed to the ground hard, landing on her back and bruised wings.

With the wind knocked out of her, Freya was barely aware of the sound of screeching brakes and a truck door opening. Still trying to catch her breath, she saw JP come running over. He was clutching his baseball bat but when he saw her lying on the ground he stopped. His mouth hung open in disbelief.

'What are you?' He kicked the side of her left wing and gasped as it moved and folded in tighter.

Freya was furious to realize her coat was wide open. Although they weren't fully exposed, JP could see her half-unfolded wings fanned out beneath her.

'What am I?' she repeated as she climbed painfully to her feet. 'I'm the last thing in this world you want to cross!'

'You're a mutant!' JP cried. 'That's what you are. A freakin' mutant!'

'No, not a mutant – a very angry Valkyrie!'

Freya started to advance on JP. He threw the bat at her and she easily deflected it away.

'Stay back, you freak.'

'Do you remember when you broke your wrist?' She stalked him slowly. 'You did that trying to hit me.'

The sudden realization showed on his face. 'That was you? You were invisible?'

Freya nodded and caught him by the coat. She pulled his face close to hers. 'Angels of Death bow to me,' she said tightly. 'Kings cry before my kind. You, JP, have just sealed your fate!'

'Freya,' Orus called, 'leave him and come quickly. It's Archie!'

CHAPTER TWENTY-FOUR

Archie was lying very still in the street. There was a pool of blood spreading from him. The raven was hopping around him frantically while Tamika took off her coat and used it to apply pressure to a large open gash on his head.

Freya shoved JP away and ran to Archie's side. He was unconscious. Despite Tamika's attempts to stop it, he was still losing a lot of blood.

'Freya, help him!' Orus cawed.

'How?' She had never felt so helpless before. Her best friend was lying in the street, possibly dying. He needed help, but what could she do? Her touch meant death to him, not life.

'Greta, here,' Tamika called. 'Be careful not to touch him, but hold this coat over his wound. I'm calling an ambulance.'

While she kept pressure on his head, Freya searched the sky for an Angel of Death. So far, none had come. Archie had a chance. But as she held the coat to his head wound, she could feel him starting to fade.

'Hold on, Archie,' she cried. 'Just hold on.'

The police and an ambulance arrived within minutes. Freya was shooed away from Archie as the paramedics started to work on him. She stood back with Tamika, watching them try to save his life.

Archie was loaded on to a stretcher and lifted into the back of the ambulance. When Freya tried to climb in after him, but the paramedic stopped her.

'I must stay with him,' she cried. 'I can keep the angels away!'

'We'll keep the angels away,' the paramedic promised. Then he looked at her. 'Were you hit too? You look a little rough. Is that your blood on your coat?'

Freya looked down at the wide, wet stain on her torn velvet coat. 'It's Archie's blood, not mine. Please, I must stay with him!'

The paramedic shook his head. 'I'm sorry, but we need to work on your friend. There will be no room in the ambulance for you. We're taking him to the hospital. You can follow behind us.'

A police officer came up to Freya. 'Let them go. I need you to tell me what happened here.'

'Not now. I must stay with Archie.' She focused on Tamika, who was standing back with a haunted expression on her face. 'Will you tell them what happened? I'm going to get my helmet!'

Freya darted from the scene before the police could stop her and ran the short distance to Archie's house. Tearing inside, she found her winged helmet and put it on. As the world turned to black and white, Orus called to her, 'Hurry, they're taking him away.'

Freya threw aside her coat and dashed outside. She opened her wings, but when she tried to fly, the swelling and pain would not let her.

'Try again!' Orus ordered. 'Hurry!'

On the second attempt Freya only climbed a few metres off the ground before her wings failed and she fell from the sky.

'I can't fly!' she cried.

'Then run!' Orus cawed. 'You can do that fast enough!'

While the raven soared above her, Freya ran as fast as she could to catch up with the ambulance. She darted around cars and wove through traffic as she followed Archie to the hospital. Her eyes never left the sky as she watched and waited for an Angel of Death.

'Archie will live,' Orus called. 'He wouldn't dare die on us.'

CHAPTER TWENTY-FIVE

Freya kept her helmet on when they reached the hospital. As she watched the doctors work on Archie, her heart was on edge. She followed, keeping out of the doctors' way as he was rushed into surgery. Orus remained at her shoulder, offering what little comfort he could.

The surgeons had only just started to work on Archie's head when an unwelcome visitor entered.

The most stunningly beautiful angel Freya had ever seen drifted into the operating theatre. He was tall and lean with immaculately groomed feathers on his neatly folded wings. He wore a soft, warm expression on his painfully handsome face.

Freya approached and held up her hand. 'Go back,' she warned the Angel of Death. 'You are not taking him.'

The angel smiled. 'I had heard that there was a Valkyrie in this place. You don't belong here, child, and you know it.'

Freya nodded. 'I do know it. And I know I've caused

some trouble with the other angels and that Azrael is going to be furious with me. But please, I am begging you. Go back. Archie means everything to me. I can't let you take him.'

The angel chuckled softly and the sound was like soft bells. 'You think Azrael will be furious?'

Freya nodded. 'That's what all the others say.'

'Well, I've heard he can be very understanding,' said the angel.

'Not about me being here. But Archie is my best friend I can't lose him.'

'I am sorry to disappoint you, young one,' the angel said. 'But it is his time. He was meant to come weeks ago, but you intervened and stopped JP from killing him. You gave him extra time. But that has run out. He must come with me now.'

Freya gasped. 'Archie was going to die that day?'

The angel nodded. 'You saved his life then. But there is nothing you can do for him now. It is as it must be. There is no future for Archie, only the past. Take your precious memories of him and return to Asgard.'

Freya opened her arms and her pain-filled wings to block the angel. 'No, I won't let you take him. He deserves better.'

'And he will have it. This you already know.'

Freya shook her head. 'No, I mean here and now, in

this life. For the first time, Archie has friends and people who care about him. I won't let you take that away.'

'You can't stop me,' the angel said softly.

'Actually I can, and you know it,' Freya said. 'Valkyries get first pick of the dying. You cannot reap until we go. I will not leave him to you.'

'But you cannot stay here indefinitely. You have your own duties to attend to and will have to go eventually. When you do, I will be waiting.'

'We'll see about that,' Freya challenged.

The Angel of Death chuckled softly, bowed and walked through the wall. Freya could feel him waiting just outside.

'I don't think he's going to go,' Orus said. 'He could still cause some trouble for us.'

Freya shook her head. 'I don't care. I am not going to let him take Archie.'

True to her word, Freya remained with Archie all through his surgery. As long as she was there, the Angel of Death had to stay away. She watched the surgeon slowly putting her friend back together again and then followed him into the recovery room.

Freya stayed with Archie as he was wheeled into the Intensive Care unit. As the long night wore on, she kept a vigil at his bedside. He was hooked up to so many machines she could barely see his bruised face under all the tubes that fed into him. The sighs of mechanical breathing mixing with the beeps of his heart monitor were the only sounds breaking the silence in the room.

Several times throughout the night his surgeon, Dr Taylor, came to check on him. Freya stayed beside Archie's bed and could feel the doctor's deep concern for his patient.

The world outside seemed to still as night turned into day and then back into night again. As yet another dawn approached, Freya still refused to leave. She couldn't risk it. Gazing towards the door, she saw Archie's Angel of Death, patiently waiting to enter. He would nod to her when she gazed in his direction. He was leaning casually against the door frame with his arms folded neatly across his chest. Never moving, always just watching and waiting.

'He's almost as determined as you are!' Orus said. 'Do you want me to go and peck him?'

'No, he's just doing his job,' Freya said tiredly. 'At any other time we might have been friends. He can't help what he is any more than I can.'

Late in the afternoon, Freya heard a voice she recognized. She looked up and saw Tamika standing outside the unit. Curtis was with her, holding her hand. The nurse pointed to Archie's bed and said, 'You can stay a few minutes.'

'Greta, are you here?' Tamika called softly.

'I am,' Freya answered.

'Where? I can't see you.'

'I'm here, in the corner up by Archie's head.'

'How is he?' Curtis asked.

'I don't know,' Freya answered softly. 'It's like this terrible waiting game. As long as I am here, Archie will live. But if I go, the Angel of Death is waiting to take him.'

'The Angel of Death is here?' Curtis asked fearfully.

'Yes,' Freya answered. 'He's standing right beside the door. He can't come in with me here. He's looking at us right now.'

Tamika looked at the doorway. 'Please go away,' she called softly. 'Archie has to live.'

The angel smiled gently at her, but shook his head.

'He still won't go,' Freya said.

'Greta, you can't stay here all the time,' Curtis said. 'You'll have to go eventually. What about food?'

'I won't leave Archie,' Freya said stubbornly. 'I will eat when the angel goes and I know he's safe.'

Curtis looked down at Archie. He was deathly pale and unmoving in the bed. It seemed that only machines kept him alive. 'Maybe it's his time,' he said softly. Tears sparkled in his eyes.

'No,' Freya shot back. 'I won't allow it. I can't lose him.'

'Has his mother been told?' he asked. 'I know this is very difficult for you, Greta, but it's probably her decision whether to turn off the machines or not.'

'She doesn't have the right to make that decision,' Freya spat. 'Not with the way she neglects him. It doesn't matter anyway; no one knows where she is.'

The nurse entered the unit. 'I'm sorry, but you must go now. Archie needs his rest.'

Tamika was reluctant to leave. She whispered, 'Don't leave me, Archie – I've had enough people die on me.' Wiping away tears, finally she called, 'Bye, Greta, see you later.'

'Who's Greta?' the nurse asked as she escorted them out, Curtis with his arm around Tamika.

Throughout the long day, others came to check on Archie. Leo Max tried to get in, so did other members of the Geek Squad, but the nurses would only let them peer at him from the doorway.

Freya waved to them, even though they couldn't see her.

As evening turned to night, Freya remained where she was. She reached out with her gloved hand and took hold of Archie's. Saying nothing, she stood still, just holding his hand.

CHAPTER TWENTY-SIX

As though the Rainbow Bridge understood the urgency of the situation, Bifröst released Maya over the central United States. It was dark out and Maya was grateful for the cover of night.

Flying as fast as her wings could carry her, she flew down into Lincolnwood and landed in the back yard of Archie's house. She stormed up to the door and shoved it open.

'Freya!' she shouted. 'Freya!'

Silence.

'Maybe she's in the city helping people again?' Grul suggested from her shoulder.

'I hope not.' Maya ran into Freya's bedroom to look for clues.

'Maya, look,' Grul cawed. 'That's Freya's coat.'

Her sister's velvet coat was tossed in a heap on the floor. When Maya picked it up, she saw that it was torn and covered in blood. She sniffed the red patch. 'Oh, no.'

'What is it?' Grul demanded.

'This is Archie's blood. I can smell it's his.'

'But there's so much of it,' the raven cried.

Panic gripped Maya's heart. Her sister was missing and her coat was covered in Archie's blood. 'Stop,' she told herself. 'Calm down. There is a reasonable explanation for this.'

Maya took several deep breaths to slow her pounding heart. She closed her eyes and opened all her Valkyrie senses, searching the house and surrounding area for signs of her sister. She felt nothing of Freya or Archie, but she did find something that might help.

'Sylt!' she said. 'Grul, Sylt is still here.'

Maya found her way to the garage and opened the door. The Reaping Mare was inside and whinnied excitedly when she entered.

Without pausing, Maya leaped on to the mare's back and directed her out of the garage. 'Find Freya,' she ordered. 'Sylt, take me to Freya.'

The Reaping Mare nickered, opened her wings and launched into the sky. Keeping low, she soared over Lincolnwood and headed towards a large building. Maya read the lit sign on the front. 'Lincolnwood Hospital.'

She looked at her raven. 'This is where they treat wounded humans.'

'Archie's blood,' Grul offered. 'He's been hurt and brought here.'

'I just hope Freya hasn't done something foolish.'

'You mean more foolish than running away from Asgard to come here?' Grul asked.

Maya had the Reaping Mare land on the roof. 'Sylt, stay,' she ordered as she climbed down. 'We won't be long.'

'Is it wise to leave a young Reaping Mare here unattended?' Grul asked.

'No it's not,' Maya admitted. 'But we don't have much choice. It's still dark out so there's little chance of her being seen.'

'You hope.'

Maya looked at her raven. 'Yes, I hope. Now, let's get in there and find that sister of mine!'

CHAPTER TWENTY-SEVEN

Archie wasn't getting any better. As the long night progressed, the surgeon came in to check up on him, but each time he looked unhopeful.

Hours before dawn, the quiet of the hospital room was broken by a familiar voice.

'There you are!'

Freya looked up and saw Maya. Her sister approached the Angel of Death and bowed respectfully before storming into the Intensive Care unit. She was wearing her winged helmet and nightclothes.

'I have been searching all over for you!' She caught hold of Freya's hand and started to pull. 'Come, we must go. Odin is in a fury. He knows you've run away. Sylt is on the roof; she will bring us home.'

'Odin?' Freya cried. 'How?'

'How do you think? Loki told him. You must come back now, before the Valkyries gather for the reaping. Odin doesn't know I've left Asgard. I told him you were out flying. But if he finds out, he'll send a Dark Searcher after both of us.'

Freya's eyes went from her sister to Archie and then to the angel at the door. 'I can't go.' She pulled free of her sister's hand and moved back to Archie's side.

'What? Why?' Maya demanded.

'Because of him!' Freya pointed to the angel. 'He's here for Archie.'

Maya frowned in confusion. 'So, let him have him.'

'No!' Freya cried. 'Archie is my friend. If I let the angel take him, I'll never see him again.'

'Then reap him and we can go.'

'I can't do that either,' Freya said. 'He won't have died in battle. Odin will never allow him to stay in Asgard. He'll send him through the Gates of Ascension and I'll lose him forever.'

Maya pulled off her Valkyrie helmet. 'Freya, you're going to lose him anyway! If Odin sends a Dark Searcher after you, you will lose everything. So will I. I begged Heimdall to let me cross Bifröst again. He'll get into trouble as well.'

Freya removed her own helmet. 'I'm sorry, Maya. Go back to Asgard. I don't want you to get into trouble for me. Tell Odin what I'm doing. Tell him I promise I'll come as soon as I know Archie is safe.'

'You are insane!' Maya cried. 'I can't tell Odin that!'

'I don't care what you tell him,' Freya continued. 'I'm

not leaving Archie!'

'But he's just a human!' Maya exclaimed. 'You hate humans! Why would you risk yourself for one?'

'Valkyries,' warned the angel at the door. 'I believe you should cover yourselves again. The doctor is coming!'

But it was too late. Freya and Maya watched Dr Taylor enter the Intensive Care unit. His eyes landed on them by Archie's bed. 'You there,' he called in surprise. 'What are you doing in here? It's late – visiting hours are long over.'

Maya stepped forward and gave the doctor her most devastating smile. The surgeon stopped in his tracks and stared at her with his mouth open.

'Wait here,' Maya told Freya. 'I'll take care of him.'

'No!' Freya wailed. 'Don't reap him. He's trying to save Archie!'

'I'm not going to,' Maya said. 'Would you please trust me?'

She approached the surgeon and placed her hand on his covered shoulder. 'What's your name?'

'Peter,' he stammered. 'Peter Taylor.'

'Well, Peter, I need to speak with my sister,' she said softly. 'Would you please check on your other patients and leave us be for just a little while?'

'I – I . . .' Dr Taylor muttered.

'Please . . .' Maya said coyly, giggling softly. 'I promise we won't be long.'

Freya watched her sister use her beauty like a weapon against the unsuspecting surgeon. His eyes grew huge and his face turned bright red. He didn't stand a chance against her. Maya's ability to charm was renowned in Asgard. No human could resist her.

'Of course,' the surgeon finally said. 'Take all the time you need.' He drifted out of the Intensive Care unit as if in a dream.

The Angel of Death took several steps into the room. 'That really wasn't very nice of you, Valkyrie. He will come out of your spell very confused. Peter Taylor is a truly gifted surgeon. It won't be good for him or his patients if he starts to question himself.'

'It's better than me reaping him,' Maya retorted. She turned back to Freya. 'Now, can we go?'

The Angel of Death took several more steps closer.

'Stop!' Freya said, blocking his way. 'I told you, you're not taking him.'

'It is his time to die,' the angel said softly. 'It grieves me that his passing will cause you pain, but it is unavoidable.'

'And I say he is going to live,' Freya insisted. 'Angel, you have so many others you must take. Go to them. Let me have Archie for a while longer.'

'I am sorry, Valkyrie,' the angel said softly. 'This is not my decision. I do only what I must.'

The angel took one more step closer and looked to Maya. 'Would you please tell your sister that there are times when we must all do things we don't want to?'

Maya reached for Freya's hands. 'I know how much you care for Archie, but you must let the angel do his job.' She paused. 'Look at him. He is suffering. The longer he lives, the more he will suffer. He wouldn't want this half-existence between life and death while you and the angel fight over him. There is no recovery for him and you know it. Let Archie go.'

'No,' Freya cried. 'Please,' she begged the angel. 'Please just give us more time together.'

'Freya, you can't stay,' Maya insisted. 'Odin is going to send the Dark Searcher after us.'

The angel inhaled sharply. 'A Searcher is coming for you?'

Maya nodded. 'If my sister does not return to Asgard with me right now, Odin will send him after both of us.'

'Child, listen to me,' the angel said. 'I have seen what the Searchers do to those they've been sent to find. They will destroy you. Please, do as your sister asks. Save yourself and return to Asgard. Your loyalty to your friend is admirable, but it will get you killed.'

Freya was desperate. 'One week, that's all I'm asking for. Please, just give us one more week.'

'Why one week?' Maya asked.

'Because that's when the school dance is,' Freya explained. 'Archie was so excited about it. All of the Geek Squad are going.' She turned imploringly to the angel. 'I know that it is within your power to grant Archie one more week's life. You must do this for him. He and the Geek Squad have been denied so much already, can't we give him this one dance?'

The angel frowned and stepped closer. 'You, a powerful Valkyrie, would risk your own life so this boy can attend a simple dance?'

'You don't understand how it is for the Geek Squad,' Freya continued. 'They have been picked on and beaten up just because they are different. They are the outcasts of the school. But they are all wonderful, caring people. This one dance may not mean much to everyone else, but it means everything to them. They are just learning to stand up for themselves and coming to this dance will prove it. If Archie and I don't go, they won't. How can we deny them their triumph over their fears?'

The angel considered a moment. Then he looked at Maya. 'One week will be but a short time in Asgard.'

'But Loki is out for blood,' Maya cried. 'There is no telling what poisonous words he is feeding to Odin right now. It is too dangerous.'

'I'm not leaving,' Freya insisted stubbornly. 'Please, Angel, give Archie one more week.'

The angel looked over at Archie. Then he approached Freya, rested his hands on her shoulders and leaned closer to her. 'If I do this, you must swear that the day after the dance, when I come back for Archie, you will not stop me.'

'Don't do it!' Maya cried. 'One week is still too long. Loki has betrayed you. Odin will send the Dark Searcher, I know he will. You must come with me now before it's too late.'

'I can't,' Freya insisted. 'I'm sorry, but you still don't understand. I must stay. Go back to Asgard. I will return right after the dance.'

'But the Dark Searcher will find you.'

The angel shook his head. 'No he won't. Not if she doesn't wear her helmet again. That is how he will track you. When he arrives, we will do what we can to distract him.'

Freya looked at the angel in shock. 'You would do that for me?'

'You are risking Odin's wrath for this human boy. How could I not? Now, do we have an agreement?'

Freya nodded. 'I swear, after the dance, I will not stop you.'

'It is agreed,' said the angel.

Freya stepped aside and let the Angel of Death pass. Her heart was pounding. She knew angels could be trusted. But seeing him so close to Archie set her nerves on edge.

The Angel of Death stood beside the bed and waved his hand over Archie's head. 'It is not your time, child. Sleep now and heal. When you wake you will grow stronger. Go to the dance. Live your whole life within this next week.'

When he finished, he looked at Freya. 'It is done. He is yours – for now. Use this time wisely, Valkyrie.'

The angel bowed and then vanished.

Maya faced her sister. 'What have you done?'

CHAPTER TWENTY-EIGHT

Moment by moment, Archie improved. Dr Taylor returned but remained under Maya's spell.

'Well?' Freya asked.

The doctor's dark-hazel eyes were only on Maya as he grinned. 'It's all good news! I'm not sure how it's happening, but he is recovering.'

'There are other forces at work here,' Maya said. She focused on Freya. 'So, the angel has done what he promised. Archie will live one more week. You are risking everything for him. Is he really worth it?'

Freya nodded. 'He is. If you could only get to know him, you'd see that for yourself.' She looked out of the window. 'It's still dark out. You'd better get going while you have the cover of night. You can't wear your helmet again or the Dark Searcher may find you.'

Maya shook her blonde head. 'I'm not going anywhere. If you are staying, so am I, and if the Dark Searcher comes, we'll face him together.'

Freya was awash with gratitude to her sister. She

hugged her fiercely. Together, she knew they could face whatever Odin threw at them.

They stood at Archie's bedside while the doctor carefully removed the breathing tube and started to disconnect him from the machines.

Archie moaned softly.

Orus flew down from her shoulder and landed on Archie's chest. He marched up to his chin. 'Come on, Archie,' he cawed loudly. 'Wake up!'

Dr Taylor tried to shoo him away but Orus nipped him sharply.

'I wouldn't try to move him,' Freya warned. 'Orus is quite fond of Archie.'

'That's because Orus has no taste,' Grul cawed from Maya's shoulder and then started to laugh.

Freya held up a warning finger to her sister's raven. 'Don't you start, Grul. I'm in no mood to deal with you right now.'

The raven huffed, but grew silent.

Finally Archie opened his eyes. They landed first on the doctor, then on Maya and lastly they found their way to Freya. 'Gee,' he rasped softly. 'What happened?'

'JP hit us with a truck. But you weren't struck very hard. You're going to be fine.'

A frown knitted Archie's brow. 'I don't remember. Are you OK? Did he hurt you?'

Freya smiled gently on her friend. 'I'm fine, Archie. But it hurt my wings again.'

'Guess this means you'll have to ride with me on Sylt.'

'Ride Sylt?' Maya asked. She looked at Freya. 'Have you been letting him ride your Reaping Mare?'

Freya nodded. 'Every night. We take her out and go flying together, don't we?'

Archie nodded. 'I love Sylt. She is so cool.' Suddenly Archie's expression tensed. 'Gee, where's your coat? You're exposed.' He looked nervously at the doctor.

'It's all right,' Freya said. 'Mia has enchanted him. He won't remember any of this when we go.'

Maya looked out the window again. The first streaks of dawn had appeared on the horizon. 'Speaking of going, we'd better get moving while it's still dark. Sylt is on the roof waiting for us. She can carry you home.'

She turned to Dr Taylor. 'Thank you so much for everything you've done for Archie. I would ask one more thing of you.'

'Anything.' The doctor blushed.

Maya walked closer to him and smiled radiantly. 'We are going to take Archie with us. Can you arrange it so there are no questions asked?'

'Of course,' the doctor said. 'This is my department. I'll take care of everything. You just take good care of young Archie here. And maybe . . .'

'Yes?' Maya asked gently.

A bright-red blush came to the doctor's cheeks. 'Maybe I can see you again?'

'Perhaps, Peter,' Maya promised. 'Perhaps.'

Getting Archie out of the hospital was more difficult than they first expected. Despite the early hour, there were still a good number of nurses on duty. With both Valkyries having no cover for their wings, they had to resort to using their helmets to get Archie to the roof.

'I hope Odin doesn't notice,' Maya said softly as they walked through the hospital corridor towards the stairs to the roof. Freya was holding on to Archie's arm to keep him invisible with her helmet's powers. 'It's this, or we expose ourselves. We don't have much choice.'

'Yes, we do,' Maya said. 'We could all go back to Asgard right now.'

'That's not an option,' Freya said as they stepped out on to the roof. When Sylt saw them, she nickered with happiness, and nudged Archie affectionately with her nose.

Archie paused and looked at Maya. 'Has something happened? Why are you here?'

Freya quickly shook her head as her eyes pleaded with Maya not to say a word about the trouble they were in.

'Nothing,' Maya finally said. 'I just came here to go to

the dance with you and my sister.'

'You want to go to the dance?' Archie asked.

Maya nodded and gave Freya a pointed, dark look. 'Why not? It's probably going to be my last.'

CHAPTER TWENTY-NINE

The sun was already up when they landed back at the house. By the time they'd settled Sylt in the garage and finished feeding the mare, Archie was already back to his old self.

Seeing his smile as he moved around their small kitchen, making a large batch of pancakes, caused a great pang of sadness for Freya. Archie was running out of time, but he didn't know it.

'What day is it?' he asked as they sat down to eat. 'I seemed to have lost track of time.'

'It's Sunday,' Freya said. 'You were in the hospital just over a week.'

'Really? I don't remember a thing. Sunday, eh? We've only got a few more days to the dance. I can't wait!'

Freya looked over to her sister, but said nothing.

Later that day, Freya and Archie convinced Maya to join them going to Tamika's house. Archie wanted to show them he was all right, and Freya wanted to

267

introduce her sister. She also wanted to quietly thank Tamika and Alma for cleaning and repairing her velvet coat. With the bloodstains gone, she didn't have to worry about Archie seeing and asking awkward questions.

When they arrived, the greetings were loud and welcoming. Everyone was shocked and delighted to see just how recovered Archie actually was.

Alma grinned at Freya. 'Angel, did you have something to do with his sudden recovery?'

She shrugged. 'What could I do? I'm just a Valkyrie.' Freya then introduced her sister, using the name Mia.

Alma smiled radiantly at Maya. 'Aren't you pretty! Two Valkyries in my home – who'd have ever imagined it?'

Maya returned the smile. 'It is a pleasure to meet you.'

Tamika was bursting with excitement and could hardly contain herself. 'We've got so much to tell you! We're moving!'

'What?' Freya said.

Tamika nodded excitedly. 'Curtis and Carol are buying a big house near here and we're all moving in together. I won't have to change schools!'

Freya frowned in confusion. 'But what about this house? You said you didn't want to leave it. We were fighting the developers to keep them away.'

Alma explained. 'Carol has got the police on to them.

They have finally opened up an investigation into their actions. They won't get away with what they've done. But this place? It's just an old, rundown house. We were fighting to protect our home. We still have that. And thanks to you, our family has grown.'

'I – I don't understand,' Freya said.

'Come into the kitchen and help me finish making dinner.'

Away from Tamika, Freya watched the old woman struggle to sit down. Instantly at her side, Freya helped her into a chair. 'What's wrong?'

'The doctor says I am weakening. Who knows how much time I have left?' Alma explained. Freya felt the oddest sensation clutching her heart. It was something she'd only experienced once before – when she'd heard the angel saying Archie's time had come. She realized that she was feeling grief. Though she had only known Alma for a few weeks, the thought of losing her was painful.

'Isn't there anything they can do?'

The old woman shook her head tiredly. 'They've done all they can. It's my time, child. It's natural and I won't fight it. You once told me there wasn't an Angel of Death standing at my side. You may not see him now, but he's there all right.'

Freya heard Tamika's laughter from the front room.

'Does she know?'

Alma shook her head. 'Not yet. She's so excited for the dance, I couldn't tell her.'

Freya dropped her head and walked over to the sink. She peered out the kitchen window at the burned-out wreck of the house next door. 'I've failed,' she said softly. 'I promised your son I would take care of his family and I have failed.'

'What?' Alma cried. 'Child, I bless the day you came to us. You have done everything you promised Tyrone and so much more.'

'But I didn't save this house – you are leaving it. The girls will be left alone without you.'

The old woman struggled to rise and approached Freya. She put her hand lightly on her arm. 'You listen to me. I was going to die whether you came here or not. But now, thanks to you, I can rest knowing my girls are safe. Curtis, Carol and I have been talking and we've made all the arrangements. They will be adopting the girls when I am gone. With the money you gave them from your jewels, Tamika and Uniik will have everything they need to live good lives.'

'But—' Freya said.

'No buts. You've fulfilled your promise to my son. Maybe not the way you intended, but you have. I know you are a Valkyrie and I know what you must do in your life. But here and now, you have saved all of us. Tamika has friends she never had before. She and her sister will grow up with parents who adore them. What more could you possibly give them?'

'You,' Freya said softly, as she peered into the old woman's fading eyes. 'I should be able to give them you.'

Alma smiled gently. 'I don't think even you could do that. It is my time. I am ready.' She reached for her cooking pot. 'Now, why don't you spend some time with Tamika and Archie, and leave me to finish dinner?'

'But I want to help,' Freya argued.

'You can help by staying out of my way.' As she shooed Freya out of the kitchen the old woman laughed. 'And tell your sister I want to take her measurements later. By the looks of things, I have another dress to make for the dance.'

Dinner was loud and filled with laughter as they all sat together enjoying their meal. At first awkward, Maya soon relaxed and sat beside her sister, telling stories of their life together in Asgard and sharing with them the details of Freya's First Day Ceremony.

'I wish I could have been there,' Archie said wistfully. 'I would have loved to see it. Asgard sounds amazing.'

'It is,' Maya said. 'But this world has its own kind of magic. I think my sister is only just starting to see that for herself.'

Freya nodded and then looked at Alma. 'When I came here, I really didn't like humans.'

'And now?'

Freya grinned. 'I really like them.'

Archie tore up a small piece of bread and threw it at her.

'I like *most* humans,' Freya corrected, as she stuck her tongue out at him.

Later that night, they freed Sylt from the garage.

'Tell me again why we're doing this?' Maya asked as she pulled off her coat and freed her wings.

'Because Sylt needs her exercise,' Freya said drawing the Reaping Mare into the backyard and helping Archie up on to her back.

'And Freya likes to play superhero,' Archie teased.

'I do not,' Freya protested. 'I just like to help people.'

Archie winked at Maya. 'See what I mean? A superhero complex.'

Taking to the sky, Freya led them into Chicago, to the part of the city that she had taken upon herself to patrol. They landed on an apartment roof and gazed down into the quiet street below.

Like he did whenever they were on patrol, Orus moved to Archie's shoulder to wait with Sylt while Freya helped people below. Maya ordered Grul to join Orus.

After a few minutes, Orus said hopefully, 'It looks like nothing is happening tonight. Why don't we all go home, make some popcorn and watch a movie.'

'Be patient,' Freya said. 'This is much better than a movie.'

'Says who?' Orus cawed.

Suddenly a scream filled the air.

'Here we go,' Archie said. He turned to Freya. 'Go get 'em!'

Freya grinned at her sister. 'Come, it feels wonderful to help people – you'll see.' She looked over to Archie. 'Follow us, but stay up on the rooftops.'

'Yes, sir!' Archie said, saluting formally as he drew back on Sylt's reins.

Freya and Maya leaped off the roof and soared over several buildings. Down below, they saw what looked like a gang of men circling a woman. She was screaming as they advanced upon her.

'Follow me,' Freya called back to her sister.

Freya and Maya touched down on the street beside them causing the men to turn round.

Freya drew her sword and charged forward with Maya following closely behind. But almost immediately, Freya knew something was very wrong. There was no fear coming from the woman and no threat towards her from the men. Instead she felt something else. It was excitement mixed with triumph.

'Gee,' Maya warned, using Archie's name for her. 'I think we should go now.'

The words were barely out of Maya's mouth when soldiers burst out of doorways behind them and the gang of men surrounding the woman drew weapons.

The woman pulled out her own weapon. 'Hold it!' she ordered fiercely. 'Shut your wings, drop your sword and don't move a muscle! You're completely surrounded!'

'You don't want to do this,' Freya warned, sensing danger all around her.

The woman's eyes moved from Freya to Maya and back to Freya again. 'This is my lucky night. I set a trap to capture one winged avenger, and here it is, I catch two.' She pulled out her mobile phone and pressed a button. 'This is Command One, send in the trucks. These birds are caged!'

Freya and Maya stood back-to-back as the soldiers aimed their weapons at them on both sides. The soldiers meant business. They could feel that they were prepared to shoot.

'What are you?' the woman demanded, stepping closer. 'Where are you from?'

'Who are *you*?' Freya asked.

'I ask the questions here, not you,' the woman shot.

'Now answer me. What are you? Why are you here?'

Maya muttered softly, 'Get ready to give them your loudest howl and then fly. If they want to know what we are, we'll show them.'

'Leave them alone!'

Freya looked up and saw Archie on Sylt. He was shouting as loud as he could while the Reaping Mare shrieked in rage. The two ravens descended from the sky and attacked the men nearest to Freya and Maya.

Sylt tucked in her wings and dove at the large group of men. Just before she struck the ground, the large mare opened her huge wings and bowled most of the soldiers over as she glided smoothly past.

'Now!' Maya shouted.

Both Valkyries let out howls that were so loud, windows shattered around them forcing the soldiers to drop their weapons and clutch their ears as the glass rained down on them.

Without pausing, they opened their wings and launched into the air. Following closely behind Sylt, they were just climbing higher when they were met with a terrifying sight.

Four large, black helicopters were hovering overhead, waiting to catch them. Their blinding searchlights shone directly on to them, lighting them up as a target.

'Stop!' boomed a voice from one of the helicopters.

'Land on the roof right now or we'll open fire! This is your only warning!'

'This way!' Freya shouted as she took the lead. She tilted her black wings and manoeuvered expertly away from the helicopters. She dipped down, close to street level, where they were protected by buildings. With the helicopters unable to follow at that level, they were able to escape into the darkness.

Back at the house, they settled Sylt in the garage. Frightened and furious, Maya charged forward. 'If that was your idea of fun . . .'

'No!' Freya cried. 'I don't know who they were.' She looked over to Archie. 'We've never seen them before, have we?'

'No, never!'

'Who were they?' Maya demanded.

'I don't know,' Archie said. 'The military maybe? They've probably heard the stories about Gee and set a trap to capture her.'

'Well they very nearly succeeded!' Maya raged. 'Do you have any idea what Odin would have done if they caught us? It would have meant war!' She focused on Freya and raised a threatening finger. 'As long as I am here, there will be no going back into that city again! Is that understood?'

Freya nodded. 'Understood.'

Maya stormed out of the garage.

Archie reached for a towel to wipe down Sylt. His hands were still shaking. 'I was really scared, Gee. I thought they got you.'

Freya smiled weakly and picked up a second towel. 'So did I.'

When Monday morning arrived Freya tried her best to convince her sister to join them at school.

'Spend a whole day with human children? No thank you!' Maya was adamant. 'After last night I have had more than enough excitement. I'd rather marry a Dark Searcher.'

Freya shot a look at her. Dark Searchers were a subject she'd rather not think about.

'Sorry,' Maya said quickly. 'My words got away from me.'

Archie looked suspiciously between the two. 'Are you sure there's not something you want to tell me?'

Freya put on a forced smile. 'Nope, everything's fine.' She waved goodbye to her sister. 'We'll be back by four.'

Outside, Archie looked back at his house. 'Will Mia be OK on her own?'

Freya nodded. 'Orus taught her how to use the television and remote. He's told her all about his favourite shows. I'm sure we'll find she hasn't moved from the sofa all day.'

Archie was met with loud shouts of greetings from the members of the Geek Squad as they all gathered round to welcome him back to school.

'Boy, I thought I'd never see you again!' Leo Max said. 'We tried to visit you at the hospital, but the battle-axe on the desk wouldn't let us in.'

'Yeah,' Kevin agreed. 'I tried to sneak past her, but she caught me.'

Freya nodded and laughed. 'I saw you there. You almost made it.'

'Where were you?' Elizabeth asked. 'I didn't see you.'

'Oops!' Orus cawed in laughter. 'Busted!'

'Who, me?' Freya stammered. 'I was hiding beside Archie's bed. The nurse didn't see me there.'

'Cool!' Leo Max said. He caught Archie by the arm. 'Did you hear? JP got away from Mr Powless right before the police got here. He stole his brother's truck. That's what he hit you with.'

'Yeah,' Kevin added. 'He busted up Mr Powless's lip good and broke his nose. He was away from school for two whole days.'

'Where is JP?' Archie asked.

Leo Max shrugged. 'No one knows. The police are

still looking for him but they think he's run away. His gang has been expelled permanently from school.'

'Finally!' Archie cried.

The bell rang and everyone headed towards their classes.

'Aren't you coming?' Archie asked as Freya stood back.

Freya shook her head. 'I'll be right there, but I've got to see the Principal first. I want to let her know that you're back and to ask permission for my sister to come to the dance with us.' She paused and looked sadly at Archie as he went off with Leo Max and Kevin. She couldn't tell him that she was also going to let her know that this was their last week at the school.

CHAPTER THIRTY

Maya waited by the window and watched the street. She needed to be sure Freya and Archie weren't coming back. When she was convinced, she picked up the large coat Alma had given to her.

'What are you planning?' Grul asked as she pulled it on.

'I don't think Freya realizes just how much danger we're in. Last night will seem like a party compared to what Odin will do if Loki convinces him that I've come here. I've got an idea, and I just hope it works.'

'I don't like that look on your face,' Grul warned.

Maya smiled at her raven as they walked out the front door. 'Then you're especially not going to like what I've got planned.'

The air was cold and it felt as if it might snow at any minute.

'Will you at least tell me where we're going?'

'We saw a park not far from here when we first arrived. There are some trees in it. I hope they are dense enough to hide in. I can't wear my helmet but I need to get back up into the air.'

'Where are we going?'

Maya grinned. 'Asgard.'

Maya paused. She had the feeling they were being followed, but hadn't spotted anyone around her. Using her senses didn't work – there were too many people in the area.

'What is it?' Grul asked.

Maya's keen eyes searched for movement behind parked cars or in bushes in people's front yards. But she couldn't see anything specific.

'Nothing,' she muttered. 'I just have the feeling that we're being watched.'

'Do you think it's Loki?' Grul asked fearfully.

Maya shook her head. 'No, he'd come at us straight on, with Odin in tow. What I'm feeling is very Earthbound. I hope it's not the same people from last night.' After a moment, she started walking again.

Reaching the park, they made their way over to a dense cluster of trees. 'Perfect,' Maya said. She pulled off her wool coat and freed her wings.

Just as she was about to take to the air, she heard movement behind her. Turning sharply, she saw a tall, stocky boy approaching her.

'Well, well, well,' he said as he casually came forward. 'What have we got here? It's another winged freak living at Daisy's house.'

Maya sensed a darkness coming from the boy. Hatred so deep and intense, she could almost taste its foulness in her mouth.

'Who are you?' she demanded.

'Don't you know? I'd have thought that other winged freak would've told you all about me. The name's JP. Who are *you*?'

'Not someone you want to know,' Maya said darkly. 'Yes, I recognize your name. You tried to kill my sister and Archie.'

'That black-winged demon is your sister?'

Maya inhaled deeply. 'I would tread very carefully, *human*,' she warned. 'I care a great deal for my sister. I won't tolerate you calling her names.'

'What are you gonna do about it, *Valkyrie*,' JP shot back. A cruel, triumphant smile rose to his lips. 'Yes, I know what you are. That black-winged freak told me, so I looked it up. I know what you do and where you're from. You kill people. But you can't kill me; this isn't a battlefield. Thor wouldn't like it.'

'Odin, actually,' Maya corrected. 'Thor wouldn't care who I killed.' She used her speed and strength to catch JP by the coat before he could move. She hoisted him in the air with one hand and slammed him against a tree. When he fell to the ground, she put her boot on his chest.

'Did your research also tell you that Valkyries can punish whomever we feel deserves it? And you, boy, deserve it more than anyone I've met in a very, very long time. I should break every bone in your body for what you've done.'

'Go ahead!' JP challenged. 'Then I'll tell everyone what you are. They'll catch you and your sister and lock you up so far away that not even Odin will find you.'

Maya was stunned by his arrogant defiance. The boy was as fearless as he was dangerous. She hauled him to his feet and pressed him against the trunk of the tree. JP struggled in her grip and tried to hit her. But Maya was faster and caught his arm.

'What happened to you, boy? How could one so young be so angry?' Her eyes bored into him, searching for answers. 'No one is born evil. Who hurt you so badly that you have become this monster?'

'No one touched me, they wouldn't dare!' JP shot. 'I do what I want. Always have, always will, and nobody can stop me.'

Maya shook her head sadly and lifted the bully until his feet dangled off the ground. 'Now, you listen to me. I don't think you fully comprehend the danger you are in. I could break your body or I could destroy your mind and make you forget who you are. Then you won't be able to hurt anyone ever again.'

For the first time, fear rose in his eyes.

'Would you like that, JP? Would you like me to destroy your mind? Because I will. Right here and right now.'

JP shook his head.

'Say it!' Maya commanded.

JP slouched in her grip. He dropped his eyes. 'Please don't hurt me.'

Maya leaned in closer to his face. 'If I didn't have somewhere very important to go, I would stay and make you beg. But I don't have time. So hear me well, human. Leave this town. Go as far away from here as you can and turn your life around. If I ever see you again, you will not survive the encounter. Whatever you think a Valkyrie is, it's only a fraction of what we truly are. Remember that!'

Maya stared into JP's eyes. The bully's emotions betrayed him. He was terrified. She shoved him away. 'Go now, and pray we don't meet again!'

JP stumbled away from her. When he was out in the open he turned back and raised his fist. 'This isn't over, freak!'

'He won't learn. Go get him!' Grul cawed furiously.

Maya shook her head. 'He's the least of our worries. If we fail and Odin releases the Midgard Serpent on Earth, he'll wish I had ended his life. Come, let's go.'

Maya leaped into the air. With the trees offering her cover, she and Grul headed straight up. Finally she changed direction in the sky and sought the entrance to Bifröst.

'Heimdall,' Maya called softly. She was standing within the brilliant glow of the Rainbow Bridge.

'Maya?' the Watchman called back. He left his post and approached the entrance of the bridge.

'Are we alone? Is it safe for me to come off Bifröst?'

When Heimdall nodded, Maya exited the bridge. It was still dark out in Asgard, but she could feel it wouldn't be long until dawn.

'Where is Freya?' Heimdall asked, looking past her.

Maya sighed. 'There's been a bit of a delay.'

'What! There can be no delays. Freya must come back right now before we are all found out!'

'It's not as simple as that,' Maya said. She stepped up to Heimdall and started to tell him about Freya's life on Earth, the friends she had made and the deal she struck with the Angel of Death.

'She is risking her life for this human boy?'

Maya nodded. 'I have never seen my sister so devoted.'

'Are they in love?'

Maya nodded. 'Of a sort, but not like you think. Archie isn't like that. What they have is a bond of friendship that runs just as deep.' She paused and looked away. 'Heimdall, if I'm honest, I envy her. She has found something so special there. Something wonderful, but tragic. Archie has only a few days left to live. The Angel of Death is going to take him the day after the dance . . .'

'And?' Heimdall asked gently.

Maya sighed. '. . . And I want to give Freya those last few days to share with him.'

'You may not have a choice. Dawn is but a short time away. Soon the Valkyries will gather for the reaping. If you and your sister aren't there . . .'

'I know,' Maya said. 'But I've got an idea to buy her some time.'

The Watchman's bushy blond eyebrows knitted together in a deep frown. 'What are you planning?'

Maya grinned. 'When I was a child, I remember when the senior Valkyrie, Broomhilde, had too much mead at Valhalla. She thought it would be fun to let the Reaping Mares out of their stalls for a long, late-night flight.'

Heimdall chuckled. 'I remember. It caused pandemonium. It took all night to catch the mares and get them back into their stalls. When Odin found out, he was furious and demoted her. Your mother then became senior Valkyrie.'

Maya nodded. 'Heimdall, I am going to do the same thing.'

'Maya, you can't! If Odin discovers it was you . . .'

'It can't be any worse than sending Dark Searchers after us or unleashing the Midgard Serpent on Earth. If I release the Reaping Mares, it might cause enough of a diversion that I can get Freya back here without anyone noticing.'

Heimdall shook his head. 'Odin is no fool. He'll know you did it and why.'

'Perhaps,' Maya agreed. 'But by then Freya and I will be back and Loki won't have any proof of where we've been.'

'But you'll be punished,' Heimdall insisted. He dropped his head. 'I don't want to see you hurt.'

Maya was touched by his concern. 'I know,' she agreed softly. 'But seeing Freya so happy will be worth whatever Odin does to me.'

The Watchman paused and rubbed his chin with a massive hand. Finally he nodded. 'Stay here a moment.'

Heimdall went back to his guard house. He returned carrying an unopened keg of mead. 'Take this. When you get to the stables, open it and spill mead around the area and then leave the opened keg where it will be found. With luck, Odin will suspect it was a reveller from Valhalla who freed the mares.'

Maya was struck silent by his generosity. 'I – I don't know how to thank you for this.'

Heimdall blushed bright red. 'I just hope Freya appreciates what a wonderful sister she has in you.'

Maya nodded and lifted the heavy keg. 'She does. She will also know what a true friend you have been to her . . . and to me.' Opening her wings, she leaped up into the air and headed for the stables of the Reaping Mares.

CHAPTER THIRTY-ONE

The week passed in a blur. Days were spent in school, while nights were passed with Freya, Maya and Archie soaring in the skies above Illinois.

With the threat of the black helicopters patrolling the skies over Chicago, they kept away from the city and soared over open farmland.

On Thursday afternoon the Valkyries, Archie and the rest of the Geek Squad helped Tamika, Alma and Uniik move into their new home with Curtis and Carol. It was in the same neighbourhood as Leo Max.

Everyone in the Geek Squad was excited that Tamika would be living closer to them and that they could all spend more time together.

'It's huge,' Archie cried as he explored the house with Freya and Leo Max. 'It's almost as big as yours, Leo Max!'

Leo Max nodded. 'This is so cool. Now we have two big yards to train in.'

'Or play football,' Curtis offered as he tossed the ball to Leo Max. 'Come on, let's take a break and try it out.'

For the first time since she'd arrived on Earth, Freya joined her friends in a quick game of touch football. Her hair was tucked up in a winter hat and every inch of skin was covered, including a wool scarf that mostly covered her face.

Maya stood on the sidelines with Orus and Grul, cheering and clapping as her sister played with the others.

The ground was frozen solid and the first flakes of snow were just starting to fall. Maya watched as Freya caught the tossed ball and ran for the end zone, slipped and fell on the slippery ground.

Despite the pain of landing on her wings, she roared with laughter as the others gathered round and made light-hearted jokes about her poor running style. 'I'd like to see you all trying to run with your wings bound behind you!' she laughed as she climbed awkwardly to her feet.

Archie and Tamika's faces showed surprise at the comment, but the others in the Geek Squad just took the remark as normal, when coming from her.

When the game ended, Leo Max invited everyone back to his house for snacks. They stayed on into the evening, playing in the games room Leo Max's father had built. Even Maya joined in. Her light laughter had the boys in the Geek Squad bewitched as they all pressed in closer to her and invited her to play against them.

Maya looked at her sister and winked as she won game after game.

Freya was used to men swooning over her sister and felt no jealousy as the Geek Squad fawned over Maya. Instead, she stood back with Archie and Tamika, laughing and teasing her.

At the end of a great day they made their way back to Archie's house, to find the lights were on.

'Mom!' Archie cried as he ran up the steps. He put the key in the lock and charged through the door.

'Archie, is that you?' a woman's voice shouted.

'This isn't good,' Orus remarked.

'I think we're in trouble,' Grul agreed.

Freya and Maya stood back in the entranceway as Archie entered the living room.

'Where have you been?' his mother angrily demanded. 'Do you know what time it is? And who were those boys who came around earlier, looking for you? What kind of trouble have you gotten yourself into this time?'

Her slurred words reminded Freya of the warriors at Valhalla who had consumed too much mead.

'I'm sorry, Mom,' Archie said. 'I was out with friends.

There was a party . . .'

'You don't have any friends,' the woman spat.

Before Maya could stop her, Freya charged into the living room and faced the woman. Her hair was just like Archie's in colour, but greasy and matted. Her eyes were red rimmed but unmistakably the same as Archie's.

'Archie has plenty of friends!' Freya cried. 'And if anyone here is a loser, it is you. What kind of mother leaves her son alone for weeks at a time? You should be ashamed of yourself!'

'Gee, please,' Archie begged.

Freya looked into his pleading eyes. All traces of fun and happiness faded beneath the cruel gaze of his mother.

'Who are you?' she commanded. 'What are you doing in my house?'

Freya could feel waves of anguish coming from Archie. He gave an almost imperceptible shake of his head, begging her not to say more.

'I'm Greta, a friend of Archie. He has been teaching me about Math. He is very good at it, not that you're ever sober enough to realize!'

'Why, you foul little cat, how dare you speak to me like that!'

She charged forward. As she came closer, Freya could smell the drink and filth on her. The woman raised her hand as if to slap Freya's face, but Freya caught hold of her wrist and bent it back.

As his mother cried in pain, Archie ran forward. 'Gee, no, please stop. Please, that's my mom!'

Freya's eyes landed on Archie. 'This is no mother. You deserve so much better.'

Drunk and unstable, the woman's knees gave out and she crumpled to the floor. Freya released her wrist. 'You have no idea who your son is, or how precious his life is to all of us. All you think about is yourself!'

'Get out,' Archie's mother wailed. 'Get out of my house and leave us alone!'

'Freya, we'd better go,' Orus said gently. 'You aren't helping Archie. Look at him – she is destroying him. Please, leave him what little dignity he has left.'

Freya took a deep breath. 'You're right,' she said softly to the bird. 'We can come back for our things later.'

She led Archie and back to the front door. 'We'll go over to Tamika's for tonight. Why don't you come with us?'

Archie was on the verge of tears. He wouldn't meet her eyes. 'I'm so sorry, Gee, but I can't.' He sighed heavily. 'She's still my mother. I have to take care of her.'

Freya ached to tell him that it should be his mother taking care of him. Instead she smiled. 'I understand. I'm just worried about you.'

He shrugged in resignation. 'I'm used to it. But did you hear what she said? Some boys came around looking for us. Do you think it could be JP again?'

'No,' Maya said knowingly. 'I'm sure we've seen the last of him. It's probably nothing.'

'Wait,' Archie cried. 'What about Sylt? She won't be able to go out flying tonight.'

'She'll be all right for one night.' Freya leaned closer. 'Just try to keep your mother out of the garage. I don't know what Sylt will do if she goes in and starts screaming.'

'She never goes in there,' he said shakily. 'She'll just eat and probably start drinking again. Then she'll lock herself in her room.'

Freya reached out and caught Archie by the hand. 'We'll be at Tamika's house. If you need anything, just call and I'll fly right over here.'

He nodded but said nothing as he turned back to the door. 'Night, Gee and Orus. Night, Mia.'

'Good night, Archie,' Maya said gently.

The two Valkyries started the long walk back to Tamika's new neighbourhood.

'Maybe it's not such a bad thing the angel is coming for him soon.' Maya tried to comfort her sister.

Freya looked back at the house where she had shared so much happiness with Archie. 'I guess so,' she agreed softly.

Before they reached Tamika's new house, Freya stopped and turned round. 'I've got to go back. I can't let that woman hurt him.'

Maya caught her arm. 'You can't. This is his life.'

'But he's only got a couple of days left. I won't let her ruin them for him.'

'Freya, stop,' Maya said. 'I understand how you feel, but we are only visitors here. We mustn't get involved.'

Freya sighed heavily. 'I know, but . . .' Her imploring eyes looked at her sister. 'Maya, what's wrong with me?'

'You know what it is. The dance is almost here. On Saturday we will lose Archie forever and it's hurting you.' Maya paused and looked at her sister as though seeing her for the first time. 'I never imagined you could feel things so deeply. Archie has really changed you.'

'It's not just Archie. It's everyone. I adore Uniik and want to see how Tamika grows up. Look how Leo Max has changed. He is brave and strong and looks out for the others. They are all my friends. I don't want to leave them.'

Maya gave her sister a powerful hug. 'And that is the tragedy for all of you. Freya, I know in Asgard you are lonely. In time, you will grow older and that will ease. But you know you can't stay here. They are human. You are a Valkyrie. The two aren't meant to mix.'

Freya dropped her head. 'I know. I also know I

shouldn't have let myself care for them. But I do. And now that I've got to go, it is tearing me apart.'

Maya kissed her on the forehead. 'Look, we still have a couple of days. Find joy in the time we have left. Let the others know that you care. Even if you can't tell them you are leaving, let them know how you feel, so that when you are gone, they will remember.'

Freya nodded. 'You're right. I'm not being fair to them or me. From this moment on, I will let them see how happy they've made me.'

'Me too!' Orus agreed from her shoulder. 'For these last few days, I promise not to bite or peck at anyone.' The raven paused. 'Except for Grul.'

CHAPTER THIRTY-TWO

The next morning Freya and Maya stood outside the school, waiting. Archie was late.

'Where is he?' Freya demanded.

'He'll be here,' Maya offered. 'Just calm down.'

'If she has done anything to him,' Freya threatened, 'I don't care what Odin does to me, I swear I will take off my glove and reap her!'

Orus leaped off her shoulder and rose in the air. 'Wait here. I'll see if I can find him.'

Several minutes later, Archie appeared down the street with Orus sitting on his shoulder. He was walking slowly with his head down. When he arrived at the school steps, they could see that his eyes were red. He looked as if he hadn't slept.

Freya leaped down the stairs. 'Are you all right?'

Archie nodded. 'Just tired. Mom won't tell me where she's been or what's happened to her. This morning she locked herself in her room and wouldn't talk to me.'

Freya balled her hands into fists. Maya came up beside her and placed a calming hand on her shoulder.

'I'm sure she'll tell you when she's ready,' Maya said. 'It's late, you'd better get inside. I'll meet you both right here after school.'

Freya remained close to Archie all day. Some of the sparkle was slowly returning to his eyes as Tamika and the members of the Geek Squad crowded round him, offering their support.

Orus too was keeping close. The raven spent most of his time on Archie's shoulder instead of Freya's.

At lunch, Archie was more himself and talking about the dance later that night. 'My mom says I can't go. But I'm going anyway. Right after school, I'll sneak back home and grab my clothes.' He looked at Tamika. 'Can I come over to your house to get dressed?'

'Of course,' Tamika said. 'Greta and Mia are changing there, so you can too.'

Leo Max put his arm around Archie. 'And we'll all come home with you just to make sure your mother doesn't try to stop you.'

'Then it's settled,' Freya said. 'Tonight we shall all have the time of our lives and dance like there's no tomorrow!'

* * *

As the clocked ticked away the final hours, Freya looked around the school with more than a trace of sadness. This was her last day here. Tomorrow she would return to Asgard. The only time she would be able to return to Earth would be to reap soldiers on the battlefield.

Each moment became a treasured memory. The noise, the crowds of kids jamming the hall, the smell of the school, all of it. This would be all she would have to take with her.

'Are you OK?' Orus asked. He was back on her shoulder.

'I guess so,' Freya said as they walked to her locker. 'But I'm going to miss this place so much.'

'Perhaps Odin will let us return,' he offered. 'If we do a good job, he may let us take a break.'

Freya shrugged and sighed sadly. 'It won't be the same. Time moves so quickly here. If we go home for a short while, most of these kids will have grown up and forgotten all about us.'

Orus moved closer to her neck and rubbed against her. 'Yes, they will have grown up but, believe me, they will never forget you.'

As the final bell rang, Freya closed her locker for the last time. She would leave everything behind.

Maya was waiting for her outside the school. Soon everyone was gathered together.

'Well, this is it!' Tamika said. 'Let's go get Archie's clothes and head over to my house. This is going to be so much fun. I can't wait!'

Freya watched her young human friends. Not too long ago, Leo Max had found the courage to ask Tamika to be his date for the dance. She had readily agreed and was now bouncing with excitement.

'Then what are we waiting for!' Maya said as she put a comforting arm round Freya. 'Tonight will be a night we'll all remember forever.'

Back at Tamika's house they were getting ready. Alma had made Freya a stunning, midnight-blue, full-length satin dress with a full, long blue cape of the same fabric mounted to the back of it. The dark colour complemented her red hair. Her sister was wearing a delicate pink silk dress that brought out her fair complexion. She also had a full long cape mounted to the shoulders. Both Valkyries had matching satin opera gloves.

Orus and Grul had been scrubbed and had preened their black feathers until they shone like new. Orus strutted around, admiring his reflection in the mirror.

'By far the most handsome of all,' he said.

'Says who?' Grul complained.

'Me!' Orus cawed.

'You're both very handsome,' Freya said as she gave

Orus a kiss on the beak. Then she whispered in his ear. 'But you are the best!'

Alma fussed with the dresses. 'They fit perfectly. No one would ever know what you two have hidden under those capes.'

Freya turned to the old woman. 'I don't know how to thank you, Alma. These dresses are stunning.'

'Stuff and nonsense!' the old woman said, though her fading eyes sparkled. 'You girls just have fun.'

Carol and Curtis watched them each appear, dressed up to the nines. 'I wish your mothers could see you all,' Carol said. 'They would be so proud.'

Freya looked down at her dress and thought about her mother. What would she say if she knew what had been going on? Her mother had had many adventures when she was growing up. Freya was sure she'd understand . . . eventually.

Moments later, Archie appeared from the spare room. His hair was neatly styled and he was wearing a dark suit. He was struggling with the tie at his neck. Curtis offered to tie it for him. 'It takes a bit of practice,' he said.

Leo Max arrived wearing a tailored suit and a new embroidered yamika. Curtis went crazy taking loads of photographs of them from every possible angle. He was behaving like an excited new father.

Standing back and watching him, Freya felt the depths of his emotions and knew that was exactly what Curtis was: a new father with a ready-made family. His joy was unmistakable.

She looked over and caught her sister smiling at her. 'You did well,' Maya softly whispered.

When they arrived at the school they could hear loud, pounding music and see colourful lights flashing from the school's gymnasium windows.

Half the school seemed to be filing into the gym. Freya's eyes were bright as she took in the sights of all her classmates dressed up in their best party clothes. The excitement was so high that for a brief moment she was able to forget the coming dawn and Archie's impending death.

Maya leaned closer. 'This is almost as good as Valhalla.'

Freya shook her head in wonder. 'No, it's much better. Look at them, aren't they all so beautiful!'

'Yes, you are,' Archie said, looking at her. He offered his gloved hand. 'Shall we go in?'

Wearing her own blue gloves, Freya accepted Archie's outstretched hand and nodded. 'Let's.'

Inside the gym, the music was pounding. Tables of drinks and snacks lined the walls while the roof of the gymnasium had been decorated with paper streamers and balloons. A single mirror ball hung from the centre and was spinning slowly, casting diamond sparkles along the walls and down on the partygoers.

Having lived among humans for several weeks, Freya had come to enjoy a lot of their music. It had seemed strange at first, but now she realized it would be added to the long list of things she would miss.

Leo Max was the first to speak as he held out his hand to Tamika. 'Wanna dance?'

Tamika grinned and followed him and soon they were swallowed into the thick of the moving crowd.

'Go on,' Maya said to Freya. 'This is your night, why don't you and Archie dance?'

Freya looked over to him. 'Want to?'

He nodded.

Together they walked into the crowd and started to dance. She studied her friends. It wasn't like any of the dancing she'd seen at Valhalla, but soon Freya was moving in time to the beat of the music. Others from the school that she knew danced past her, calling her name and commenting on her lovely dress.

'It's great to see you finally out of your coat!' called Kevin as he danced with Elizabeth. Their eyes were sparkling with the thrill of actually being there.

Soon the whole Geek Squad had found their way to the centre of the floor. Song after song, they continued to laugh and dance together. Even Orus joined in, hopping from shoulder to shoulder as he bobbed up and down to the rhythm of the music.

Eventually Maya made her way on to the dance floor and the two Valkyries danced together, surrounded by their closest friends. Freya felt an overwhelming sense of belonging. For this one night, she was truly one of them. There wasn't the separation of human and Valkyrie. It was simply friends sharing in the joy of each other.

When the next song ended, the lights in the gym were turned up. There were cries of protest from the dancers as their Principal took to the DJ's podium.

'Good evening, everyone,' Dr Klobucher called as she raised her hands in the air to get their attention. 'I hope you are all having a wonderful time.'

All the students cheered and shouted. Up on the DJ's stage, Dr Klobucher's eyes sought out Freya in the crowd. When they found her, she smiled. 'I hope you will forgive me, but I would like to ask a favour. I'm sure some of you have heard what a wonderful voice Greta has. But I've never heard her sing.'

The crowd cheered and roared as the Principal's eyes focused only on Freya. 'Would you please come up here and sing for us?'

Freya shook her head. 'I can't,' she said.

'Sure you can,' Archie said as his face glowed with

pride. 'Go on – I've never heard you sing either. Please do it for me. Just this once.'

That comment cut right through to her heart. Archie was making a final request. How could she say no? This would be her final gift to him.

Freya looked over to Maya. 'Will you join me?'

'But this is your school and your night,' Maya protested.

Freya held out her hand. 'Please – just like we do at Valhalla.'

'Come on,' Orus cawed. 'Let them hear you sing together.'

Even Grul joined in and prodded Maya to sing with her sister.

Finally she surrendered and took Freya's hand. Together they walked up to the stage and joined Dr Klobucher.

'I promised I wouldn't tell anyone you were leaving,' the Principal whispered to Freya. 'But I couldn't let you go until I heard the song of the Valkyries. Please . . .' She stood back and indicated the microphone on the stand.

Clutching Maya's hand, the two sisters approached the microphone. Without musical accompaniment, they both started to sing at the exact same moment. Freya was melody while Maya automatically took harmony.

The song poured over the crowd.

Not a sound was made from the gathered students as the two Valkyries raised their voices high and clear and sang as they did at Valhalla. The mournful melody drew tears from the students and teachers as they were enchanted by their voices. Finally, when the last notes were sung, a long silence filled the gym. Archie and the Geek Squad were the first to break it by clapping their hands wildly and screaming. Soon the entire gym burst into roaring applause.

Maya squeezed Freya's hand and leaned closer. 'And you were afraid they'd forget you? Now they will remember this moment for the rest of their lives!'

Freya's heart was beating fast as she felt the love surrounding her from everyone.

Everyone, but one.

JP stood at the entrance to the large gym. At first no one noticed, as all eyes remained locked on Freya and Maya. But when JP and his gang shoved their way into the room, word spread of his arrival and the crowds parted fearfully to let him through.

The moment the Principal caught sight of JP, she shouted to another teacher, 'Call the police!'

JP stalked closer to the stage and shouted, 'Valkyries!'

He was wearing Freya's silver breastplate over his shirt. In his hand he was clutching her sword. He pulled it from its sheath and the lights in the room glinted off the polished steel. He pointed the tip of the blade at Freya. 'She's a black-winged freak! A Valkyrie, an Angel of Death sent here to kill all of you!'

Freya and Maya both looked at JP. Suddenly they realized what he and another member of his gang held in their hands. It was their winged helmets.

'No!' Freya howled as JP lifted the one he was holding and pulled it on his head.

CHAPTER THIRTY-THREE

There was no reaction from the humans in the room – their ears could not pick up the high-pitched squealing from the two distressed winged helmets. But the Valkyries could.

Freya put her hands to her ears and tried to block out the terrible sounds. Her sister was bent over and crying in agony. Both ravens cawed and shrieked in pain.

'We've got to go!' Maya screamed, reaching for Freya. 'Odin will hear that! He'll come for us!'

'Odin?' Dr Klobucher demanded. 'What will he hear?'

Freya pointed a shaking finger at JP and shouted over the sounds. 'It is forbidden for living humans to wear our helmets! Odin will hear their cries of distress and come for them.'

Both Freya and Maya were being deafened by the sounds from the helmets, but for everyone else in the hall, there was only silence. So they heard Freya's shouted response to the Principal.

'See what I mean!' JP cried. 'They're both monsters!'

Confused expressions turned to fear as the students moved away from the DJ's podium.

'He's lying!'

Freya heard Archie's voice rising above the sound of the helmets. She looked into the crowd and saw him, with the Geek Squad, charging forward. 'They're just causing trouble.'

JP turned the sword on him.

'What are you going to do?' Archie demanded, facing the bully. 'Kill all of us? Go on, try it, in front of all these witnesses! Use the sword. But I swear you won't get out of here alive.'

'Archie, stop!' Freya shouted desperately. Was this it? Was this how Archie was to die? Murdered by JP, using her sword?

Archie looked up to her. 'No, Gee, for too long we've all been terrified of JP and his gang. But not any more. I won't be bullied by him or anyone else!' Archie advanced on the bully. 'Take off the helmets. Right now!'

'No, Archie!' Freya howled.

'Who's gonna make me?' JP spat as he advanced on Archie. '*You?*'

Archie nodded.

'And me!' Leo Max added. 'C'mon, everyone, let's get him!'

JP took a frightened step backwards. 'Stay back!' He

raised the sword in the air and swished it back and forth. 'I swear I'll kill anyone who comes near me! Just stay back.'

Suddenly all the windows in the gym shattered. Ferocious howling screams came from the entrance doors. Everyone turned and started screaming in terror at the sight.

Two creatures stood at the doors. They were dressed in long, flowing, hooded cloaks that covered their heads and obscured their faces. Black armour could be seen beneath their dark cloaks. Huge black wings extended from their backs. In each gloved hand they carried a sword with a black blade. If it were possible, they were blacker than the darkest night and seemed to absorb light.

Both creatures threw back their heads and howled again.

'Dark Searchers!' Maya screamed. 'Odin sent the Searchers after us!'

Freya had never seen one before, let alone two. They were so much worse than she'd ever imagined.

Freya shouted to the room. 'Everyone get out of here! They are after us, but will kill anyone who gets in their way!'

The two Dark Searchers stormed into the gym. Their heads were panning back and forth over the crowds, searching, searching, and searching until they found JP and his friend, wearing the Valkyrie helmets. They raised their swords and charged forward.

'Take off your helmets!' Freya cried frantically. 'They are calling them!'

JP and his friend shrieked in terror as the two monstrous creatures ran at them.

'The helmets!' Maya shouted. 'Take them off!'

JP's friend was the first to understand. He pulled off his helmet and cast it aside. One of the Dark Searchers followed it as it rolled away. But for JP, it was too late. The Searcher caught hold of him before he could remove it.

The Dark Searcher held JP by the neck and hoisted him easily off the ground. The bully screamed and tried to break free, but the Searcher's grip was too tight.

Freya pulled the blue cape free of her dress and exposed her wings. Opening them wide, she leaped from the podium and flew full speed at the Dark Searcher holding JP.

She struck him and they tumbled to the ground. Freya was the first on her feet. She turned to the students in the gym and opened her wings fully, letting out a loud Valkyrie howl. 'Go!' she roared to the crowds. 'Get out of here! Go now!'

Up on the podium, Maya shouted, 'You heard her,

go!' She freed her own wings and unleashed a flying tackle on the second Dark Searcher.

Everyone in the gym followed their instructions and ran for the door, clambering over each other in their desperation to get out.

Freya was struggling to get JP free of the Dark Searcher but his grip wouldn't loosen. The Searcher was so much stronger than she'd imagined. Much stronger than her.

It was as though the Dark Searcher suddenly realized who she was, and that he had found his true target. He released JP and reached for Freya. But she was faster. She moved just before his brutal grip caught hold of her arm.

Freya dashed for the weapon in JP's hand. The bully was unconscious and she couldn't tell if he was alive or dead. But before she could reach her sword, the Dark Searcher rose and blocked her. The monstrous creature raised his two black swords and advanced on her.

She only had seconds. Freya glanced over her shoulder and saw that the other creature was focusing on Maya. Both Dark Searchers now recognised their true targets. The remaining students in the gym were safe.

Freya opened her wings and cried, 'Fly, sister, fly!'

With no time to say goodbye to Archie, Freya lifted off the ground and flew straight at the gymnasium's shattered windows. She pulled her wings in tight and slipped through an opening too small for the Dark Searchers to follow.

Moments later, Maya was behind her in the sky. Orus and Grul quickly caught up with them as they headed away from Lincolnwood.

'Faster, Freya, they're right behind us!' Orus cried as they rose higher into the sky.

Freya stole a glance back and saw the two Dark Searchers gaining on them. Even though she was the fastest flyer in Asgard, Freya's wings were only half the size of theirs. There was no way they could ever hope to out-fly them and get to Bifröst.

Their only hope was to lose them. Freya called over to her sister. 'They're too close. Follow me. We'll try to lose them in Chicago!'

'Freya, no!' Maya cried. 'The soldiers are waiting for us in Chicago!'

'That's what I'm hoping for!'

Freya took the lead. With her sister close at her side, she reached over and caught Orus in her hands and pulled him to her. 'Hold on, this is going to be rough.'

She took them lower in the sky and flew only a few metres above the ground. Darting in and out of traffic, car horns blared as drivers caught sight of the two Valkyries and the two monsters chasing behind.

No matter what they tried, Freya and Maya could not lose the Dark Searchers. They were able to get further ahead by manoeuvering around tight corners and hiding behind buildings. Then they heard the Searchers' massive wings clip the corners and blast huge chunks out of the buildings, gaining on them once more.

As everyone in Asgard knew, once a Dark Searcher was after you, there was no escape. They would find you. The only thing to do was to give up and hope that, if they'd been ordered to kill, death came swiftly.

Freya was not ready to die but was quickly running out of ideas. No amount of dipping or dodging could get the Dark Searchers off their tails. Suddenly she heard a sound that on previous nights would be a warning to flee. But tonight, she welcomed it.

High above them in the sky, four black helicopters had arrived. The beams of their intense searchlights panned the ground.

'Here!' Freya called as climbed to meet them. She looked over to Maya. 'Follow me!'

Freya flew into the beam of a searchlight. At once the other helicopters focused their searchlights on her and Maya. Freya squinted and tried to see the pilots. But all she saw was white light.

'Stop!' announced one of the helicopters. 'Stop or we'll open fire!'

Freya pointed back behind her. 'Shoot them!'

The Dark Searchers had also been caught and blinded by the beams of light. The monstrous creatures were howling in pain and dropped their swords as they shielded their unseen eyes from the light. Their wings faltered and they began to fall from the sky.

But the blinding light was burning the Valkyries' eyes too.

Freya tilted her wings to try to fly out of the beams but there were too many of them. Trapped and unable to see, both Freya and Maya flew headlong into the side of a building.

Stunned from the impact, they both started to fall.

CHAPTER THIRTY-FOUR

Freya crashed to the ground with a deafening impact. She landed on her wings and, without her breastplate for protection, she felt many of the fine bones snap. The pain drove the wind from her lungs and left her unable to move.

'Freya, are you all right?' Orus cried as he landed beside her.

Freya shook her head. 'I've broken my wings.'

'You can't fly?'

'I can't move . . .'

'Freya . . .' Maya moaned. She was lying crumpled on the ground not far from her. Her left leg was at an odd angle and bone could be seen sticking out of it. The feathers on her open wings were bent and frayed and she was bleeding.

'Orus, where are they?' Freya weakly asked.

'Several streets away. They landed just as hard as you did. I hope they're both dead.'

'Don't count on it,' Grul cried. 'Nothing can kill a

Dark Searcher. Maya, Freya, please, you must get up. They will come for you.'

Above them, the helicopters continued to shine their lights down. But with the closeness of the buildings, they couldn't land. However, the sounds of sirens and heavy vehicles could be heard getting closer.

'Please get up!' Orus howled. 'The Searchers will get you.'

'Or the soldiers,' Grul added as he stayed with Maya. 'Gee!'

'Archie?' Orus called.

Freya looked to her left and saw Sylt in the beam of the bright searchlights. Archie, Tamika and Leo Max were jammed on her back and struggling to climb down.

'What are you doing here?' Freya cried.

'We came to give you these.'

Archie held up Freya's sword and breastplate. Leo Max and Tamika were holding their helmets.

'How?'

'It was Sylt,' Archie explained. 'She knew how to find you. Now, get up.'

'I can't,' Freya moaned. 'I'm broken. I can't move.'

Grim determination rose on Archie's face. 'You're not giving up, Gee. I won't let you. I said, get up!' He caught hold of her hand and hauled Freya to her feet. 'We don't have much time. Put this on.'

Freya looked at her armour. 'What happened to JP?'

'He's dead,' Archie said. 'That thing killed him.'

'It was a Dark Searcher,' Freya explained as she struggled to stay upright. 'Odin sent them here to get us. They crashed on another street. But they will be here soon.'

'Then you'd better be ready,' Archie called.

He was still wearing his gloves as he helped Freya put on her breastplate. She howled in agony as he moved her broken wings aside so he could fasten it closed around her.

But once the armour was in place, Freya found the pain faded and with its support she could move again. She stepped over to her sister. Without her armour, Maya was too battered to move.

'Leave me,' she moaned. 'Take Sylt and go home. Maybe Odin will forgive you.'

'I'm not going to leave you here for them,' Freya said. 'Sylt, come.'

Leo Max walked beside the winged Reaping Mare as they approached Freya. He shaded his eyes as he stared at her in disbelief. 'Greta?'

'I'm sorry I couldn't tell you,' Freya said to him. She looked over to Archie. 'Can you help me get my sister up on Sylt's back? Maybe they can out-fly the Searchers.'

Archie and Freya managed to get her wounded sister

up on Sylt. Maya was fading in and out of consciousness. Her leg was bleeding, she had a deep cut on her head and both her wings were badly broken.

Archie tore pieces off Maya's dress to bandage her leg. 'You've both got to go,' he shouted above the roar of the helicopters. They were trying to manoeuvre closer to the ground.

Suddenly the sound of machine-gun fire spiked the air. They looked up and saw flashes coming from the circling helicopters. Following the line of fire, their hearts sank. The Dark Searchers were moving steadily down their street, and the bullets from the helicopters did nothing to slow their advance.

'They're coming!' Orus cried.

Freya looked back at her friends. 'They are here for us. Stay back. They won't hurt you if you aren't a threat to them.'

'But they'll kill you!' Archie cried.

Freya reached for her sword. 'Not without a fight.' She inhaled deeply. 'Thank you, Archie, for everything. You've shown me what it is to be human, if only for a little while, and I will treasure those memories forever.'

'Freya, don't do this!' Orus cawed.

Freya handed the raven to Archie. 'Stay with Archie, my sweet Orus. I can't watch you die.'

'No!' the raven cawed.

'Don't go, Gee,' Archie begged, clinging to the raven. Tears were rimming his eyes. 'Stay with me, please. I'm nothing without you.'

'You're wrong, Archie,' Freya said, controlling her wild emotions. 'You are everything. I won't let those things hurt any of you.' Unable to say more, Freya turned from him and started towards the two Dark Searchers. She heard Orus calling after her, but she ignored his pleas.

The pain of leaving them was tearing at her heart. But she turned that pain into rage as she faced the Dark Searchers.

'You want me?' she cried furiously. 'You're going to have to fight!'

Raising her sword, Freya charged at the two creatures. All her fury rose to the surface as she used the skills she'd been taught since birth to fight them. Swords flashed and sparks flew as Freya's one sword fought against their combined four.

But even as her fury carried her forward, she was wounded and badly outmatched. The tip of a Dark Searcher's sword grazed down her leg. Freya cried out in pain as the blade sliced through her beautiful long dress and into her flesh. A second blade cut deeply into her arm.

Her breastplate offered her protection from human weapons, but little against the Dark Searchers. Moment by moment, Freya was losing ground. As she focused on one advancing creature, she could not defend herself against the other.

With each cut and swipe of their blades, Freya cried out in pain. She realized they weren't going to kill her quickly. These Dark Searchers wanted to draw it out slowly, to hurt her as much as possible.

As she stumbled backwards, a powerful blow knocked the weapon out of Freya's hand and hurled her through the plate-glass window of a large department store.

Without pausing, the creature stormed forward and followed her through the broken glass. The second Searcher returned his attention to Maya.

As Freya struggled to untangle herself from a rack of expensive clothing, the sounds of her sister's weak cries tormented her.

'Fly, Sylt!' Archie was shouting. 'Get out of here!'

Gaining her feet, Freya's heart pounded as she looked for the Dark Searcher. She could hear his furious movements knocking sales displays over as he searched for her.

With her leg badly damaged, Freya kept low as she limped back to the window. Being as quiet as possible, she carefully climbed out.

Just before she jumped down from the window ledge, a fearsome hand flashed out and caught hold of the edge of her broken wing.

The Dark Searcher screeched in triumph as he drew her back to him.

Freya screamed in agony. Her wing exploded in pain as the creature pulled the broken bones in his vice-like grip. She was powerless to stop him as he came forward – a terrifying, black monster looming above her.

Moments before his other hand went round her neck for the final snap, Archie screamed, 'Let her go!'

He was holding Freya's sword and brought it down on the hand clinging to Freya's wing. The blade sliced through the creature's black gauntlet and down to the bone of its ghostly-white wrist.

The Dark Searcher howled and released her.

Freya fell forward and hit the ground hard.

'Run!' Archie cried as he caught hold of her bleeding arm and pulled her forward. 'C'mon, Gee, get up and run!'

Freya was dragged alongside Archie for a few steps, but the wound in her leg slowed them both down. 'I can't – my leg is hurt. Archie, go. He'll kill you if he catches you. Just go and leave me.'

'Stop complaining and run!' Archie screamed. He half dragged and half carried her into the street. 'What kind of Valkyrie are you? You're stronger than this. Now, run with me!'

She looked up, searching for her sister. 'Where's Mia?' She was careful, even now, not to use Maya's real name so as to protect Archie.

'She's gone,' Archie answered. 'Sylt took her away, but the Dark Searcher followed right behind. We tried to slow him down but he got away from us.'

Leo Max and Tamika ran forward to help Freya, but Freya warned them back. 'No, you're not wearing gloves. You'll die if you touch me!'

As they ran further down the street, police vehicles came to a screeching halt before them. 'Stop!' an officer shouted as he opened his door and drew his weapon.

From all around, more police and military trucks arrived, pulling right up on to the pavement. They were surrounded.

'Run!' Freya warned them. 'The Dark Searcher will kill you all. Your weapons are useless against him!'

'Look!' Tamika howled.

Behind them, the Dark Searcher was moving again. He focused his attention on Freya and charged forward.

'Keep moving,' Archie called as he released Freya and lifted her sword. 'I'll slow him down.'

'Archie, no!' Freya screamed. 'Stop!'

Orus cawed. 'Come back!'

Their cries could not stop him. Archie held up her weapon and charged forward.

The Dark Searcher only held one sword as his right hand was all but useless due to Archie's cut. But the creature raised his weapon and took him on.

The fight was brief.

Beneath the bright helicopter lights and surrounded by police and military, Freya saw Archie try to block a cut from the skilled Dark Searcher. But at the last moment, the creature changed tack. He brought his weapon up and stabbed it deep into Archie's stomach.

'No!' Freya howled.

'Archie!' Orus cawed.

Archie stood motionless as the Dark Searcher's sword struck through to his back. When the wretched creature pulled the weapon out, Archie collapsed to the ground.

'Archie!' Tamika screamed.

The police and soldiers opened fire on the Dark Searcher but their bullets could not stop him. Instead, Orus, Tamika and Leo Max ran at the creature as he kicked Archie away and focused on Freya. Orus dived at his head, while the others ran to his rear. Both Leo Max and Tamika jumped on to his massive black wings.

'Get away!' Freya howled at them. 'He'll kill you. Get down and run!'

'Save Archie!' Orus cawed.

Holding on for their lives, Tamika and Leo Max were madly spun around as the Dark Searcher fought to bat Orus away while trying to shake them off. Black feathers filled the air as Tamika did all she could to pluck them out of the monstrous creature's wings.

While the Dark Searcher was occupied, Freya limped as fast as she could over to Archie. He was still alive but bleeding heavily from the wound in his stomach.

From somewhere behind them, a distant clock chimed the hour. It was midnight. The start of a new day – the day after the dance. Freya collapsed beside Archie and pulled him into her arms, knowing what was about to happen. There was nothing she could do to save him. She had made the bargain. Soon the angel would come to collect.

'I'm so sorry, Archie.' Freya stroked his young face with her gloved hand. Tears filled her eyes. 'I can't save you.'

'It is over, child.'

Freya looked up into the face of Archie's Angel of Death as she cradled her best friend.

'Gee?' Archie whispered.

'I'm here.'

'I wanted to stay with you,' he said softly. 'I wanted you to show me Asgard.'

'You're going somewhere much better,' she struggled

to say. 'I wish I could go with you . . .' Finally the loud sobs she fought to contain escaped her.

'Please don't cry, Gee, not for me. I'm not worth it.'

'Yes, you are,' Freya whispered.

Archie shuddered as pain tore through him. He shivered as he clutched her arms. 'I'm so cold. Please make me warm.'

Freya looked up pleadingly into the angel's eyes. 'Please,' she wept, 'I'm begging you, end his pain. Take him now.'

The Angel of Death shook his head and smiled gently. 'He has fought valiantly to save you, Valkyrie. Archie is a brave warrior who has earned his rightful place at Valhalla. Take him, he is yours.'

Freya inhaled sharply, disbelieving.

'But you'd better hurry. Archie's time grows short, if you want to give him your name.'

Freya was shaking as she looked down into Archie's fading eyes. 'Archie, listen to me. You can stay with me. Just say my name. I'm Freya. I give you my true name. Please, accept it. Say it now.'

'Gee?' Archie whispered.

'Not Gee,' she pleaded. 'I am Freya. Fre-ya, please say it!'

With his final, gasping breath, Archie uttered, 'Freya . . .' and closed his eyes.

Freya leaned forward and kissed him tenderly. The moment her lips touched his, Archie died. She pulled him closer and rocked her friend in her arms.

CHAPTER THIRTY-FIVE

Archie was hers. But for how long? Freya put his still body gently aside and rose to face the Dark Searcher. Archie's spirit stood at her side, looking just the same. He had a huge grin on his face. 'Thanks, Gee,' he whispered. 'Thank you so much.'

'It's Freya,' she corrected.

Archie grinned. 'Nah, you will always be my Gee.'

Freya lifted her sword. She had to get Orus, Tamika and Leo Max away from the Dark Searcher before he hurt them. 'Stay here, I must surrender to him.'

'Child, wait,' the angel said. He pointed up. 'Look.'

The Dark Searcher was shrieking in fury as Angels of Death descended from the sky. Holding hands, they formed a tight circle around him, imprisoning him.

Shocked by their sudden appearance, Orus fled as both Leo Max and Tamika fell from the Dark Searcher's wings. They landed on the ground in stunned silence.

'This way, children,' urged an angel as she opened the circle a fraction to allow them out.

The searchlights shining from the helicopters above illuminated the brilliant white of the angels' open wings as they surrounded the midnight-black Dark Searcher. Around them, police were ordering everyone to remain where they were. Soldiers piled out of their trucks and, with their weapons held high, they surrounded the circle of angels. Others raised their weapons on Freya, but stayed back a safe distance, as if they already knew who or what she was.

Trapped within the angels' ring, the Dark Searcher shrieked and charged furiously forward, but could not break through them.

Freya looked back at the angel in confusion. 'I don't understand.'

'Just wait a bit and you will.'

'Greta!' Leo Max called as he and Tamika ran towards her. Soldiers tried to catch hold of them but they tore free of their grip. They approached Archie's body.

'Archie!' Tamika shrieked as she knelt down beside their fallen friend.

'He's not there,' Freya called. 'He's right here, beside me.'

'Where?' Leo Max said.

Freya offered her arm. 'Touch me, but only where I'm covered.'

Both Leo Max and Tamika touched her arm. They

gasped in shock when they saw Archie's smiling face.

'It is really you?' Tamika sniffed.

Archie nodded. 'Gee reaped me. That means I can stay with her. Please don't be sad for me; I couldn't be happier. We're going to Asgard together.'

'If we survive this!' Orus cawed as he landed on Freya's shoulder.

'I don't think we will,' Freya said darkly. 'Once he breaks free he'll come after me. There is no escape from a Dark Searcher.'

'Perhaps not,' the angel said. 'But he can be called off.'

As more soldiers surrounded them, they stood together and watched the circle of angels holding the trapped Dark Searcher. The creature's enraged howls could be heard throughout the city.

Suddenly a sound Freya knew all too well filled the air around them. She looked back at the soldiers. 'Please go! The Valkyries are coming. You can't fight them – go now and save yourselves!'

The soldiers heard the sounds too and started to back away. 'There!' one cried fearfully. 'What is that?'

Freya looked up. '*Odin* . . .

Odin, in full battle armour, was tearing through the night sky, riding Sylt. Thor was beside him on another Reaping Mare, wielding his hammer in his hand. On the other side of Odin flew the second Dark Searcher. In his arms he clutched Maya and Grul.

Behind them flew the Valkyries of Asgard, led by Freya's mother.

Freya looked over to Archie in regret. 'I'm so sorry it's going to end like this. I shouldn't have reaped you. It's not fair.'

'Whatever happens,' Archie said, 'we'll face it together.'

Above them, Thor waved Mjölnir in the air. All the helicopters were driven away as though blown by a thousand winds. And when he touched down on the ground he slammed his hammer down so hard that all the windows in the buildings around them exploded and rained glass on to the street. The police cars and military vehicles were blown backwards and the men sent flying away.

Beneath the pressure of the hammer, the ground cracked and a large pit opened. Ferocious, deafening roars could be heard coming from the newly opened hole.

Freya put her hands to her mouth. 'Oh no!'

'What is it?' Leo Max asked.

'Thor has freed the Midgard Serpent!' Freya cried. 'Odin is going to destroy Chicago because of me!'

CHAPTER THIRTY-SIX

'Valkyrie!' Odin roared as he climbed down from Sylt.

A large eagle touched down beside him. Moments later it changed. Freya's heart sank at the sight of Loki's grinning face.

Freya turned back to Tamika and Leo Max. 'Whatever happens, stay here with the angel; he'll protect you. Odin does not forgive. It won't matter that you are young and human. He'll punish you too.'

She looked at Archie, pulled off her glove and offered him her bare hand. 'We may not have much time left together. But I don't regret a moment of what we've had.'

Archie pulled off his glove as well and for the first time they actually held bare hands. He nodded. 'Me neither.'

Together they walked to Odin. They both knelt before the leader of Asgard.

'You were warned,' Odin boomed. 'You know the punishment for running away.'

Freya raised her head. 'I do, Great Odin. But I beg you, please don't punish Maya. She has done nothing wrong. She came here to bring me back to you. Not to stay. She did not run away. And Orus could not stop me, though he tried. This isn't his fault.'

Odin looked back at Maya as she struggled in the Dark Searcher's arms. 'Your sister is far from innocent in this. She released all the Reaping Mares from the stables in a futile attempt to delay the reaping. They have caused havoc in Asgard. Even now, half of them are still flying wild. She tried to disguise her crime, but there was a witness.'

Freya looked at her sister in shock. 'She couldn't have done it. She was with me. Who saw her?'

'Me,' Loki said proudly. 'I knew she would try something to protect you. But she made a terrible mistake.'

'He's lying!' Freya shouted.

Odin's face went red with rage. 'She has confessed her crime! That she convinced Heimdall to go along with her is further evidence of her deceit.'

Freya was left speechless. Her eyes sought her sister in the Dark Searcher's arms. Maya had endangered herself for her sake.

'As for your raven,' continued Odin, 'he will be punished with you.' His harsh blue eyes blazed as he drew his sword. 'Open your wings!'

Freya struggled to open her badly broken wings. She dropped her head and bent forward to offer them up to him.

'No, sir, please don't!' Archie cried.

'Archie, no!' Freya warned. 'I knew the penalty for breaking the rules. Odin must take my wings.'

'No!' Archie shouted. 'It's not fair. Gee isn't a runaway, she came here to help. She's helped Tamika's family and she helped me!'

'Archie, be quiet!' Orus cawed.

'She helped you to your grave, boy!' Odin spat. 'If you think I am going to allow you to stay in Asgard, you are sorely mistaken!'

'I gave him my true name,' Freya said softly.

'What?' Odin shrieked.

'Freya, no!' her mother cried, coming forward. She was still dressed in her nightclothes. 'Tell me you didn't!'

Freya raised her head. 'Yes, Mother, I did. And I don't regret it.'

'Freya,' Orus warned.

'Impudent child!' Odin shouted. 'If you have given him your true name, so be it. He will join you in your banishment!'

Odin raised his sword higher. Just as it was swinging down to cut off Freya's wings, the Angel of Death blocked the blow with Freya's sword.

'What is this?' Odin roared. 'Azrael, you have no right to halt my justice!'

'In this case, Odin, I believe I do.'

'*Azrael?*' Freya was in complete shock as she gazed up at Archie's Angel of Death. 'You are Azrael?'

The angel's gentle, warm eyes sparkled and he chuckled. 'Fooled you, didn't I?'

'I don't understand,' Freya said.

Azrael bent closer to her. 'I wanted to meet the Valkyrie that was causing so much mischief and interfering with my angels' work. You were so passionate, so determined to help these people.' He rose and faced Odin. 'She has done you proud.'

'She has betrayed me,' Odin spat. 'Broken the rules. *My* rules.'

Azrael shook his head. 'You are Odin, leader of Asgard. Freya is a Valkyrie. That is understood. But she is much more than that. She came here with good intentions. She has saved lives and enriched the existence of all who know her.'

'What does that matter to me?' demanded Odin.

'It should mean everything,' Azrael said. 'For too long we have resented each other. We serve the same purpose and yet there is animosity between us. This one Valkyrie has changed that. Look . . .'

The angel pointed to the others encircling the Dark Searcher. 'I did not command them to do that. They wanted to. They all know what Freya has done. Though she has interfered with their duties, she did it for the right reasons. They have come here to protect her. We are all pleading on her behalf. If you will not allow her back in Asgard, I will gladly claim her for my own.'

Odin looked at Azrael in disbelief. 'You would claim a Valkyrie?'

Azrael smiled lovingly on Freya. 'I would gladly ask her to join us and be grateful if she did. You should be proud of her, Odin, not punish her.'

From beneath the earth, the roaring increased. The ground trembled and the street cracked further as the Midgard Serpent shot like an erupting volcano to the surface. It looked like a giant snake, but with long, sharp fangs and flaming red eyes. It loomed several storeys high as it pulled itself from its prison deep within the earth. Slithering through the streets, its long tail grazed a tall building. Within moments, the building collapsed to the ground in a demolished heap.

The Midgard Serpent roared in delight at its destructive freedom. Its red eyes blazed and its long fangs dripped acid on to the ground. It slid through the streets of Chicago, biting huge chunks out of buildings and devouring the military trucks like they were sweets.

'Send him back, Odin,' Azrael ordered. 'There has been no crime committed here. The world has done nothing to deserve this punishment.'

'Only Loki can command his child,' Odin said.

Loki stepped forward. 'And I won't stop him until this place is in ruins.'

Freya pointed an accusing finger at Loki. 'But it was Loki who helped me come here. He's just as guilty as I am. He should be punished too.'

'What?' Odin demanded. 'Explain yourself!'

'Go on, Loki,' she challenged. 'Tell him, if you dare.' She turned to Odin. 'I would not have come here if it weren't for him. He suggested I see the World of Man for myself. It was Loki who gave Heimdall the sleeping powder that allowed me to cross Bifröst. He said he always does that whenever he wants to come here.'

'*Loki?*' Odin repeated.

'It is true,' Azrael agreed. 'Loki is the one who has betrayed you, not Freya or Maya.'

Odin's face went red with rage as he faced Loki. 'Explain yourself!'

'They're lying to you,' Loki cried as he backed away. His eyes were wild and desperate. 'You know I would never betray you.' After several more steps, Loki transformed into a hawk and flew away.

Odin turned to Thor. 'I will see to him later. Go get

the Midgard Serpent. Without Loki here to stop him it's up to you to drive him back to the pit! And don't be too gentle.'

Thor nodded to his father. He raised his hammer and gleefully chased after the disappearing serpent. As everyone stood together, they could hear the roaring sound of destruction at the fight starting between the two.

'They've always hated each other,' Freya whispered to Archie. 'I just hope there's something left of Chicago when they are finished.'

'Silence!' Odin commanded. 'Rise, Valkyrie.'

Freya climbed painfully to her feet. Archie stood at her side, holding her hand tightly while Orus remained loyally at her shoulder.

'Azrael has pleaded for mercy on your behalf,' Odin started. 'I will grant that mercy. But you cannot go unpunished.'

Freya dropped her head. 'I understand.'

'I am stripping you of your powers,' Odin continued. 'They will not be returned until you can prove to me that you have earned your place among the Valkyries. From this moment forward, you and your human companion will work in the stables of the Reaping Mares. You will be servants to the Valkyries, but not hold any of their privileges. You are banned from Valhalla and will not be welcome at any of the reapings or celebrations. Until further notice, you are nothing more than a simple citizen of Asgard.'

He turned back to the Dark Searcher holding Maya. 'You have served me well, Searcher. Release her, your duty is finished. You may return to your home.'

The Dark Searcher released Maya and Grul. Her mother and sisters flew instantly to Maya's side to support her.

Odin then faced Azrael. 'Your words hold power. Perhaps it is time we considered working together and not against each other. Will you release my Searcher?'

Azrael bowed. 'As you wish, Odin. Release him,' he called to his angels.

The angels encircling the Dark Searcher nodded their heads and separated. Opening their wings, they took to the sky and disappeared.

'You are also excused,' Odin called to the Searcher.

The dark creature growled at Freya and Archie and raised a threatening hand. Then he opened his massive wings and took off.

'It is time we left this place to the humans and returned to Asgard,' Odin continued. He walked back to Sylt and caught her by the reins. He handed them over to Freya. 'From the look of your wings, you are going to be grounded for some time. I will allow you to keep your reaping mare.'

Freya's heart was pounding so ferociously she was sure Odin could hear it. 'Thank you,' she said respectfully.

Odin came forward and touched Freya on the head. 'I remove your powers, Valkyrie. Your touch is no longer lethal and your senses are dulled. You are no better than a human.' Odin turned abruptly and approached another Reaping Mare. Climbing up, he ordered the mare into the sky. 'To Bifröst!'

Freya's mother gave her a disapproving look as she helped Maya up on her Reaping Mare. 'Do not test his generosity,' she warned as she opened her wings and launched into the sky. 'Follow us! We have much to discuss.'

'Yes, Mother,' Freya said softly. She looked at the angel. 'Thank you, Azrael. Thank you so much.'

He smiled warmly and kissed Freya lightly on the cheek. 'There is no need to thank me. Remember, my invitation is always open to you. Just call my name and I will come to you.' His smile broadened as he looked from her to Archie. 'Have fun in Asgard, you two.'

Freya grinned as Azrael opened his wings and vanished.

Moments later they were alone. Shattered glass and rubble surrounded them. Fires blazed while dust was still settling from the collapsed building. The sounds of Thor fighting the Midgard Serpent could be heard in the distance while police and fire sirens blared.

Tamika and Leo Max ran up to Freya. 'Are you going to be all right?'

Freya nodded. 'Odin has removed my powers. I'm just like you now.'

'Except for the wings,' Leo Max commented, grinning at her.

'Is Archie still here?' Tamika asked.

Freya offered her arm, but when the others touched it, they couldn't see him. 'I guess without my powers, you can't see him any more. But I promise you, he's right here with me and always will be.'

'Freya, we had better go,' Orus warned. 'It won't take much to get Odin angry again.'

Freya nodded. She inhaled deeply and looked at her two friends. 'We must go.' Once again, pain clutched her heart at the painful goodbye. 'Will you be all right getting home?'

Tamika nodded. 'I've called Curtis. He'll be here soon.'

'Just stay hidden until he comes,' Freya warned.

Tamika nodded again. 'We will.'

Freya inhaled deeply. 'I am going to miss you both so much.'

Forgetting the danger, Tamika threw her arms around her and hugged Freya tightly. She kissed her on the cheek.

Terrified at first, Freya now realized she could touch her friends. She pulled Tamika closer. 'You take good care of your little sister and give Alma a big kiss from me. Please let her know I will treasure every moment we had together. And say my farewells to Curtis and Carol.'

Tamika sniffed. 'I will.'

Leo Max's face went bright red as he faced her. 'Bye, Greta. I'm sure going to miss you.'

Freya pulled him close and held him tight. 'I'll miss you too. Take good care of the Geek Squad – I'm counting on you.'

Leo Max nodded. 'I will.'

Freya smiled and gave him a big kiss, right on the lips.

'Wow!' he sighed as he staggered back. He grinned at Tamika. 'My first kiss and it was a Valkyrie. How cool is that!'

'Freya, we must go,' Orus prodded.

Freya nodded and reached for Sylt. Archie was the first to climb up. It took Freya longer, as every part of her ached. Finally she took her place right behind him. 'Archie and I will remember you both always.'

Tamika and Leo Max waved and chased after Sylt as

the Reaping Mare opened her wings and started to run.

Archie and Freya waved back as they climbed higher in the sky. Rising above Chicago, they could see that Thor had managed to trap the Midgard Serpent on the edge of Lake Michigan and was driving the monstrous beast back underground.

More police and military vehicles surrounded him.

'Will Thor be OK?' Archie asked.

Freya slipped her arms around his waist and rested her weary head against his back. 'He'll be fine. With Thor's temper, it's the humans we should worry about.'

Archie burst into laughter as he whooped happily. Before too long, his eyes went wide at the sight of the shimmering Rainbow Bridge.

'Is that Bifröst?'

Freya peered over his shoulder and nodded. 'Welcome to Asgard, Archie,' she said gratefully. 'Welcome home.'

ACKNOWLEDGEMENTS

This has been the hardest book of my career to write. Normally I love to visit the places I write about. For the *Pegasus* series, I enjoyed going back to New York, then to Las Vegas and, finally, I was thrilled to visit Greece.

Then I started *Valkyrie* and planned to go back to Chicago for research – I lived there as a kid, but I couldn't remember it enough to write about.

But just before I was meant to fly out there, my father became seriously ill. In fact, he needed three critical operations. During that time I couldn't write, let alone go on a research trip.

Were it not for the skills and care of my father's amazing surgeon, Professor Peter Taylor, and the staff at St Thomas' Hospital in London who pulled him through, this book would not have been finished.

'Prof', I am eternally grateful to you! (And I hope you enjoy your appearance in this book.)

I would also like to give a very special thanks to Dr Linda Klobucher – who at the time of writing *Valkyrie* was a principal in a Chicago area school before being promoted. Linda became my long-distance tour guide and a good friend. While I stayed in the United Kingdom while my father recovered, she was always available to talk to guide me through the school system and answer any questions I had about what a Principal would and wouldn't allow – especially if a Valkyrie showed up on her doorstep!

You were invaluable, Linda. Thank You! And look, you're back in a school!

Finally, I would like to give extra special thanks to my dad, for surviving the operations that would have killed a lesser man. He is still my biggest supporter and best friend.

I love you Dad . . .